PRAISE FOR

THE WILD LANDS

"This fast-paced book contains all the hallmarks of a classic wilderness
survival novel (deadly terrain, vicious predators, literal cliff-hangers)
and the best of the postapocalyptic genre . . . The author's
decades of Alaskan wilderness experience is evident throughout . . .
A great high-stakes wilderness survival tale."
—*School Library Journal*

"This rugged survival story places a group of teens in a dark, burned-out
postapocalyptic nightmare. Your heart will pound for them as they face
terrible dangers and impossible odds. Gripping, vivid, and haunting!"
—*Emmy Laybourne, international bestselling author of the Monument 14 trilogy*

"A compelling story that wouldn't let me stop reading. Greci has created both
a frightening landscape and characters you believe in and want to survive it."
—*Eric Walters, author of the bestselling Rule of Three series*

"A brutal vision of things to come. Greci delivers an apocalyptic
odyssey that's honest, relentless, and backed by his firsthand
knowledge of the wilderness."
—*Lex Thomas, author of the Quarantine series*

"Heart-racing . . . A rugged wilderness lover's post-disaster survivalist tale."
—*Kirkus Reviews*

"Heart-thumping suspense for readers who liked Rick Yancey's *The 5th Wave*."
—*Booklist*

"Raw and accessible. Offering hints of *Hatchet* with markedly
more manmade danger."
—*The Bulletin*

"The themes of teamwork, choice, and free will are incredibly
well done . . . an intense and thrilling ride."
—*TeenReads.com*

HOSTILE TERRITORY

ALSO BY PAUL GRECI

THE WILD LANDS

SURVIVING BEAR ISLAND

FOLLOW THE RIVER

HOSTILE TERRITORY

PAUL GRECI

[Imprint]
MAKE YOUR MARK

NEW YORK

[Imprint]
MAKE YOUR MARK

A part of Macmillan Publishing Group, LLC
120 Broadway, New York, NY 10271

Library of Congress Control Number: 2019941084

ISBN 978-1-250-18462-7 (hardcover) / ISBN 978-1-250-18463-4 (ebook)

Our books may be purchased in bulk for promotional, educational, or business use.
Please contact your local bookseller or the Macmillan Corporate and
Premium Sales Department at (800) 221-7945 ext. 5442 or by
email at MacmillanSpecialMarkets@macmillan.com.

Book design by Carolyn Bull

Imprint logo designed by Amanda Spielman

First edition, 2020

1 3 5 7 9 10 8 6 4 2

fiercereads.com

This book remains in the owner's possession.
Swipe it and you'll be met with severe aggression.
With bears at your heels and fire in your face,
It's likely you'll disappear without a trace.

For my father, Joseph Greci (February 4, 1927–September 5, 2018),
an Army and Navy veteran, and a person who cared deeply
for his family and his community.

CHAPTER 1

I UNZIP MY TENT, SCOOT forward through the door, and slowly stand up. The breeze blowing down from the high mountains keeps the mosquitoes away. Clouds stained pink block the early morning sun and give the landscape a reddish tinge. I put my binoculars up to my eyes to check on the others. Derrick is a couple of miles away on a rocky ridge, higher than the one I'm camped on. I can't make out his tent, but I can see a green triangular flag flying close to his campsite—just like the flag at mine.

Derrick's on the same side of Simon Lake that I'm on. The two girls are on ridges that rise above the lake on the opposite side. I guess it's the camp director's way of keeping us from hanging out together while we're supposed to be by ourselves. I look up and across the lake and spot Brooke's flag, and then a couple of miles beyond hers I see Shannon's flag, too. Both green, which means everything is okay.

Below us all, at the head of Simon Lake, sits the main complex of the Simon Lake Leadership Camp. I can't see the camp's flag right from this spot, but I can from where I've got my food stored about a quarter mile away, and last time I checked it was green, too. We haven't even had one red flag, which orders everyone back to camp immediately.

After this solo experience ends tomorrow and the four of us hike down to the camp and join up with everyone else, we've got a few more days until the floatplanes come to haul us all back to civilization. Back to the land of buildings and roads—and people. And back to the trees. Living above the tree line this past month has been cool. It's like there are no obstructions. You can see forever. And if you want to see farther, all you need to do is climb higher.

Part of me wishes I could stay in the mountains. That I could take my backpack and keep hiking deeper into the wilderness. But another part of me is ready to go back to Fairbanks. Ready to start my senior year of high school. Ready to run cross-country and see if we can take State this year just like we did last year. My coach was concerned about me missing a month of summer training by doing this Simon-Lake-Leadership-Camp-thing, but I've been running up and down steep mountainsides to stay in shape so I'll be ready for the season. You can't run up the slope right from the camp because it's so rocky and almost vertical, but if you jog down the lakeshore for a mile or so then you can go up. One of the counselors, Theo, runs college cross-country, and I'd been running with him almost every day until it was my turn for a solo experience. Theo's pushed me hard, but I like that because it's the only way to get faster.

I set my binoculars down just inside my tent and bounce on my toes a couple of times. I could take off running right now, but part of the solo experience is staying put and seeing what comes up in your head. Instead of filling your time with activities, you're supposed to fill it with silence. Besides clothes, food, and binoculars, I've got a journal to write in and that's it. So far, I've written *Josh Baker*—that's my name—on the inside cover, plus a list of things I've been thinking about.

Running. How can I get faster and stronger?

My parents. How can I keep them from splitting up?

Brooke. How can I get to know her better?

Control. What do I really have control over?

I added that last one because of Theo. Not only does he push me to run faster, he really gets me thinking and challenges me to, as he says, *go deeper*.

On our last run, Theo said, "Josh, you can't change other people. You can only change yourself."

"But I can do things that will make other people change, right?" I asked.

"Someone might change," Theo said. "Like your mom might decide to stay with your dad. But that's still her choice. It's an illusion to think you can control her. You can only control your own actions—not what other people do in response to them."

Now I'm thinking about control and what Theo said. I mean, I don't really want to control anyone. I just want them to do certain things.

Like I want my parents to stay together. But that doesn't mean I want them to be unhappy. I want them to be happy together. I want them to stay together because *they* want to stay together.

I want Brooke to like me. But I want that to come from her. I don't want her to pretend she likes me. She hasn't been that easy to get to know. Out of everyone in camp, she's probably been the most reclusive. Besides being beautiful, there's something about her that makes me want to get to know her better. What is going on in her head when she's silent? Or when she chooses to sit by herself instead of with the group? What's she thinking about? There's this mystery there that I want to solve. I mean, she lives in the same town that I live in, but I'd never met her until now.

I want to be the fastest cross-country runner in Alaska. I don't want other people to slow down so I can win. I want them to run their best and still beat them.

None of those things, like Theo said, are things I can control. I can still want them, but all I can do—all I can control—is what I do and how I do it.

When Theo says it, it sounds easy to remember, but it isn't.

I reach my arms over my head to stretch, and that's when I lose my balance, when my feet are swept out from under me and I fall on top of my tent, which is bouncing up, down, and sideways. I'm tossed off the tent onto the ground and feel a stab of pain, like a knife has been shoved into my calf. I roll onto my stomach and grip the ankle-high tundra plants, trying to ride out the earthquake, but the shaking grows stronger. Then the ground starts to split apart directly under me.

CHAPTER 2

I ROLL TO THE RIGHT, toward my tent, which is tipped upside down, and reach for it. Now I'm lying on my side with my hand wrapped around the base of one of the tent poles. Another jolt pitches me forward—like the earth is a trampoline that I've just made contact with. I grab the base of another pole of my inverted tent and hang on, draping my body on top of the flimsy nylon.

Then the ground is still. I let go of the tent and slowly stand up, keeping my knees bent in case I have to ride out another wave. I turn and look behind me. There's a gap in the ground, about five or six feet wide and seven feet deep, that didn't used to be there. My flag is still upright, but it's in the gap so only the top foot of my flagpole is aboveground. There's no way anyone else could see it now.

I reach for it and feel this pain in my calf, like someone hit it with a hammer. I can still move but it hurts. I remember the stab I felt when the quake threw me to the ground, so I twist my body around and work my pant leg up to my knee. There, in the middle of my calf, is a black bruise about as big around as a silver dollar. It'll heal, I think, in time for the first cross-country meet of the season. It'll have to.

I set my flag up so it's flying again. Then I flip my tent over. I fish my binoculars out of the mess and peer across the lake. Both Brooke's and Shannon's flags are flying. I turn and search behind me and see Derrick's flag flying as well.

I walk a few steps, testing out my calf. It throbs but I can tell it'll be okay for the few miles I'll need to hike down to camp. I keep walking, picking my way through the rocky tundra for a quarter of a mile, until I get to my food cache. We keep our food in these black plastic bear-proof canisters that screw closed. Down at Simon Lake we've got camp stoves to cook on, but on our solos we only bring simple food. Raisins, peanuts, dried fruit, cheese, and tortillas.

I unscrew the top half of the canister from the bottom half, pull out the peanuts, and munch down a couple of handfuls. I screw the two halves back together, and then I look down toward the lake, scanning with my binoculars, but I don't see the camp's green flag. It could've fallen like mine did and they just haven't put it back up yet. I limp a little farther along the ridge, knowing that eventually the whole camp complex will come into view, the outdoor kitchen with the low blue tarp and the dome tents for sleeping.

I keep walking and looking, walking and looking, but when the end of the lake comes into view all I see is a massive pile of boulders and smaller rocks and a brownish-gray dusty haze. When I scan the slope above the pile, I see a monstrous scar on the mountainside.

And then I realize that somewhere under that massive pile of rocks lies the Simon Lake Leadership Camp.

Four staff. Twenty participants—minus us four on our solos, which makes sixteen.

I scan the boulder pile, searching for movement, for a color of clothing different from the gray-brown of the rock. And then I notice the rock slide is so huge that the bottom end of it is actually in the lake. Like a new peninsula has been created from the slide.

And the camp had been thirty or forty feet back from the lake-shore.

I let my binoculars hang from my neck, and I take a breath. I swallow the peanuts that are trying to come back up. I jog back to my food canister, unscrew it, and stuff my binoculars inside. I can't take them with me right now because I need to move as fast as I can.

Then I start picking my way down the mountain. The wind is blowing from behind me. A dull ache settles into my calf but doesn't stop me from pushing on. At this pace, in a couple of hours I'll be down there, searching for survivors.

CHAPTER 3

NOW THAT I'M AT THE lakeshore and walking toward it, the rock pile from the avalanche is even bigger than I imagined. It's as long as two or three football fields and a couple of stories high.

"Josh," I hear a faint voice call. "Josh."

I scan the massive mound of rocks and dirt but see no one.

"I'm coming!" I yell back, and pick up the pace. My calf throbs but doesn't slow me down. Now I can see a person scrambling down the mountain of rock toward me. If there's one survivor, I think, there must be more. But as we approach each other at the base of the slide, I shake my head.

"Brooke," I say. "I thought maybe you were, you know, someone who was actually in the camp." Don't get me wrong, I'm happy to see Brooke. But I figured she was okay since she was up high in a mostly flat area and I saw her green flag.

"I've been screaming your name," Brooke says, "since we both started walking toward the lake. Didn't you hear me?"

"No," I say. "The wind was at my back the whole way down. It was pretty strong up there."

Brooke nods. "The wind. Duh. I didn't even think of that." She points behind her to the ocean of rock. "What are we going to do?"

We're standing next to each other now, staring at the slide. The scar on the mountainside above it—where it all came from—is like the inside of a huge brown bowl that's been tipped on its side.

I turn to Brooke. "We need to search for survivors. Maybe people are trapped under there. Maybe when the rocks settled there were spaces left." I pause, trying to picture it in my mind. "You know. If two huge rocks ended up like this." I put the tips of my fingers together to form an inverted V. "If a tent was squished between them, and then more rocks piled on top, then the tent and whoever was in it would get buried but not squished."

"Josh," Brooke says. "Are you looking at the same thing I'm looking at?" She makes a sweeping motion with her hand, and that's when I notice that it's all cut up. "The pile is like thirty feet tall. And, it's long." She points. "It's sticking into the lake. The camp might be underwater *and* covered with rocks." She shakes her head. "How are we going to search?"

I look her in the eye and say, "We crawl all over the rock pile. We yell. We listen. If we hear something, we try to move the rocks."

"And if we don't hear anything?" Brooke asks.

"Then we move the rocks we can move and keep searching," I say softly. "If there's someone alive under there, we need to find them. They might be injured. They might die if we don't get to them in time."

"Josh, I'm just trying to be real." Brooke brushes her hair back, and I see a bruise on her forehead and scratches on her cheek. "I climbed over that rock pile to get to you and there's not one scrap of clothing or a food canister or anything visible. Nothing."

"With Derrick and Shannon there'll be four of us to move rocks," I say. "Their camps are farther away than ours, but they've got to be on their way down by now."

"What makes you so sure of that?" Brooke says. "My tent was swallowed into a crack that opened up, and I was inside it. While I was clawing my way out, a rock fell and hit me on the forehead. I thought I was going to die right then."

"I saw your flag flying, so I knew you were okay," I say. "I saw Derrick's and Shannon's, too."

Brooke shakes her head. "I never touched my flag. It stayed up through the whole quake. I could still be in that hole, but my green flag would be flying. This little flag system only works if someone can actually get to their flag to change the color."

I start telling Brooke about how I almost got swallowed as the ground split beneath me when I hear a humming noise in the distance. I stop talking and we both look skyward.

We yell and wave our arms when we realize what we're seeing, but the planes are so high up we must look like specks of dust to them down here. The camp buried under a pile of rocks must make us an even harder target to spot.

"I counted twelve planes or jets or whatever they were," I say.

"Who cares?" Brooke says. "They didn't see us." She's got her arms crossed over her chest like she's angry.

"It must mean lots of people are helping out," I say. "Think about places where people actually live. The quake probably caused a lot of damage. Maybe whole houses were swallowed like your tent was."

Brooke shivers. "I hear you, Josh. I just want to get out of here and see if my parents are okay."

"Our parents will make sure someone comes for us. But right now, we've got to search for more survivors."

The wind is starting to chill me now that we've been standing around talking. I glance up the ridge. I have warmer clothes and rain gear up there, but it'll take at least three hours to get back up. Maybe longer with my injured calf.

I turn my attention to the rock slide. "Let's crawl around on top of it and listen. And yell into the rocks and see if we hear anyone yell back or make a noise." Last night I kept trying to think about a way to stay in touch with Brooke after the Leadership Camp ends, a way to have her want to spend time with me once we're back in Fairbanks, but right now all I can think about is Theo and everyone else buried under this enormous pile of rocks.

Brooke and I walk side by side and then start climbing on top of the rock slide. Brooke puts her face into an opening between two giant rocks and yells, *"Hello,"* and then puts her ear into the opening and listens. After several seconds she shakes her head and moves on.

We spread out, each yelling into small openings and then turning to listen for responses. Every time I have to use my right foot to boost myself up higher, my calf throbs, but I keep going. I'm starting to warm up from the movement but my voice is going hoarse from all the yelling.

My mind jumps to Derrick and Shannon. Their solo camps were at least twice as far away as mine and Brooke's, but if they're okay they should be showing up soon. I stand up straight and turn toward the high ridge where Derrick's camp is. I put my hand above my forehead to shield my eyes from the glare of the sun, which is growing brighter by the minute.

Before I can really focus, Brooke shouts, "Josh, I think I found something!"

CHAPTER 4

I SCRAMBLE ACROSS THE ROCK slide to where Brooke is. She's lying on her stomach and peering into a small opening.

I sit next to Brooke. "What is it?"

She pushes up into a sitting position and her shoulder brushes mine. "Just look." Frowning, she points toward the opening.

I lie down and press my face into the gap but it's too dark to see anything, so I shift backward to let some light in, and then I see it. Several feet down, but it's there. "Okay, I see the flag." I sit up and face Brooke. "It was on the highest point down here, so it makes sense it'd be closest to the surface."

Brooke shakes her head. "It's more than just the flag. Didn't you see the orange pole? Didn't you—"

"Yeah," I say. "I saw the pole, too."

Brooke turns her head sideways, then thrusts her face back into the gap with her shoulder pressing against my thigh. "There," she says. She pulls on my arm. "Look."

I scoot in next to her, and she shifts her head away from the hole to make room for mine.

Now I'm looking down the hole.

"Okay," she says. And I can feel her breath on my ear. "Look just below the flag. You see the orange pole, right?"

"Right," I say.

"Then you see a little break or space, and then more orange pole. Right?"

"Right," I say.

"Look at that space."

I focus on the dark space between the two segments of orange, and at first all I see is nothing. Like maybe a rock smashed the pole. But then I see something else. Movement. A dark-skinned hand is barely opening and closing around the pole. There's only one person at the camp whose hand that could be.

"Theo!" I shout. "Theo. We're here. Are you okay?" I press my ear to the hole and listen but hear nothing, and my heart sags. Maybe he's unconscious. Or maybe his face is so trapped that he can't yell. But his fingers—they moved—so he's got to be alive.

I sit up and turn to Brooke. "Help me. We've got to get him out of there."

"Brooke. Josh."

Brooke and I turn toward the voice, and there's Shannon, almost on top of us.

I stare at the side of her face. "Are you okay?" Some of her hair, which is usually tied back in a ponytail, is plastered to her cheek—anchored there by blood.

"I'm fine. I took a fall and landed on my face." She motions at the buried camp with her hand. "I've got nothing to complain about."

When I look closely at Shannon's eyes, I can see that she's holding back tears, just like I was when I first took in the quadrillion tons of rock that now cover the camp and everyone who was down here.

I point down and say, "Theo's under there. Brooke spotted his hand through this hole. We've seen it move. We've got to get these rocks off him now."

"I'm surprised there's no one else here," Shannon says. "With all the planes and helicopters flying around, I was sure that a helicopter would've landed down here."

"Helicopters?" I say, looking at Brooke. "All we saw were planes flying super high."

"There were helicopters lower down. Lots of them. You probably didn't see them," Shannon explains, "because of the steep slopes surrounding the lake."

"Helicopters or no helicopters," I say, "we've got to help Theo."

For the next few minutes we work together, trying to move the smaller of the two rocks on either side of the opening. If only there were some trees around, we could use a big branch to create some leverage. Instead, Shannon and Brooke are pulling on the rock from behind and I'm pushing on it. We've gotten it to move maybe a foot, but it keeps sliding back to its original spot whenever we let up. It must weigh at least two hundred pounds, and it's mostly wedged in place.

If Derrick were here, it might make a difference. He's the biggest of the four of us. And that gets me wondering where he is and if he's okay. I mean, his camp is about as far away as Shannon's.

"What if we all push it?" Shannon says. "But not in the direction we're trying right now." She points. "Let's push it down the hill instead of across."

Brooke says, "There's not much space for all of us on the uphill side, but it's worth a try."

We regroup so we're three across on the uphill side. I'm in a half squat, and I've got my arms and chest pressed up against the rock like I'm trying to tackle it. Shannon and Brooke are on either side of me, pushing on the rock above where I am, their sides pressing into the tops of my shoulders.

"Okay," Shannon says, "on the count of three."

But she doesn't even get to *one* before the ground starts to shake with a strong aftershock.

"Hang on." I hug the rock and feel Shannon and Brooke collapse onto it as well. My feet slide backward, and now I'm on my knees and my head is being jostled between Shannon's and Brooke's hips, but we're all leaning onto the rock, riding out the aftershock. I don't know if it's because of the aftershock or in spite of it, but I can feel the rock starting to give. Starting to slide downhill.

CHAPTER 5

HIS GRIP IN MY HAND is weak. "Theo," I shout. "Theo. Hang on. We're going to get you out." I drop his hand and turn to Shannon and Brooke, who are moving smaller rocks away from where we think Theo is buried, based on the angle and position that his hand is in. We're trying to clear where we think his head is in case he's having trouble breathing. The big rock that slid during the aftershock has made removing other rocks easier, but there's no telling what got rearranged under the surface.

"Help me with this one," Shannon says, her hands under one side of a rock the size of a daypack.

I squat and put my hands under the opposite side of the rock, and on *three* we lift it enough to tip it out of the way.

"I need both of you for this one," Brooke says. The rock she's working on is easily twice as big as the one Shannon and I just barely moved.

The three of us work at it and manage to move it about a foot and a half, and by doing that we can see another part of Theo.

Only it's not the part I was expecting.

"He must be curled up or twisted or something," I say.

I touch his newly exposed knee but don't feel any response. I grab his hand and feel his weak grip in return, so I know he's still with us.

"Maybe his head is over there." Shannon points a few feet away and back from his knee. "Maybe his leg was slammed forward. Picture him in a lying position instead of standing straight up."

"The quicker we expose more of him the better," I say. My mind scans the rock pile, picturing twenty people buried under here. We haven't heard one voice. But we didn't hear Theo's either, and right now he's alive, so maybe more people are, too. Maybe everyone is.

We keep moving more rocks, concentrating on his hand because his arm will eventually lead to his shoulder, which has to be close to his head. I don't know if his body is vertical, horizontal, or something in between.

After we remove a bunch of medium-sized rocks the size of shoeboxes and expose Theo's arm up to the elbow, Brooke says, "It looks like his arm is going straight down, but with his knee right there, it's like he's lying down but holding his arm straight up."

"Theo," I yell. "We're coming. Hang on."

"We've got to make the area wider," Shannon says. "If he's hurt, we can't just yank him out of there."

"Let's get to his head"—I point to the spot where I think it should be—"in case he's having trouble breathing. Then we can make the hole wider to ease him out."

The next rock we dislodge is red and sticky on the bottom side.

I get this sick feeling in my stomach. Not like I'm going to puke, but more like dread. How are we going to deal with injuries, with bleeding, when we've got nothing? I think of the small first aid kit back up in my tent, hours away. We each have one, but none of us brought it down here.

Shannon's voice snaps me back to the bloody rock cradled in my arms. "We've got to be careful," she says. "The rocks may be keeping him from bleeding because of the pressure they're exerting."

"We still have to get him out of there," I respond.

"I know," Shannon says. "But we might have to try to stop some bleeding along the way. I think—"

"How?" Brooke breaks in.

"Pressure." Shannon pauses. "Clothing for bandages."

I toss the rock aside, rip my pile jacket off, and then pull my T-shirt over my head. "We can start with this." I set my T-shirt down and put my pile jacket back on.

Shannon kneels next to Theo's exposed forearm. "I can't see where the blood came from."

Brooke and I dislodge a large rock and haul it away while Shannon holds Theo's forearm.

"I think I see his shoulder," Shannon says. "His arm got twisted behind him. I see where he's bleeding. Just above the elbow. Josh, hold his arm just like I am."

I take Theo's arm, and Shannon reaches into the small opening Brooke and I created by moving that large rock.

"Brooke," Shannon says, "hand me the shirt."

Brooke picks up the shirt. "Couldn't he get infected? This shirt is all sweaty. Gross."

"Can't be too choosy right now," I say, keeping my grip on Theo's arm. Brooke doesn't say anything back. We both keep our eyes on Shannon.

After a minute Shannon says, "I've almost got it. I just have to make it a little tighter."

She does something, and I feel Theo's grip tighten.

"It's okay, Theo," I say. "We're just patching you up." I don't know if he can hear me, but after I say it, his hand relaxes a little bit. I wish he would say something, anything. Even a muffled groan so we'd know where his head is.

Shannon shifts her body and tilts her head toward me. "I should keep putting pressure on this wound while you and Brooke move more rocks."

"Is it bad?" I ask softly, not wanting Theo to hear.

"It's not good," Shannon responds. "But keeping pressure on it will slow down the bleeding."

I nod, and as I'm gently releasing Theo's arm, Brooke says, "You guys, there's something moving along the edge of the rock slide."

I stand up and see a big grizzly bear walking on all four legs, coming our way.

"I left my bear spray in my tent," I whisper.

"So did I," Shannon says.

Brooke takes a step toward me and says softly, "Me too."

CHAPTER 6

THE MASS OF BROWN FUR is about two hundred yards away from us. I don't know if it came down the mountainside like I did or if it came up from the lowlands and walked the lakeshore. Either way, here it is—way too close for comfort.

We watch as the bear climbs up on the landslide. It keeps stopping and sticking its face into the rocks. Then it starts pawing at the rocks, like it's trying to dig.

I glance down at Theo's arm and knee. He'd be an attractive meal for a grizzly.

We talk quietly about what to do.

Brooke wants to yell and scream at the bear to try to scare it away before it comes any closer. "We should let it know we're here."

Shannon thinks that since the bear is still pretty far away we should just keep working on getting Theo out.

And I think we should do a little bit of both.

I say, "What if the bear is digging toward a person who is alive, like Theo? We can't let that happen. I—"

Brooke cuts me off. "Didn't you see all that blood on Theo? And now, with that bear so close, we're risking our lives for a lost cause. You really think he has a chance?" She shakes her head.

"Yeah, I do. He's alive," I say softly, staring her down, when really I want to shout into her face. "What if it were you?"

"Look," Shannon says, pointing toward the bear.

More rocks clatter as the bear digs. Now it has its whole head in the landslide, and all we can see are its massive shoulders and body straining as it pulls and tugs.

Some orange starts to show, and then the bear stumbles backward with a big orange dry bag in its jaws. At the bottom of the rock slide the bear drops the bag and starts pawing at it.

"The bear found our kitchen," I say, "or, at least part of it."

We had an electric fence around the kitchen area, powered by a couple of batteries hooked up to some small solar panels, but that system must be smashed up.

In no time the bear has shredded one side of the dry bag and is now pulling out smaller bags with its jaws.

Shannon says, "Let's keep working on Theo while the bear is busy."

I try to forget about the bear and what Brooke said about Theo and just focus on digging him out.

We all keep moving rocks, and we uncover Theo's other elbow and then the rest of his arm. And under his bent arm, we get the first glimpse of the top of his head.

"Careful," I say as we move small rocks and uncover the rest of Theo's head. I put the back of my hand in front of his mouth and nose and feel a tiny stream of air run across my skin. "He's breathing."

"That's great," Shannon says, "but he's still bleeding. It's hard to tell how much, but there's more blood since I stopped applying pressure and started moving rocks again."

Shannon kneels and then sits beside Theo's arm and applies pressure to the wound.

I glance at the bear. Luckily, it is still busy devouring our food.

Brooke starts moving more rocks, and I do the same. We work in silence. I'm still pissed that she thinks Theo is as good as dead. She was here when he squeezed my hand. Clearly he was alive then and still is now.

We uncover his torso. He's got a pile jacket on, and we don't see any blood seeping through it. It appears that he's in a sitting position with one leg scrunched up. Shannon is supporting him with her body while keeping pressure on his arm wound.

"We need to free his other leg," Brooke says, acting like it was her idea to dig him out.

I don't argue with her because I agree. As I move more rocks, my mind pounds away.

Maybe she's figured out that she was wrong.

Maybe I should drop the whole thing.

But how could she even question whether we should try to dig him out?

We're going to need to deal with that.

If there's one thing they drilled into us at this camp, it's that you need to deal with the big things.

But right now, the biggest, most immediate thing is getting Theo out of the rocks.

Still, at some point, we've got to talk about what Brooke said. Her words—*we're risking our lives for a lost cause*—replay in my brain.

We keep working in silence and now have most of Theo uncovered. Just one leg from the knee down remains trapped, but one of the rocks over it is a big one—too big for just the two of us.

Brooke is already reaching under the rock, trying to get a firm hold.

"Shannon," I say. "We're going to need your help with this one."

She nods and eases Theo into a lying position, and then lets go of his arm where she's been applying pressure.

As she starts to stand up, I hear a clattering sound from the bear's direction.

We all turn and look. I can feel the wind directly on my face, blowing up from the valley.

And below the bear, about a quarter mile down the lakeshore, we see him. "That's got to be Derrick," I say.

"He must not know about the bear," Brooke says.

The bear is now standing on two legs and facing Derrick's direction. I think about the wind hitting my face and say, "It knows about him."

Then the bear drops back down onto four legs, turns, and starts running away from Derrick and directly toward us.

CHAPTER 7

"BROOKE, SHANNON," I SAY. "STAND with me in front of Theo. We have to appear big."

We've all been taught what to do in case we encounter a bear. It was drilled into us the first couple of days of camp, but now that it's happening, my mind is racing and my body is shaking.

We're bunched up shoulder to shoulder. I'm guessing Shannon and Brooke are both wishing they hadn't left their bear spray behind just like I am. We were taught to never go anywhere without it. *Got to get out of your tent to take a leak, well, don't forget your bear spray.*

The bear is already agitated. Catching Derrick's scent obviously spooked it, but because of the direction the wind is blowing, there's no way it'd catch ours. Will it feel trapped between the three of us and Derrick? Will it fight or flee? Luckily, the rock slide is so jagged and slanted that even a bear can't run full speed across it—but the bear is moving in our direction.

"If it doesn't back off," Brooke says, "we may have to."

We were taught to back away slowly from a bear but to stand your ground if it was pursuing you—but that didn't take into account protecting an injured person.

"We can't back off," I counter. "Only three of us can walk."

"What would Theo want you to do?" Brooke asks. "Get mauled because of him?" She shakes her head.

"I don't care what Theo would want me to do," I say. "I know what he would do if the situation were flipped. He wouldn't abandon us."

Shannon doesn't say anything, which I take to mean that she's not planning on leaving Theo.

The bear has halved the distance to us—it's only one hundred yards away—but has slowed down. Still, with Derrick continuing his forward push to get here, the bear isn't going to be turning around.

"Would Theo want you to die defending him while he has almost no chance of survival himself?" Brooke says. "He's lost a lot of blood. He can't talk. He's barely breathing, and he's still stuck in the rocks. He's—"

"Hello. Hello." Derrick's voice echoes off the steep mountain walls surrounding the lake and seems to come at us from all directions. But the bear can smell where he is and keeps moving away from the smell. I still don't know if Derrick knows there's a bear. I don't know if he's even spotted us yet.

"We need to make some noise," Shannon says. "The bear might not know we're in its path."

"You two can yell and shout all you want," Brooke says. "I'm moving out of the way."

"And what if the bear comes at you?" Shannon asks.

Brooke scowls. "Why can't we all move out of the way?" She takes a step sideways, like she's going to abandon us, but doesn't go any farther.

Maybe she's mustered up an ounce of compassion for Theo. Maybe she's realized that his life is worth just as much as hers. Or, maybe it's the thought of being alone and confronting the bear that is just too freaking scary for her. Maybe she realizes she has more of a chance of saving herself if she stays put.

"Hey, bear," Shannon yells, just like we were taught. I join in and so does Brooke, and now we're all yelling the phrase in sync.

Maybe it's the strong headwind that keeps the bear from noticing our voices.

Maybe it's Derrick's scent that keeps pushing it forward.

Or maybe it's the smell of Theo's blood.

Whatever's driving it, the bear just keeps on coming like it's set on autopilot.

CHAPTER 8

THE THREE OF US KEEP yelling. I pick up the orange wand that used to hold the green flag—the pole that Theo's hand was clutching when the landslide buried him—and start waving it in front of me. It's flexible but it's also strong; it will bend a lot but not break easily.

The bear pulls up about thirty feet from us and stands on its hind legs. It wags its head back and forth a couple of times, drops back down on four legs, comes forward about ten feet, and then stands up again.

We've all stopped yelling because the bear obviously knows we're here. If it weren't for Theo, right now we would all take a step or two backward, and if the bear stayed put, we would continue to slowly back away. If the bear advanced, we would stop retreating so we wouldn't look like prey.

"Don't look it in the eye," I whisper. Standing our ground is definitely challenging it, but staring it down could make the situation worse. The end of the wand is bouncing gently. I've stopped waving it, but it's still extended toward the grizzly.

I hear some rocks clattering, and so does the bear because it turns in the direction of the noise. Derrick is at the edge of the landslide now, where the bear had been tearing through one of our food bags.

I don't know if he sees the standoff we're in, but now he's yelling, "Hey, bear," just like we were.

My mind is a confused fog. None of the bear encounter training has prepared me for this. Do we continue to shout? Do we remain quiet? Do we wait to see what the bear does now that Derrick is yelling? But if we wait and the bear charges, it'll be on us in less than a second.

I wonder what Shannon and Brooke are thinking. I glance at each of them and raise my eyebrows.

"Rocks," Shannon mouths, then points down. I don't know if Brooke can see what Shannon said, but she definitely saw where she pointed because she quickly bends forward and picks up a fist-sized stone. Shannon and I do the same. Now I've got the wand in one hand and a rock in the other.

Do we throw them while the bear is focused on Derrick? Is that Shannon's plan? Or do we use them only if the bear advances on us?

Shannon cocks her arm back and waits for us to do the same. Derrick is still yelling, "Hey, bear," and the bear continues to look in his direction. And the wind is still blowing in our faces.

Shannon lets her rock fly, and Brooke and I follow with ours. Shannon's rock hits the bear square in the back, and as the bear turns, Brooke's rock nails it in the side of the head and my rock hits its shoulder.

The bear drops to all four legs and scrambles straight over the rock slide toward the lake. When the bear gets to the edge of the lake, it splashes into the water and starts swimming toward the opposite shore, which is steep and shaded, with pockets of last winter's snow still present.

I drop the wand and let out a breath that I didn't know I was holding. Brooke takes a couple of steps in Derrick's direction.

Then I hear Shannon's voice behind me. "Theo. Theo. Stay with us."

CHAPTER 9

"HEY," DERRICK SAYS.

I look up from where I'm kneeling next to Theo and shake my head. Shannon and Brooke are sitting on either side of me.

Shannon says, "We lost him."

Derrick takes off his pack and sets it down. "Did a bear get him?"

"The avalanche did," I say. "It might've gotten everyone"—I pause because I can feel my voice starting to crack—"except us."

The wind is still blowing, and now that we're just sitting and not moving around, I'm starting to cool off. A shiver runs up my spine.

"What do you mean, everyone?" Derrick asks.

"Look around," Brooke says. "The whole camp is buried under tons of rock. It took forever to dig Theo out. And it was all for nothing. We almost got mauled by a bear, too. You chased it right toward us." Brooke frowns.

"I didn't know there was a bear until I saw the mess down there." Derrick points to the edge of the landslide where the bear tore into the food bag. "Even then, I didn't know it was still around. Don't blame me."

"No one is blaming you." *Except maybe Brooke*, I think but don't say. "I—"

"We have to bury him," Shannon says softly. "Or else scavengers will get him. Ravens. Wolverines. Bears."

"No way. We just unburied him," Brooke says. "I don't want—"

"You are so sick," I shout. "Don't you care about anyone but yourself?"

"I worked for hours moving rocks when he was barely alive," Brooke shouts back. "I stayed here when the bear approached. I put his life before mine just like you did. But now that he's dead, what's the point?"

"The point," Shannon says softly, "is that the more scavengers are attracted to this spot where the camp used to be, the more likely that we'll keep having encounters like we just had."

"Plus," I say, "it's the respectful thing to do. Eventually his body is going to get hauled out of here. His parents are going to see it."

"Dudes," Derrick says, "let's quit wasting time and energy arguing and get the job done." He sets his bear spray down. "Now, how do we want to do this?"

We decide to cover Theo with small rocks and use the wand as a marker for where he's buried. As we work, Derrick recounts what happened to him during the earthquake, which is pretty different from what happened to the rest of us.

"I was finally asleep after being awake most of the night when the quake rolled me around and threw me up toward the ceiling of my tent," Derrick explains. "I thought maybe a bear was batting me around. I was fighting to get out of my sleeping bag so I could reach for my bear spray. Then I thought I should just stay in my bag because it'd offer a layer of protection against the bear, so I curled up and pulled the drawstring tight. The ground kept rolling under me, and that's how I figured out it was an earthquake."

After the rolling stopped, Derrick stuck his head out of the tent and then stood up. The ground hadn't gotten all split up around his campsite like it had at mine and Brooke's. Through his binoculars he saw that all three of our flags were still flying green. Since he was dead tired from last night, he went back to sleep for a while. He remembers hearing some jets and maybe some helicopters while he tried to get back to sleep. When he finally got up and hiked to the spot where he could see the camp, he saw the monstrous collapsed mountainside of rocks, so he packed up as fast as he could and headed down.

We are all sharing a moment of silence around Theo's temporary grave when it starts to rain lightly. Derrick is the only one with his pack and bear spray.

"We need to get our supplies," I say, "before we freeze."

Brooke points across the lake and up toward her camp. "I'm beat. I don't want to hike all the way back up there right now. Besides, someone will rescue us. Our parents will make it happen."

I think about having Brooke stay here while we pack up her camp, but we've got one canister of bear spray among the four of us and we know there's at least one bear in the area. Plus, with the rain, it'd be easy to freeze to death even in the summer if the temperature dropped.

"We all need to go," I say. "You stay here with nothing, and they could be recovering your body instead of rescuing you."

"Easy for you to say," Brooke responds. "You live to run."

"He's right," Shannon says. "Right now, without any of our gear, we need to move to just stay warm."

"Let's do it this way," Derrick says. "We all hike to Brooke's camp. Once we have her bear spray, two of us hike to Shannon's camp and two of us hike to Josh's camp. And then we all meet back here."

"I'm game for that." I nod once. The rain is starting to chill me, and I want to get moving.

"Good idea," Shannon says. She stands up.

"Whatever," Brooke mumbles. "Like any of us have a choice."

We are about halfway across the rock slide when a set of jets screams across the sky. Then in the distance both to the left and right of the jets we see squadrons of helicopters. They are far enough away that we can't see how many there are, but they make that unmistakable *whop-whop-whop* helicopter noise. Then another set of jets flies overhead.

"The quake must've been pretty widespread," Derrick says, "for the military to be getting involved."

"See," Brooke says, "we're going to be rescued. They're already out looking for people."

"Maybe my dad is flying one of those choppers," Derrick says. "But if he is, that means they're already coming back from somewhere, because they're flying west to east." Derrick takes his pack off, wrestles out his binoculars, and scans the horizon. "They're too far away for me to tell what kind they are, but they don't look like the kind my dad flies."

CHAPTER 10

WE REACH THE EDGE OF the landslide and walk single file on the narrow trail along the lakeshore in the spitting rain. After a mile or so, we start heading up the ridge toward Brooke's campsite.

The pain in my calf is knotted, and stings with every step. If I were home, I'd need to rest it for a few days to let it heal so I could be at my best for cross-country races, but now I'm probably doing more and more damage, not that I have a choice. Even with the pain, I could go for miles and miles. I'm starting to outdistance everyone on the climb, so I stop on a flat spot and wait. With one canister of bear spray among the four of us, we need to stay close to each other.

When we're all together, Shannon says, "When we get back down to the landslide, we should try to find the satellite phone. Then we could just call for help."

"How are we going to know where to dig?" Derrick asks.

"We know where the flag was. And, thanks to the bear, we know where the kitchen was," I say. "So, we should be able to map it all out. Plus, they put our cell phones in with the satellite phone. Maybe they would work, too. You know, from a high spot."

"I doubt it," Shannon says. "We are way out here. Hundreds of miles from nowhere."

"Then why would they collect the phones from us?" I ask. "If they didn't work, then they wouldn't have bothered collecting them."

Derrick responds, "They didn't want us listening to music, looking at pictures, playing video games. All the crap my parents said it'd be good for me to get away from."

Brooke hasn't said anything for a while. The rain has washed most of the blood off her face, exposing the scratches that were bleeding. They look like they sting. Maybe because she can tell I'm looking at her, she turns toward me.

Then she says, "Cell phones." She brushes her hair out of her eyes. "I've still got mine."

"You snuck it back?" I ask. "Gutsy."

"I never turned it in," she responds. "Well, I turned in *a phone*, it just wasn't *my phone*. And they only work up high, and even up there"—she nods toward where we are going—"just barely."

"Bringing two phones," Derrick says. "I wish I'd thought of that."

"My dad," Brooke says. "He made me do it. Told me to use it just for emergencies. He gave me a solar charger, too." She shakes her head and says softly, "My dad. The *gadget guy*—that's what he calls himself—comes through."

The rain lightens up as we pick our way toward Brooke's camp. A pale outline of the sun shows through the thinning clouds, but the wind is still blowing.

We top the first ridge above the lake and stop again.

"Too bad they didn't let us use this ridge," I say, staring up to the next one, where Brooke's camp is.

"Self-reliance," Derrick says. "They didn't want us so close that we could just run back to camp if we got scared or whatever."

Shannon turns to Brooke. "Did you use your phone? Did it really work?"

"One bar. I sent my dad a text last night," Brooke says. "It was delivered, but I never heard back from him."

Another squadron of jets screams over us, just specks in the sky. "Can you call a jet on a cell phone?" I ask.

Derrick laughs. "Only if you know someone on the jet and their number."

"What about the satellite phone? Can you call a jet with that?" Shannon asks, looking at Derrick.

"I don't know." Derrick shrugs. "Just because my dad's in the military, it doesn't mean I know everything." He looks away. "He barely talks to me."

"Who cares," Brooke says. "When we get to my tent, I'll just text my dad again. He'll know what to do."

"I just hope all of our parents are okay," I say.

Everyone nods and we keep walking.

I picture our house in Fairbanks. If the quake could crumble the rocky slope above Simon Lake, it could easily collapse a house.

I just hope it wasn't as strong in Fairbanks as it was here.

When we get to the ridge with Brooke's tent on it, there's a series of cracks in the ground. I turn to Brooke. "The exact same thing happened on my ridge." I point across the lake to land approximately on the same level as where we're standing.

"At least your tent didn't get swallowed," Brooke says.

In the distance we can all see her green flag, but there's no sign of her tent. I try to imagine what it would've been like to be inside my tent and have the ground open up and swallow me. Maybe that's why she was so much more freaked out than Shannon and me. Maybe that's why she was acting so selfish, like she didn't care if Theo lived or died and didn't even want to try to save him.

Maybe.

Or, maybe that's the way she is.

"The ground split right below me," I say. "After I was tackled by the first tremor, I rolled onto my back to get away from the split. But being in a tent, that must've been scary."

"I was like a cat in a bag that had been tossed into a lake." Brooke pauses. "I was drowning. At least that's how it felt."

No one says anything for a few seconds, but then Shannon says,

"It's hard to believe the quake just happened this morning. It already feels like a long time ago. I mean, so much has gone on since then." A tear spills down her cheek and she wipes it away.

We all nod in silence. With digging Theo out and then facing the bear, we haven't really dealt with the reality that there are probably a lot of dead people down there. People we were living closely with until this morning. It just as easily could have been one of us, or all of us, buried down there. Everyone had a couple of days for a solo experience, and ours just happened to fall when the quake struck.

"After we get our supplies, so we can, you know, not die," I say, "we need to keep searching for survivors. Just because Theo died"—I can feel my voice starting to crack—"doesn't mean everyone else did."

CHAPTER 11

"YOU WERE IN THAT THING when the ground opened up?" Derrick points to Brooke's tent, which is sitting on its side at the bottom of a crack that opened up during the quake. "Unbelievable. What are the chances?"

Brooke nods. "Climbing out wasn't easy." She touches the bruise on her forehead.

"Let's haul it out of the hole," I say, wanting to keep us moving since we have my camp and Shannon's to dismantle after this one.

I lie down on my stomach at the edge of the hole. I can feel moisture being absorbed by my shirt and pants from the wet ground, but I've got a set of rain gear at my camp so I don't care. I reach into the hole but can't quite make contact with the tent.

Derrick takes his pack off and lies next to me, which is good, because out of the four of us, he's got the longest arms. He reaches down and grabs a corner of the tent and starts pulling. "Josh, as soon as you can, grab part of it," he says.

"I got it," I say. And together the two of us keep pulling.

Shannon and Brooke, who've each knelt on either side of Derrick and me, grab the sides of the tent as it gets higher, and before you know it, we've got Brooke's tent on the ground next to us.

We roll it over so it's sitting the way it's supposed to, and Brooke sticks her head in the unzipped door. After a few seconds she comes out with her cell phone.

She peers at the screen. "My dad never wrote back. Or if he did, the message didn't get to me." She types something with her thumbs, then frowns. "It didn't go through."

"Maybe the system is overloaded," Shannon says. "You know, because of the earthquake, people are probably calling and texting their families all over the state to see who is okay and who needs help."

"I guess." Brooke types something else and hits send. "It still won't go through."

"People will come for us anyway," Derrick says. "This whole leadership-camp thing was supposed to be over in like two more days. Even if we have to wait that long, they'll come."

Brooke takes all her stuff out of her tent. While she starts loading her pack, Shannon and I take the tent apart and Derrick goes to get Brooke's food, which is stashed nearby.

"I know you and Theo were close," Shannon says. "Maybe if I had kept the pressure on his wound instead of standing up and helping keep the bear away, he would've made it."

"Shannon, we all did what we had to do. He wouldn't have lasted as long as he did if it weren't for you." I keep stuffing the tent into its bag. "I still can't believe he's gone."

"I think he was with us." Shannon stops breaking down the tent poles and looks me in the eye. "The way he would squeeze your hand when you talked to him. I think he could hear you. And that probably brought him some peace. He didn't die alone. You gave him that."

A tear runs down my cheek and I wipe it away. "Thanks," I say. "His parents are going to be devastated." I think about all the others down there, and my stomach clenches up. They *all* have parents. "Let's finish this so we can get back and search for more survivors."

After Brooke's camp is all packed up, Brooke and Shannon head for Shannon's camp up to the next ridge, and Derrick and I head for mine.

We walk fast side by side on the tundra, deciding not to go down to the lake and back up, but to stay up high to circle around to my camp.

The sun is breaking through the clouds, and I'm squinting to keep it out of my eyes.

"We've got some big rocks to move down there." I point to the buried camp as we walk.

"I get what you're saying," Derrick says. "I mean, I want to find anyone who is alive, too. But think about it." Derrick stumbles on a rock but regains his balance. "Theo had the flag wand in his hand. He was on the high point of land in the camp." Derrick pauses. "Remember how that little spot was like ten feet higher than the rest of the camp?"

"Yeah," I say. "I remember."

"Dude, that means everyone else was probably ten feet lower than him when the mountainside cut loose."

"I know all that," I say. "But how do you explain the food bag that the bear found pretty close to the surface?"

"I don't know." Derrick shrugs. "Maybe some stuff got pushed along by the slide before more rocks fell on top of it?"

"So," I say, "maybe a tent with a person in it got pushed like that food bag did. Maybe that happened to more than one tent. We owe it to everyone to search. The fact that we survived is just dumb luck."

"Hey, man," Derrick says. "I'm not saying we shouldn't search. I'm just not that optimistic about what we'll find."

CHAPTER 12

SIX DAYS LATER AND WE'VE got four more shallow graves all in a row next to where we buried Theo. We've built rock cairns at the head of each grave.

"Why hasn't anybody come?" Derrick asks. "My dad would be on this in a heartbeat if I didn't show up on time. If we *all* didn't show up."

"We don't know what it's like anywhere but here," Shannon says. "Maybe there was widespread damage. And mass casualties."

I point at the shallow graves and say, "There's no reason to stay anymore. I mean, if I thought there was still a chance that someone was alive, I'd keep digging." I feel my eyes getting hot. "We need to leave this place."

"But if we leave," Brooke argues, "and they come after we've gone, they'll just give us up for dead, too. They won't even look for us."

"We'll write them a note," I respond. "We can put it in one of the empty bear-proof food containers and we can plant all of our flags around it so there's no way they can miss it."

"What are we going to do after that?" Brooke says. "Walk out?" She shakes her head.

"There was a plan," Derrick says. "Remember? We were all briefed on the routes to follow if there was an emergency and we had to evacuate on foot. West to Talkeetna or east to Lake Louise."

"They were about the same distance," I say, remembering Theo describing part of the plan.

"Yeah," Derrick agrees. "Both long as hell."

Brooke huffs. "They spent five minutes showing us on a map,

and then they were on to where to dig the latrine. Does anyone even remember which way to go? Everything looks the same. We'll get lost if we leave."

"So," I say, "we stay here when obviously no one is coming?" I raise my voice. "That makes no sense."

Before Brooke can respond, Shannon says, "One of us has hiked up the ridge every day to try to send a message with your cell phone. None of them have gone through. We should try to send one more message, saying that we're walking out and which way we're going, and even if it doesn't go through now, it could go through as we get closer to civilization. It might save our lives."

No one says anything. I'm just waiting for Brooke to come to her senses. She's grudgingly helped dig for survivors and rebury the dead bodies we've found, but out of the four of us she, by far, complains the most. Even though Derrick made it pretty clear that this felt more like a recovery than a rescue effort from the start, he's worked as hard as Shannon and me and never complained about the work—just about being hungry, like the rest of us have.

I point at our four tents in a row in the sunshine on the lakeshore. "At least we'll have some shelter for the journey. Whichever way we go, it'll take seven to ten days. That's what I remember. But for us, it might take longer. I mean, we know generally where we're going but not exactly. I wish we had the maps."

"Shoot," Derrick says. "I wish we had the satellite phone, a GPS, the camp first aid kit, a cook stove, and a water filter so we don't all get diarrhea." He pauses, then shakes his head. "They always at least drop you a note, and maybe some supplies, from the sky. Or they'll fly low and buzz you so you'll know you've been seen. But every helicopter and jet we've seen has been flying high. It's obvious we're not on their radar. What puzzles me is why."

I nod in agreement. "This camp system seemed pretty organized.

What about the people in Fairbanks who work for the camp? They should be on this. They're four days late. I know it's a long shot to make the walk, but to stay here now is an even longer shot."

Brooke takes a step toward me. "Here's what I remember from that *walk talk*. Mountains, rivers, and swampy valleys to cross. We won't make it. I—"

"Brooke," Shannon cuts in, "I don't know why nobody came for us. Did *all* our parents die in the quake?" She makes a sweeping motion to take in the whole landslide. "There were twenty of us. Plus four adults. Are things so bad that we're a super-low priority?" Shannon shakes her head. "I don't know the answers to any of these questions. But I do know one thing. They're not coming for us anytime soon. We're on our own."

CHAPTER 13

Dear Rescuers,

On June 25th, an earthquake caused a massive landslide that buried the Simon Lake Leadership Camp. We recovered five bodies and buried them in shallow graves to keep animals from scavenging them. The graves are marked by rock cairns. An additional fifteen bodies are under the landslide. The four of us, who were away from the main camp during the earthquake, survived. It is now July 1st and no one has come to our assistance. We've decided to hike west to Talkeetna. We are in good health, but have limited supplies and no map.

The Survivors,

Josh Baker (Fairbanks, Alaska), Shannon White (Fairbanks, Alaska), Derrick Anderson (Fairbanks, Alaska), Brooke Simpson (Fairbanks, Alaska)

In the end, after we secure the note in the empty food canister and put the flags up, we decide to take almost everything else with us.

Not that it's that much stuff.

The camp was pretty strict about what we could take on our solo experience, and almost everything else is buried under the landslide.

We each have a backpack, a tiny one-person tent, a blue foam sleeping pad, a sleeping bag, a raincoat and rain pants, a canister of bear spray, a pair of binoculars, a one-liter water bottle, and one set of clothing.

Brooke has a cell phone and a solar charger.

We also each started our solo experience with small blue stuff sacks. And inside the blue sacks we had the following items:

One lighter

One small bottle of insect repellent

One writing journal

One pen

One package of Band-Aids

One small bottle of water purification tablets

At camp there were three large water filters in the kitchen. And one of the jobs was to haul water from the lake and pour it into the holding tanks, which then released the water so it'd flow through the filters and be purified for drinking. On our solo trips we used the tablets, which make the water taste like liquid rust. You basically use one tablet per liter of water. And we've been using the tablets since the earthquake, so we don't have that many left.

"We're supposed to each drink about a gallon of water a day if we're hiking," I say. "I've got ten tablets left. Enough for about two and a half days."

"Some water sources are a lot more likely to be clean than others," Derrick says. "Creeks from snowmelt, or any fast-moving water, are going to be better than drinking from a lake or pond where bacteria can build up."

"Maybe we shouldn't use the tablets when we've got water that we think is clean," Shannon suggests. "We could save them for when we've got to get water from lakes or ponds or puddles."

"I'm not drinking from a puddle." Brooke huffs.

"You might," I respond, "if it's the only place to get some water."

No one else says anything but I'm pretty sure Shannon, Derrick, and Brooke are all thinking about the same thing I am, and how little of it we have.

Food.

CHAPTER 14

"IT DIDN'T GO THROUGH," BROOKE says, staring at her phone. "Big surprise."

We're on top of the ridge above Simon Lake that I was camping on when the quake struck. My calf muscle seems to be healing up because it barely hurts from the steep climb to get up here.

Brooke sent the message to all her contacts. Maybe at some point on our journey we'll get to a spot with a little bit of reception and the message will go through, and someone will do something about us.

I take one last look down at what used to be the Leadership Camp and then turn away and face the rest of the group. I worked up a sweat from the climb, but now I'm cooling off in the breeze. Clouds are stacking up in the distance to the west, the direction we need to go, and where the wind is coming from.

Brooke turns her phone off to save power. "Now, where to?" she says to the three of us.

"That way." I point toward the clouds.

Derrick says, "We should stay up high if we can. I mean, I know we'll have to go up and down a lot, but the walking is going to be easier on these ridges."

"And," Shannon adds, "we'll have a better chance of being spotted."

"The best chance we have of being spotted is to stay right here," Brooke says.

I wish she would let this die. We already decided we'd leave if the message didn't go through, and we've taken everything with us because we didn't want to waste time and energy going back down to the lake if the message failed, but Brooke just can't drop this.

But a small part of me believes that she might be right. I mean, this is where someone *would* come to look for us—*if* someone were to come.

And, if we had more food, I'd want to stay. But we don't.

We've got three days' worth of food for a hike that's supposed to take seven to ten days. We've already figured out how to ration it so it'll last about five or six days, but all that means is that we'll be eating significantly smaller portions than we have since the earthquake.

Like today. We each had about a quarter cup of granola for breakfast—that's half of what we've been eating. For lunch, we each get a stick of beef jerky. And for dinner, our last meal of the day, a package of dry ramen noodles. You can choose to soak them in cold water or not, but that's what you get. A pretty simple recipe for starvation when you add in that we'll be hiking through the trail-less wilderness. I wish we had some fishing gear, or a gun for hunting, but we don't.

The only weapon we have is defensive. Bear spray. And hopefully we won't have to use it.

I look Brooke in the eye and say, "There's no choice here, Brooke. If we stay, we starve." Then I start walking toward the cloud bank, already hungry.

CHAPTER 15

"WHAT TIME DO YOU THINK it is?" I ask. We've come to the end of this high ridge we started walking on after our last attempt to send a message with Brooke's phone, and now we need to make a decision about which way to go. Simon Lake is a speck in the distance. We had to leave our watches behind for our solo experiences, so they're buried under the landslide.

"My guess?" Derrick says. "Sometime after three."

Shannon points toward the towering clouds. "Whatever time it is, we're in for some weather soon."

"I could turn my phone on and check the time," Brooke says, "but I'd rather save the power."

I shake my head. "I don't even know why I want to know. I mean, I wanted to know how long it took us to walk this far, but it doesn't matter. I'm just so used to timing myself for running. Forget it. We just need to figure out what to do from here."

Shannon takes her pack off, pulls out her raincoat, and puts it on. "That wind is cold."

We all copy her, and then I say, "We have to go down before we can go up again." I point to the route right in front of us. "We could go down into that saddle and then up to the next ridge. Or, we could turn to the north a little and go down to that saddle and then up."

"Let's do the first one," Derrick says. "It'll keep us heading west. At least, I think it will."

Shannon and Brooke agree, so we all start picking our way down the slope. Little white and purple flowers carpet the hillside, interspersed with lichen-covered rocks poking out of the mountain.

Theo and I ran up slopes like this on the opposite side of the lake. I took it all for granted. Do a hard workout. Come back to camp sweaty as hell and then jump in the lake to cool off. And then eat a ton of food.

By the time we reach the saddle, the first drops of rain are falling.

Brooke takes off her pack. "We should set up camp."

"I say we keep walking." I take off my pack, pull my rain pants out, and put them on. Then I fish out my backpack cover. "We can keep all our stuff dry by using our pack covers." I fit mine over my pack.

"You're not in charge," Brooke says, "so quit acting like you are."

"I was just responding to what you were saying," I counter. "Whether we all decide to camp or not, it's better to stay dry."

Derrick and Shannon already have their rain pants on and their packs covered. I wish one of them would step in and say something to Brooke. It seems like it's always me having to confront her.

I think about that line I wrote in my journal about wanting to get to know Brooke more, about liking her, about wanting to hang out with her when the camp ended. I wanted to know what was behind that quiet aloofness. I wanted to know what she was thinking as she stared off at the mountains. Of course, I put my own thoughts into her head. *She must love wild places just like I do.*

Now I just want her to quit putting up roadblocks to our survival. Basically, I want her, as Theo would have said, *to suck it up.*

"Wet is wet." Derrick throws his arms up in the air. "Both options basically suck. But I guess I'd rather walk than sit in a tent with nothing to do."

Shannon says, "We should use our energy while we have it."

Big fat drops of cold rain pelt us as we work our way across the saddle. With my hood on I can see forward but have to turn my head to see anything else.

When we start up the ridge on the far side of the saddle we hear the first crack of thunder.

Shannon stops and says, "We shouldn't go up higher when it's thundering. My mom treated a lightning victim last summer." She pauses. "If we get struck by lightning out here, we're basically dead."

"What's the chance lightning will strike one of us?" Derrick asks. "We should keep going."

"The chance of it hitting you is the greatest," I say, "because you're the tallest."

"I told you guys we should've made camp back there." Brooke points behind her. "Now we've all got wet feet and when we set our tents up, they'll get soaked too."

"I didn't say anything about setting up tents," Shannon responds. "I think we should wait it out and then keep going."

Another clap of thunder shakes the ground. I start counting and get to four before the lightning flashes.

"I'll set up my tent," I say. "And we can all squish inside until the storm passes. Then we keep going. Deal?"

"Let's do it," Derrick says.

Shannon nods.

Brooke says, "Okay."

I take my pack off, remove the cover, and pull out my tent. Then I put the cover back on my pack and lay it down with the cover side up. Derrick and Shannon do the same with their packs and help me set up the tent. Brooke takes off her pack and watches as Derrick, Shannon, and I stretch the rainfly over the tent and stake it down.

I unzip the door and say, "Pile in."

Then another crack of thunder fills the air, followed instantly by the brightest lightning I've ever seen.

CHAPTER 16

I'VE GOT THIS NARROW WOODEN box that my grandfather made me before he died of a heart attack a few years ago. In the box, I keep some trophies I won for running in elementary and junior high school. There isn't enough room in the box for each trophy to sit upright, so I have to tilt the ones up on either end of the box to make them all fit. That's exactly how it is trying to cram four of us into a tent designed for one person. Derrick's on the far end of the tent, and I'm on the end with the door. Brooke and Shannon are squished between us. I'm riding up one wall, and Derrick is riding up the other.

The side of Shannon's thigh presses against mine, and our shoulders are smashed together. We've all kept our rain gear and hiking boots on. My boots are really just high-top running shoes made for trail running. We were required to have something with ankle support at Simon Lake.

The thunderclaps and lightning strikes seem to be right on top of one another, which basically means they're right on top of us.

The rain picks up, and now it's pounding the tent like it's under a high-pressure hose in a car wash. But the sound it's making has changed, too.

"Hail?" Shannon guesses.

"Right," Derrick says. "It would suck to be out there right now."

"This whole situation sucks," Brooke says. "It was almost over. I was so looking forward to going home. To having a hot shower. To collapsing on the couch." She sighs. "Why didn't anyone come for us? I hate this."

Brooke has a point. I mean, someone should have come, or at least dropped a message from the sky saying they would be coming. I think about my parents. They were in the process of splitting up. Were they under the same roof when the quake hit? Are they working together to try to find me? Are they hurt?

"Things must be bad everywhere from the earthquake," Shannon says. "At least we're not hurt."

My stomach lets out a rumble that challenges the thunder.

Derrick laughs and says, "I second that."

Our food is out in our packs, and it's a good thing it is because right now I feel like mowing through it all. When you're walking, your body is doing something and you're focusing on it, so even if you're hungry—even if you are living on almost no food—you've got something to do. But sitting in a tent in a storm with nothing to do, the hunger asserts itself front and center. And then it starts working on your mind, and you feel even hungrier than you are. At least that's how it is for me.

I lean away from Shannon and try to stretch one of my arms but am stopped by the tent wall. "As soon as the rain or hail or whatever it is lightens up and the lightning goes away, we should keep going. I mean, it doesn't really get dark, so we could put in a lot more hours before we stop to rest."

"What about just staying here for the night?" Brooke suggests. "We could set up the rest of our tents after the storm passes." She lets out a sigh. "I'm beat."

"Seriously?" My voice cracks. "We can't stay here any longer than the storm that's pinning us down. When it leaves, we should make some tracks. You just feel tired because of the stale warm air in the tent. Once you're back outside, you'll wake up."

"I don't know, man," Derrick says. "I mean, I'm feeling pretty sleepy, too."

"Trust me," I say. "Every time I had to ride on a warm bus to a cross-country or track meet, I'd get sleepy. The whole team did. But once we got off the bus and moved around, we were fine."

"Josh," Brooke barks, "Just because you're some all-American athlete, it doesn't mean the rest of us are." She huffs. "You're not in charge here. No one is."

"Think about it." I lean toward her. "We've got almost no food. We need to move while we still have energy from everything we've eaten the past several days." I take a breath. "The longer we wait, the weaker we'll get. And, if you're really tired, I'll carry some of your stuff. No problem."

"I'll carry my own stuff," Brooke says. "But you're not going to be the only one who decides *when* I carry it and for how long before I rest."

"Enough." Shannon leans forward so her face is just inches from Brooke's and mine. "We can't be using our energy arguing. If we don't work together, we'll have almost no chance of surviving long enough to be rescued."

"Maybe we should each take turns being in charge for a day," Derrick suggests. "You know, like we did at the Leadership Camp."

"I like your idea in theory," I say, "but I'm not sure it's a good one for the current situation." *And the mix of people*, I think but don't say.

"So, you think you're the only one who should make decisions?" Brooke asks.

"No, that's not what I think." I shake my head. "We should make them together—either by consensus or majority."

"Consensus will take too long," Shannon says. "Maybe if we had more supplies, that would work. Majority is the only way to go."

"But there's four of us," Brooke says. "What if we try to make a decision and it's a tie? Two to two? Then what?"

"Then we'd flip a coin or pick a number or do something random to make the decision and move on from there," I say. "Agreed?"

"Sure," Derrick says.

"Yes." Shannon nods.

"Okay," Brooke says.

The pelting on the tent starts to slow down. And the phase between the thunder and lightning lengthens.

It's time to put our new leadership system to the test.

CHAPTER 17

"TWO TO TWO," DERRICK SAYS.

I can't believe Derrick voted in favor of staying, especially since the rain has slowed way down and we haven't heard any thunder in like five or ten minutes.

Part of me wants to abandon Brooke and Derrick and keep heading toward Talkeetna with Shannon. I mean, do you stick to an agreement even when you think it's dangerous and might result in everyone dying?

But I'm getting ahead of myself. It's tied, so we might still win. "Okay," I say, in as even a voice as I can muster. "Now we need to somehow break the tie. Any ideas?"

"Easy," Derrick says. "One of us could pick a number between one and ten, and then two people—you and Brooke—guess what the number is, and whoever is closer is the winner. Pretty random. Right?"

"Sure," I say. "Let's do this."

"For this to be fair," Derrick goes on, "we need two people to agree on the number. Shannon and Brooke should trade places so me and Shannon can quietly agree on a number and then you and Brooke can guess."

"Sounds good," I say, just wanting to get this whole stupid process over with. *Pick a number. If you lose you might die. You might not die for a few days. But you still might die because of the number you chose. Great.*

"Not so fast," Brooke says. "It's not fair. The person who goes first has the advantage."

I swear I feel my heart skip a beat. "I don't care who guesses first," I say.

"Actually," Shannon says, "Brooke's right. And, this isn't really random. Derrick and I are going to decide on a number, and then you and Brooke are going to think of a specific number and tell us what you think it is. Random doesn't really involve thinking and strategy. But this guess-the-number contest does. It does matter who goes first or second. The second person to guess will be influenced by the first person's guess. And the two people who come up with the number are picking it. That's not random either."

"Where'd you come up with that?" Derrick asks.

"Biology class." Shannon stretches her arms out straight and yawns.

"I get your logic," I say.

"Shot down." Derrick sniffles. "Don't worry. I don't bruise easily," he says in a fake crying voice, with a couple more sniffles thrown in. That gets a smile and small laughs from everyone, and for a moment, it's like we're not in a survival situation where there are twenty bodies buried under an avalanche and we're the almost-out-of-food survivors.

"We still need to do something to decide," I say. "Unless someone wants to change their vote?" After no one responds to that invitation, I go on. "Anyone have any ideas that are more random?"

"We could flip a bottle cap from one of our water purification tablet bottles," Shannon suggests. "And we could decide before the flip what each side of the cap stands for. That's probably about as close to random as we're going to get out here."

I lean forward and turn my head toward Brooke. "What do you think?"

Brooke moves her head from side to side and then says, "It sounds pretty fair. Except for the one flip. I think it should be the best of five."

"One, three, five, seven, nine," Shannon responds. "It won't matter. But can we all agree on best of five?"

We all nod.

"It's barely raining," I say. "We should pile out of here, get a cap, and get this over with." I've still got a sick feeling in my stomach from having to do anything but keep walking. Or maybe that's just my hunger resurfacing now that the discussion is over. Then a humming noise invades my ears followed by the *whop whop whop* of helicopters.

"Unzip this thing," Derrick says, leaning across Brooke and Shannon toward me and the door I'm sitting in front of. "Maybe we won't have to flip that bottle cap at all."

CHAPTER 18

"BIG GRAY BIRDS." DERRICK POINTS.

Four groups of at least six helicopters each are flying overhead. They are pretty high in the sky, but low enough that we can count individual choppers.

We all jump up and down and wave and shout, but the helicopters don't change direction.

Now Shannon's got her binoculars trained on them as they grow smaller. "It's hard to see much detail from this distance. Some writing or numbers, but I can't make it out to actually read it. And some red emblem." She lowers her binoculars. "Not that it matters. They obviously didn't see us."

"The red emblem. Could it have been a maple leaf?" I ask. "You know, from the Canadian flag?"

"Maybe Canada is helping with recovery from the quake," Derrick chimes in. Then he shakes his head. "If they are, then things must be bad."

"Why?" Brooke says.

"According to my dad," Derrick responds, "the old US of A doesn't take help from anyone these days."

"You've lived in Alaska for like three years, right?" I say to Derrick. He nods, and I go on.

"Up here, people help each other out. The United States might be the United States, but Alaska is Alaska. It wouldn't surprise me if Canada was helping."

"Whatever," Derrick says. "Alaska is still part of the United States.

And if the Feds are taking over the recovery, they take their orders from Washington. It doesn't matter what part of the world you're stationed in, my dad says, his ultimate boss is still in the White House."

I feel a shiver go up my spine. The rain has let up, but the wind is blowing. The last of the helicopters disappear in the distance, and it's just the four of us again. It's weird how you can feel like you're coming so close to being rescued, and then it turns into nothing. It just reminds me that waiting around for someone to save us is the exact opposite of what we need to be doing.

"We can put some miles behind us," I say, pointing at the sky. "It's not raining or thundering or anything."

"Not so fast," Brooke says. "We haven't flipped the bottle cap yet. Remember?"

I nod. "I just thought maybe you and Derrick might have changed your minds now that the reason we stopped in the first place isn't an issue anymore." I look over at Shannon, hoping she'll back me up, but she's still staring in the direction the helicopters went.

"Not me," Brooke says. Then she turns to Derrick and smiles at him.

"I'm into some rest," Derrick says. "For sure."

Shannon turns toward the three of us. "Do you think they're following a flight path?" She points to the sky in the direction the helicopters went.

"I doubt it," Derrick responds. "I mean, according to my dad, in general their flight plans are to get from point A to point B using the least amount of fuel possible, so they take into consideration the wind speed and direction at different altitudes."

"The farther we get from the lake," Brooke says, "the less likely that we'll be spotted."

"You don't know that," I say. "We sat there for six days, and no one came for us."

"This is turning into the same old argument," Shannon says. "Let's just flip this bottle cap and get the decision over with." She reaches into her pack, pulls out her blue stuff sack, and searches until she finds her small bottle of water purification tablets. "We said the best of five, right?"

This is so idiotic, I think. Four survivors from a major catastrophe and we have to flip a freaking bottle cap to make a decision.

Derrick walks a few steps and stands next to Shannon. "Since you two have the strongest opinions on this *should we stay or should we go* dilemma, me and Shannon will be in charge of the flipping. Agreed?"

"I don't care," I say. "Let's just get this over with." I'm bouncing on my toes. I don't know what I'll do if I lose this. I mean, I'll try to rest, but I'm so ready to go.

"So," Brooke asks, "one of you flips and one of you calls?"

Shannon shakes her head. "We should decide which side means go and which means stay and do five flips, and the one with the most is the winner."

"Does it matter what side is up when you start the flip?" Brooke asks. "That cap isn't the same on both sides."

"This isn't going to be perfect," I break in. "Let's just get this over with."

"I just want it to be fair," Brooke counters.

"Sure you don't want to change your mind?" I say to Derrick.

He laughs softly. "I want to see this through."

Sometimes you've just got to let go of what you're trying to control, I remember Theo saying on one of our runs when I was talking about my parents and their problems. *Okay*, I think, *I'll quit trying to get people to change their minds even though I still think setting up camp is a waste of time and energy.*

I turn to Brooke. "You pick whatever side you want for staying, and the other side will be for going."

"Right side up for staying," Brooke says, "because staying is the right thing to do."

"Sounds good," I say, still baffled by how much she wants to stay here and starve instead of make tracks toward Talkeetna. She seemed like a basically normal person until the earthquake. I mean, I was even attracted to her. And weirdly, I still am. She's beautiful. And I still want to know what went on behind all the silence and aloofness during most of the month we were in camp together. But at the same time, I'm also furious with her.

"Okay." Shannon unscrews the cap to the bottle.

I look at my tent, which I sacrificed for the group. It's drying out in the wind, but I'm guessing it's still pretty wet inside.

If I lose the flip, I won't even have a dry place to rest.

CHAPTER 19

I WON. BUT IT'S THE most bittersweet victory I've ever had. Brooke has been sulking and complaining every step of the way. We've come maybe six or seven miles from where we waited out the storm, and we're up on another high ridge, staring down into a forested valley.

"We'll have to go down and cross." Derrick points. "No way around that."

"Maybe we should rest here," Shannon suggests. "That way we'll be more visible for anything flying overhead."

"Canadians, Americans, aliens from outer space, or creatures from the center of the earth," Derrick says. "At this point, I'll take a lift from pretty much anyone."

We filled our water bottles in a snowmelt stream a few miles back. I also drank at least a liter of water back there—drank until my stomach ballooned out—but I know under that bloated feeling is hunger. All told, we've probably hiked ten or twelve miles—all on a quarter cup of granola and a piece of jerky each. But I know if we'd stayed put, I'd be feeling just as hungry now.

Brooke takes off her pack and sits on top of it. The bruise on her cheek from the day of the quake is fading, but it's not gone. She stretches one leg out in front of her and lets out a moan as she sets her foot down heel-first. She does the same thing with her other foot and moans again when her heel hits the ground.

"What's up with your feet?" I ask.

Brooke shrugs, keeping her eyes averted.

"Take your boots off," I say.

"You can't tell me what to do," she fires back.

"Brooke," I say. "Even if we disagree on some things, we're all in this together. Just take them off." It's obvious to me that there's something wrong, and having foot problems with what we're up against is serious business. "I want to help you."

Brooke huffs, but then unties one of her boots, loosens the laces, and lets out an even louder moan, almost a scream, as she starts to tug on it. She grits her teeth and pulls it off.

By this time Derrick and Shannon have joined me.

Derrick points and says, "That's quite a bit of blood." Brooke's sock has blood spots across the tops of her toes, and her heel is bloody, too.

"Why didn't you say something?" I ask.

"I did," Brooke responds. "You and Shannon wanted to keep going, and I wanted to stop. Remember?"

"You didn't say your foot was getting torn to shreds. You only said you were tired." I shake my head. "I could have prevented some of this if I'd known." I kneel down in front of her. "Does the other one hurt just as bad?"

Brooke nods. "Maybe worse."

I reach out and gently touch the top of Brooke's boot and feel her toes pressing against the front of it.

"Your boots are a little small," I say. "But if we loosen the laces right in front of your toes"—I point to the spot—"it'll help a little bit when you're walking."

"I don't think I can take another step," Brooke says.

My first cross-country coach taught me that most people buy their shoes too small if they're planning on covering any type of long distance. Our feet expand during the day, and if your foot is already filling your shoe, you'll most likely be in some pain if you try to do anything extensive.

"Shannon, Derrick. Get your first aid kits out." I reach for my pack and get mine out, too. "If we pool our resources we should be able to make this a lot better."

"We should let the wounds breathe," Shannon says, "before we patch them up. They'll heal faster."

A wind rips across the ridge, and I feel the hood of my raincoat flapping against the back of my head. I turn in the direction of the gust and see dark clouds piling up on the next ridge, maybe a mile away. "We've got to get the tents set up, too."

Shannon opens all three of the first aid kits and pulls out the small tubes of antibiotic ointment. "We should wash the wounds and put a little ointment on them and leave them uncovered for as long as possible."

The wind is still making my hood flap. "Okay," I say. "I'll wash Brooke's feet, but can you two set up the tents? That storm is coming."

I fish my water bottle out of my pack. "Brooke, I'm just going to trickle some water onto your feet where the broken blisters are. Do you want some help with your other boot?"

"I'll get it." Brooke winces as she undoes the laces. Then she grits her teeth and pulls her boot off, and I see another bloody sock.

At least we're on tundra and not mud. Once I wash the wounds, Brooke should be able to get inside her tent without getting her feet all dirty. Shannon and Derrick have two tents up when the rain starts falling.

"You and Brooke use that tent." Derrick points. "Me and Shannon will hang out in this one until the storm passes. Then we'll set up the rest of the tents."

I stuff all the first aid supplies back into the bags and cover my pack with my backpack cover. Brooke stands up, and I get her backpack cover out, but before I cover her pack I pull out her sleeping pad and say, "It'll give us something to sit on once we're inside."

Brooke nods and hobbles toward the tent. Derrick and Shannon are already inside one tent with the door zipped up. I can hear them talking but can't make out what they're saying. I take the sleeping pad, the first aid supplies, my canister of bear spray, and my water bottle and head toward the other tent. Brooke is down on her knees, crawling in with her feet up in the air to keep them from dragging on the ground. I toss the supplies in behind Brooke, and out of the corner of my eye catch sight of her boots and bloody socks on the tundra, so I run over, grab them and bring them to the tent, toss them in, and then crawl in.

Brooke has spread out on half of the sleeping pad with her legs stretched out. I sit down opposite her with my legs stretched out so her feet are next to my thighs and my feet are next to her thighs. The rain is pounding, but the tent is doing its job and keeping us dry.

"You're going to be okay," I say. "Your feet, they'll heal." What I don't say is that they're going to hurt like hell and she is still going to have to walk on them. "I wish you had said something earlier."

Brooke bends her legs and sits so her arms are resting on her knees. "I didn't want to complain. I'm always the one holding people back. With my sisters, it was always me saying, *wait*. Always me. Whenever we'd do something physical as a family, I was always the slowest. All I wanted to do today was to keep up."

I kind of get what she's saying. With Theo, I always told him the pace was fine even if I was killing myself to keep up with him. But I never faked being tired as an excuse, or to cover something up.

Brooke goes on, "I hate myself. I hate the person I am."

"Brooke, you've survived an intense tragedy. Give yourself a break." I look her in the eye. "You dug up bodies for a week. And now we're hiking with almost no food. Not many people could do what you've done."

"Yeah," she says, "but look at you. You could travel twice as fast if it weren't for me. You all should just leave me here." She points at her feet. "Especially now. See, I screwed up again. I was ashamed of the blisters and didn't want anyone to see them."

I think about all the anger I've felt toward Brooke the past week, and then before that how I was kind of attracted to her. And now, I don't know what to think. I mean, maybe all her behaviors that were rubbing me the wrong way weren't really about who she is but more about what she was struggling with.

"Brooke," I say, "I may not agree with how you want to do things all the time. Lately, I haven't agreed with much of anything you've wanted to do. But that doesn't mean I don't care about you. That doesn't mean I won't do all I can so you'll be okay—so we'll all be okay. We've all got to do that for each other, even if we're pissed off."

You've got to be willing to work with people, I remember Theo saying. *All kinds of people. Don't put up with discrimination of any kind, but other differences, you've got to be willing to be open to. You've got to stay open.*

"That's easy to say when you're the strong one," Brooke says, "the one who's helping or doing more. Put yourself in my shoes."

Brooke and I both glance at her boots.

"I don't think I'd want to go that far." I smile.

Brooke laughs out loud.

The pounding rain on the tent has slowed down some.

"There are things we can do"—I point at her feet—"to lessen the pain and speed the healing."

"Like what?" Brooke asks.

For the first time since the quake it feels like we're talking to each other in a normal way. There's no edge to her voice. And I'm not stuffing down anger so I don't say something mean.

"You'd have to be willing to accept some help," I say. "If you do, we could all keep moving forward."

"Go on." Brooke nods.

"We could carry your stuff," I say. "Me, Derrick, and Shannon could divide it up. Without the weight on your back, the pressure your toes and heels take on with every step would be less. It'll still hurt, just not as much. And you'll heal faster."

"I want to do my part," Brooke says, raising her voice slightly. "I already feel bad enough."

"So," I say, "you'd rather tear your feet up and slow the group down more than accept a little help and have the group move faster? Given the current situation, this is the best way to do your part."

"You mean that *you think* it's the best way." Brooke points at me. "You can't just give an opinion and say it's the best thing to do just because you think it. Do you get what I'm saying? You sabotage your chances of people agreeing with you when you say stuff like that."

The noise from the rain on the tent is almost nonexistent now.

I know Brooke is right about the way I communicate sometimes. I just get an idea in my head, and if I think it's a good one, then I can't see how anyone would question it. That's partly why I felt like a loner on the cross-country team last year. Yeah, I was the fastest runner, and I worked hard to achieve that, but I also sacrificed some close friendships. I stayed longer and ran after the official practice was over. I basically told everyone that it was the best way to ensure that we'd win State.

"I know what you're talking about," I say.

I tell Brooke about my experience on the cross-country team, and she says, "At least you knew what you wanted and you went after it. I always feel like I'm reaching for something someone else has done, something I envy them for doing. This camp was the first time I felt like I was doing something of my own choosing. And I didn't even want it that badly. I chose it mainly because there was no one else I knew who had done it. It was something none of my sisters had done."

I nod. "I don't know what I'd do if I didn't have goals I set for myself." I put my ear against the tent door. "I think it's stopped raining."

"Open it up," Brooke says. "It's getting kind of stuffy in here. All the hot air." She smiles. "From both of us."

I unzip the door and see why we're not hearing any rain on the tent. Big white flakes are floating down and sticking on the ground.

CHAPTER 20

I ZIP THE TENT DOOR up partway, grab my water bottle, and take a drink. "Want some?" I say, holding the bottle toward Brooke.

"Are you sure?" Brooke says. "I mean, you only have so much, and you just used some to wash my feet."

"Drink," I say. I don't think it'll be too hard to find another water source up here.

Brooke takes the bottle and drinks. I watch her neck contract a little. She takes another gulp. "I guess I was thirsty." She hands me the bottle. "Thanks. I'll give you some of mine. It's in my pack."

I nod. "I hope we don't get too much snow. We must be up pretty high for it to be sticking. If we hike down to that valley tomorrow, there shouldn't be any snow there."

Brooke curls her toes a little bit, and now with the added light from the door being partially open I see that the broken blisters have turned a little red.

"We should finish working on your feet," I say. "If you keep them just like that, I can put the antibiotic ointment on them."

"You sure you want to touch my feet?" Brooke asks. "They're mine, and I don't even want to touch these bloody stumps."

"Before I learned to buy bigger running shoes, I had to drill holes in my toenails because blood vessels would break underneath them and the blood would pool up, and the pressure from the blood beneath the nail was really painful."

"Gross," Brooke says. She glances down at her feet. "I'm glad I don't have that problem. No way would I let you, or anyone, drill a hole in one of my nails." She shudders.

"You might," I say, "if it meant you'd be out of pain."

"Not a chance," Brooke counters.

I get one small tube of antibiotic ointment out of the first aid supplies. "We'll put a little bit on every open wound. But first, I need to wash my finger." I stick my hand outside the tent door into the heavy snowfall, palm open. In a few seconds I've got enough moisture for a quick washing. "I hope you're okay with this. I mean, the ointment is supposed to kill the germs anyway."

"It's fine," Brooke says.

I lean forward so my face is close to Brooke's toes. "Lucky I washed your feet first. Otherwise, I think they'd smell pretty ripe."

"Shut up," Brooke says. Then she laughs.

"This might hurt a little." I dab some ointment on the end of my index finger.

Brooke doesn't say a word as I rub the ointment on her blisters until I get to one that extends between her toes. When I stick the ointment-covered tip of my finger between her pinky toe and her fourth toe, she lets out a giggle.

I look up at her and say, "Really? It's a freaking blister."

"Honest," she says. "That one tickled."

I get back to work. I scoot closer to her so I can see her heels. My head is right next to her thigh. It's tight quarters, but I manage to get the ointment on both blisters that have taken over her heels.

I work my way back to my side of the tent and stretch my legs out and say, "I don't know how long you can sit like that, but it'd be good for the ointment to kind of glaze over. You don't want to move around because anything you touch will stick to your heels and toes now."

"I'm good right here for now," Brooke says. "But at some point, I'll have to go pee."

I point at the Band-Aids laid out in front of me. "Between the three kits we'll have more than enough. Plus, your kit is still in your pack."

Brooke nods. "Josh." She pauses. "Thanks." Then she smiles.

"No problem," I say. "We should check in with Derrick and Shannon." I unzip the tent a little more, stick my head out into the snowstorm, and shout, "Hey, you two! How's everything?"

I hear some rustling, and then the sound of a zipper. "All good," Shannon shouts. "Just waiting out this crazy storm."

I can't see her because of the way the tents are set up.

Then Derrick's voice booms out, "We're going to just stay in this tent. Get our sleeping bags. You should do the same. Less wet gear that way. Plus, you've got someone to hang out with."

"Body heat," Shannon yells. "The warmer we stay, the fewer calories we'll burn."

"Got it," I yell back. Then I turn to Brooke and say, "Are you okay with all this?"

CHAPTER 21

I DASHED OUTSIDE, WRESTLED OUR sleeping bags and our dinners out of our packs, tossed them into the tent, pulled our packs closer to the tent, and then crawled back inside, and now we're about to eat.

"I wish we had a hot meal," Brooke says, holding her unopened package of ramen noodles in one hand.

"At least ramen noodles are already cooked," I say. "This would really suck if we had regular pasta and had to eat it raw."

"I didn't know they were already cooked." Brooke sniffs the package. "Still, I'd rather eat them hot and soft than cold and hard."

I know we're breaking a rule eating in the tent, but it's still snowing wet, sloppy snow, and the drier we can stay the better.

The two of us crammed into this little tent are creating body heat, just like Shannon said. I unzip my raincoat and take it off. Then I pull my rain pants off. My nylon hiking pants are just barely damp, unlike my socks, which are wet. Not wet like you need to wring them out but wet like if you touched them you'd want to wipe your hand off.

I hold up my unopened brick of ramen. "I think I'll skip the spice packet. Too salty by itself."

Brooke laughs. "You mean you were actually considering eating it dry?" She scrunches up her nose. "Yuck."

"I'd eat it if I had more water," I say.

Brooke rips open her package. "Now the trick is not to spill noodles all over the place."

I take my raincoat and spread it out on my lap. "It's a ramen catcher."

"Good idea," Brooke says. She copies me.

I don't know if Brooke's just been pissed at me because I always want to do the exact opposite thing she wants to do. Or if, maybe, she hasn't really been angry with me at all. I'm starting to get to know and understand her a little bit. And she seems appreciative for all I've done to help her with her feet. But there's still some stuff I want to know, like why she was so reluctant to search for survivors, and why she didn't want to stand by Theo, who was still alive when the bear was approaching us.

After we finish our gourmet meal, I say, "I think we should put Band-Aids on your blisters. Once you get in your sleeping bag, you don't want those open sores rubbing against the fabric."

Brooke uses her hand as a fan. "It's so warm in here, I don't know if I'll need to get all the way in my bag. Maybe I'll get partway in but make sure my feet are sticking out." Then she yawns. "I'm beat."

I'm not exactly beat. I'm just glad we've got the storm coinciding with her blisters because if we had stopped in good weather I'd be hating this right now. Well, I wouldn't be hating hanging out with Brooke in a small tent, I'd just be hating that we could've been making progress on getting somewhere while we still have our strength.

"At least put Band-Aids on your heels so if you lie on your back and stretch your legs out those blisters will be protected," I say.

Brooke sticks Band-Aids on her heels without my help.

I pull my sleeping bag out of the stuff sack. "I think we should sleep head to toe, you know, like we've been sitting, otherwise this tent will be bursting at the seams even more than it is."

"I don't know." Brooke waves her hand in front of her nose. "Your feet in my face? And, my bloody feet in your face?"

"I'm definitely getting the raw end of the deal. Especially if you keep your feet in the open air." I pinch my nose.

She laughs and then takes her sleeping bag out of her stuff sack, and I press myself against the wall of the tent so she can spread it out.

Now we're both lying on top of our sleeping bags.

"I'll do it," Brooke says.

"Do what?" I ask.

"I'll let you three carry some of my stuff," she says softly, "if that's the best thing for the group."

"Okay," I say. "Cool." I don't want to say anything more about this because I don't want her to change her mind. I glance at my watch-less wrist and say, "I wish I knew what time it was. Not that it matters, but I'm so used to always knowing."

"Can you reach my pack from the tent door?" Brooke asks.

"Yeah," I reply.

"In the top pocket," she explains, "there's a small waterproof bag with my phone and solar charger."

"Duh," I say. "It's got a clock. I keep forgetting." I sit up, unzip the tent, and stick my head outside. The snow is still falling. I reach for Brooke's pack, and as I'm brushing the new snow off the top of her backpack cover, I catch some movement out of the corner of my eye and what I see sends a jolt to my heart.

I slowly retract my head into the tent, look Brooke in the eye, and say quietly, "We've got company."

CHAPTER 22

"I COUNTED FIVE IN ALL, but there could be more," I whisper.

Brooke scoots forward, and now we're kneeling side by side. I reach across her legs, grab the can of bear spray, and say, "Just in case."

"Would that stuff really work on wolves?" she whispers.

"I'm guessing if it'll work on a bear, it'll pretty much work on anything," I whisper. "It's not a hundred percent certain, but it's all we've got."

Through the falling snow about forty feet away, five wolves mill around like they're unsure of what to do. I don't hear any voices coming from Derrick and Shannon's tent, so either they're asleep or they've seen the wolves and are watching, too.

Should I call out to them? If I do, will that bring the wolves toward us or will it scare them away? Right now, they aren't a threat, but that could change in an instant.

I think about being inside this tent. Yeah, it's dry, but it's also like a trap if the wolves decide to make a meal of us. And then there's Brooke's feet. I don't want her to shove those open sores into her boots unless it's an emergency.

Movement jolts me back to what's right in front of me. Three wolves are working their way closer to the tents, and the other two are moving off to one side.

"I'm going to stand up," I say to Brooke, "so I can see the other tent and tell them what's happening. I pull my boots on but leave them unlaced, unzip the tent all the way, and scoot forward.

I plant my feet outside the tent and stand up. The snow hitting my face instantly melts. The three wolves stop when they see me. I turn and look over our tent to the other tent. "Shannon, Derrick," I say. "Wolves. Five of them. They're close."

I hear some rustling in the other tent, then a zipper, and in an instant Derrick is standing up. The three wolves remain still. I look behind me and see the other two wolves have halved the distance to our tent. "Do you two have bear spray?" I say to Derrick while keeping my eye on the closest wolf.

"I got mine," Derrick says to me. Then he yells, "Shannon! Shannon!"

"What are you—"

Derrick cuts me off. "We were both falling asleep, but she went out to relieve herself and she's not back."

"Stay here," I say to Brooke. I grab her pack and pull it into the tent. "Get out your bear spray."

"Hey, wolves!" I yell. "Go! Beat it!" I take a step toward the three wolves in front of me and clap my hands. Then Derrick is next to me doing the same thing. The wolves move sideways away from us, but that still keeps them within striking distance of the tents. And the two wolves that circled around are behind the tents.

It's in their genes. Hunting as a pack. But they don't usually hunt humans. Maybe they're testing us. Maybe they can sense that we're hungry and a little weak. Maybe they smell the blood from Brooke's wounds. Maybe they've never seen humans. Maybe all three of those things are true.

"Shannon! Shannon!" Derrick yells.

"We should follow her boot prints," I say. And then I think of Brooke and her injured feet, and say, "One of us should go and one of us should stay."

"We shouldn't split up," Derrick says.

I hear rustling behind me, and there's Brooke with her boots on but with the laces taken out. "Let's go," she says. And then she shouts, "Shannon! We're coming!"

CHAPTER 23

WE FOLLOW SHANNON'S FOOTPRINTS IN the snow. With three of us together, the wolves keep their distance but don't turn and run. Shannon's tracks lead straight toward where I first saw the five wolves.

All three of us continue to shout her name, but then I say, "We should be quiet and give her a chance to answer."

We are flanked by wolves. Two on the right and three on the left. We each have a canister of bear spray in our hands. We keep following the tracks, and then I see movement through the thick falling snow, straight ahead.

A big black wolf crosses our path about forty yards away, increasing the wolf count to six. And that makes me wonder if there are even more wolves that we haven't seen.

Why hasn't Shannon called anything back to us? Is she hurt? Did she fall and hit her head? Did the wolves already get her? Or did she get lost?

"Shannon!" Derrick shouts again. The he scoops up a rock, throws it at the black wolf, and yells, "Get!"

The rock sails over the wolf, and the wolf just stands there, not looking directly at us but not backing away. I pick up a rock and throw it, and it skids to a stop right in front of the wolf, but all the wolf does is trot a dozen steps to the right.

The wet snow has penetrated my shirt and pants, and I'm starting to feel the moisture since I didn't take the time to put on my rain gear.

"Did Shannon have her rain gear?" I ask Derrick.

"I think so," he says. "What she didn't have was this." Out of a big side pocket in his cargo pants he pulls out a canister of bear spray. "She left it in the tent." He tucks it back in his pocket.

Oh man, I think. All these wolves around and not an ounce of protection. Where is she?

Shannon's tracks start angling to the left slightly.

"How far did she go to relieve herself?" Brooke asks. "In this weather, I wouldn't have gone very far."

"Me neither," I say.

"Do you think the wolves will mess with our camp since we're not in it?" Brooke asks.

"I doubt it," Derrick says. "They're interested in meat. And right now, the nearest meat is *us*."

The tracks angle back to the right. The black wolf continues to watch us but hasn't come any closer since we threw the rocks.

Now we're at the edge of the ridgetop where there's no place to go but steeply down.

"Shannon!" I yell.

I wait.

No response.

"Shannon!" I yell.

I wait.

No response.

"That girl sure likes her privacy," Brooke says.

"This just doesn't make sense," I say. "She must've gotten turned around in the heavy snowfall." I look back and can't even see our tents from this spot. But I could follow our tracks back in the snow, and so could Shannon. She's super smart. Not that you even need to be that smart to follow your own tracks.

Something must've happened to her.

"Down there." Derrick points. "More movement."

And then I hear a voice. It's faint, but I hear it. Coming from the direction Derrick is pointing.

"Over here." Shannon's voice sounds small. Maybe it has something to do with the wet, thick snow that's still falling.

"We're coming," I yell.

I start to work my way toward her voice, following her tracks down the steep slope.

I hit a patch of thick blueberry bushes. They form a waist-high wall and are wet with snow, but her tracks lead right into them.

I turn and see Derrick and Brooke closing the distance behind me, sidestepping down the slope. This must be killing Brooke's feet. Slaying them.

"The tracks end here," I say, standing at the edge of the berry bushes.

Through the falling snow, I see movement at the far end of the berry bushes. Then Shannon is moving through the thick brush toward us.

"Are the wolves gone?" she asks.

"Not exactly," I say. "I mean, I'm pretty sure they're still around the camp, but we won't know until we climb back up the hill."

Derrick holds a canister of bear spray out to Shannon. "Forget something?"

She takes the canister and says, "Never again." Then Shannon tells us about how after she peed, it felt so good to be outside in the fresh air that she decided to walk to the edge of the ridge, but when she turned around to go back, there were wolves between her and the tents. The wolves were so focused on the tents that she was able to slip out of sight.

She wanted to yell to us but didn't want to draw attention to herself, especially when she realized she didn't have her bear spray. So she picked her way down the steep slope until she found the first opportunity for cover—the thick patch of berry bushes—and waited.

"If it weren't for the stink from Derrick's gas"—Shannon smiles—"I may not have decided to go for a walk."

"Hey," Derrick says, "it wasn't just *my* gas stinking up that place."

"Well, it was mostly yours," Shannon replies.

"Just remember your bear spray next time," Brooke says. "We're all getting soaked out here because we don't have our rain gear on, except for you."

Then I remember Brooke's feet. It must've been pretty painful for her to hobble down here. She probably set herself back in terms of healing.

"Sorry," Shannon says. "The last thing I thought would happen would be getting separated from camp because of wolves."

"Speaking of wolves," I say, "we need to head back and see what's going on."

CHAPTER 24

"WE SHOULD STAND SIDE BY side," I say. With my thumb, I remove the safety clip from my bear spray. "Better to be ready than wishing you were ready."

Shannon, Brooke, and Derrick all remove their safety clips, too. Then Derrick says, "If we do need to use the bear spray, we've got to take the wind into account. Down here, below the ridgetop, it feels pretty calm, but up there, I remember it blowing pretty hard."

"Let's just get up there and get this over with," Brooke says. "My feet are killing me."

I glance down at Brooke's feet, then look her in the eye. "We'll fix them up when we get back."

Shannon doesn't say anything. I don't know if she's still feeling bad for forgetting her bear spray. But the truth is, even if she'd had it with her on her walk, one person is no match for six wolves. Who knows what would've happened.

And we're all here now. That's what matters.

I lead the way to the lip of the ridge and wait until everyone lines up next to me. The snow is still falling, and it's probably blowing sideways up on top—where we'll be in a matter of seconds.

With Shannon on one side of me, Brooke on the other, and Derrick next to Brooke, we make our way in unison to the top of the ridge.

About a quarter mile away through the blowing snow I see our tents, still standing. At least the wolves haven't torn them up.

We're all looking around. I notice the wind is blowing from our right and quietly point that out in case we have to use our bear spray.

"Anyone see anything?" Shannon says softly.

Brooke, Derrick, and I shake our heads.

"Let's start walking," I say. "Toward the tents."

We've taken about ten steps when a shrill whistle pierces the air and stops us dead in our tracks.

"What was that?" Derrick asks. "It came from somewhere off to the left."

We all turn and focus our attention in that direction.

"It's a person," Brooke yells. "What else could it be?"

Then another, fainter whistle comes from straight ahead. "It sounds like that one came from the tents or beyond them." I point.

"Maybe it's a rescue crew and that's how they're communicating with each other," Derrick says. "We're here!" Derrick shouts. "We're here!"

Shannon says, "I think—"

"I won't have to walk in these boots anymore," Brooke says, cutting her off.

Another whistle splits the air, coming from somewhere beyond the tents.

"How did we not hear the helicopter or plane or whatever?" I say.

"They must've landed when we were down in the brush," Brooke says. "And they must've scared the wolves away. That's why we haven't seen any. This nightmare is almost over."

Another whistle pierces our ears from off to the left.

Brooke turns her head toward the sound and shouts, "We're here!"

The snow is still blowing, but the ridgetop area isn't all that big. I mean, we can see the tents straight in front of us a quarter mile away, and off to the left we can see at least that far.

Another whistle invades our ears from straight ahead, and we all look that way.

"Let's just walk to the tents," I say. "There's obviously someone over there. They've probably spotted the tents and are whistling to tell the rest of their crew that they found something."

"And the rest of the crew"—Brooke points to the left—"is whistling back to say they heard them."

"I'm game," Derrick says. "Let's go meet these people. I'm curious who they are. They can't be military. They would use radios if they were."

Shannon says, "I think—"

"Let's just get over there," Brooke cuts in. "Before they think the place is abandoned and leave without us."

Brooke starts limping toward the tents, and we all fall in a couple of steps behind her.

"Hello!" Brooke calls. "Hello!"

I see movement off to my right and catch a glimpse of a wolf slinking away from us.

"The wolves are still here," I say, pointing. "Don't let your guard down."

Derrick and Shannon turn their heads in the direction I point, but Brooke just keeps shouting and plowing forward like she'd step directly onto a wolf to get to whoever is whistling.

We reach the tents and hear another whistle.

"We have to keep going," I say, "beyond the tents." I point through the blowing snow. "Maybe the people haven't gotten this far."

Another whistle sounds off to the left and behind us. It's fainter than it was when we were at the edge of the ridge.

"Hello!" Brooke shouts. "Hello!"

"Over here!" Derrick yells.

Another whistle sounds beyond the tents.

We all step past the tents and keep going in the direction of the whistle.

My clothes are starting to soak through from being out in the wet snow, but I don't care. Not if it means being rescued.

"Do you think they've heard us yet?" I ask. "I mean, why haven't they shouted back?"

Shannon says, "I think—"

Derrick cuts her off. "Maybe it's some weird search-and-rescue protocol."

"Who cares?" Brooke says. "They're here. That's all that matters."

Brooke keeps limping forward. Her blisters must be throbbing with pain.

The next whistle is so close it makes my heart skip a beat. It's almost like the whistle traveled from the ground up and then through me.

I turn in a circle, searching for its source. Brooke, Derrick, and Shannon are also searching.

Another shrill blast sends a jolt up my spine. And then I see the source of the whistling, and it's not at all what I expected.

CHAPTER 25

"MARMOTS?" BROOKE SAYS. "BIG FAT rodents?" She lets out a scream. "No!"

"I tried to tell all of you," Shannon says. "Three times actually. I just kept getting cut off. This is their habitat. And they live in colonies."

As we make our way back to the tents, I say, "How do you know all this stuff?"

"Am I the only one who's taken an Alaska wildlife class?" Shannon responds.

"But what about their whistle?" Derrick asks. "You must've heard that somewhere. Do you live out in the sticks?"

Shannon smiles. "I live in an apartment with my mom, not out in the woods. This is the first time I've heard them in the wild, but they sound just like the recordings I heard in class."

The snow is still falling, but the sky seems to be lightening up a little bit. I'm thoroughly soaked and looking forward to crawling into my sleeping bag and letting the storm snow itself out.

Brooke is lagging behind the three of us. Her feet must be killing her, especially since there are no rescuers. It's like if I put my *all* into a race, knowing I'd be able to rest afterward—only to discover I had to run another race ten minutes later: I'd be psychologically as well as physically spent.

Shannon says, "You know, it's possible that those wolves were just interested in the marmots. Maybe we camped right on one of their main hunting territories."

"Still," I say, "wolves are wolves. They may not attack people very often, but they're hunters and meat eaters. And we're meat. The wolf would be like, *Wow, a really big marmot for a meal, cool.*"

At the tents, we wait for Brooke to catch up. She's got a frown on her face a mile wide. If my feet were in her condition, I'd be feeling the same way. I hope I can patch them up enough for tomorrow's hike to make it at least a little less painful for her.

"Brooke," Derrick says. "How about we see if you can get any reception?"

Brooke peels back the cover on her backpack and removes a small green waterproof bag.

We all crowd around Brooke as she powers up her phone. In the top center of the screen the time reads 11:23 p.m. In the upper right corner the battery power reads 43%. But the most surprising reading is the two solid bars in the top left.

"You must feel pretty strongly about your favorite color," I say, pointing at the completely red screen, aside from the time, bars, and battery reading.

Brooke doesn't respond, just presses the home button. She presses it three times, but the screen remains the same solid red.

"I don't understand," Brooke says. "I mean, I had a picture of me and my sisters as my wallpaper."

"And there are no apps," Derrick says.

Brooke turns her phone off and powers it back up, but the result is the same.

"Could be the military," Derrick says. "My dad says they have tools to use for every imaginable situation. And if they're big into the rescue and recovery from the quake, they can probably take over any and all civilian systems."

"Maybe the red screen has something to do with the Canadians helping us," I say. "Maybe they need a certain network for their communications."

"But how would we get a signal way out here?" Shannon says. "And why would Brooke's apps disappear?"

"The apps disappearing," Derrick says, "that could be something internal in her phone. But the signal? Who knows? Maybe they've got some small, lightweight towers floating from weather balloons so they can talk to each other over large areas?"

"For real?" I say. "They can do that?"

"All I know," Derrick says, "is that my dad is always bragging about systems they have that the public has no clue about. They can do anything."

"Whatever they're doing," Brooke says, "it's not helping us." She turns her phone off and puts it back in the bag.

"At least it shows that they're out here even if they haven't found us yet," Shannon reasons.

Another whistle pierces our ears, followed by the howl of a wolf, reminding us that we're not the only residents of this ridge.

A shiver runs up my spine. I'm freaking freezing, and wet. "I think we should all warm up and get some sleep because tomorrow we'll be walking again."

Back in the tent, Brooke and I get settled in.

"I'll help bandage up your toes tomorrow." I pull off my soaked shirt and pants, scoot into my sleeping bag, and turn away from Brooke to give her some privacy.

I hear her moan and groan and imagine her pants rubbing against the tops of her toes as she pulls them off. "I'm not looking forward to wearing wet clothes tomorrow," she says. "I'm not looking forward to anything tomorrow."

"If the weather clears, we could always wear our rain gear and tie our wet clothes on the outside of our packs to let them dry. We're going to be going down into that valley tomorrow, and it should get warmer the lower in elevation we go."

"Whatever," Brooke responds. "I'll be lucky if I can walk at all."

I think of how she walked all the way down to the berry bushes searching for Shannon, and then back. And then beyond the tents and back. I think she'll be able to walk tomorrow. It'll hurt, but she'll be able to do it.

I hear another wolf howling somewhere in the distance. I roll over and lie on my back. My toes still feel clammy, but in general I'm warming up.

And then I think, *Yeah, we've got what it takes to stay warm even when we get our clothes sopping wet. But will we all have enough energy to make the hike?* I glance over at Brooke, who is also on her back but has her eyes closed. And when I think of her trying to cover mile after mile through trail-less wilderness with those blisters, I sure hope we see some more helicopters soon and that we can flag one of them down—because right now the deck is stacked against us.

CHAPTER 26

MY RAIN GEAR IS STICKING to me like a second skin, but at least I'm not freezing. We're just getting into the first spruce trees in the valley. I patched up Brooke's toes when we woke up and made sure her laces weren't too tight, and true to her word, she let the three of us carry most of her gear. She's still wearing her pack with her phone and some food inside it.

I'm sure every step hurts, but she hasn't complained since we started walking this morning.

My mantra for walking is *step, step, step*. The more I can keep that one word in my head the less I'll remember that I'm a starving wreck with maybe ten times as many miles to cover as I've covered so far. The only way to win with this journey is to take it one step at a time. My calf started tightening up about halfway down to the valley. Hopefully it won't explode.

"I'm beat," Derrick says. "Starving, too."

We've all eaten our ration of granola and our sticks of jerky, but both just made me feel hungrier. Just a tease to my stomach.

"The sooner we get where we're going, the less we'll have to deal with the hunger." I point ahead. "Once we get into the trees we've got to make sure we keep going in the right direction."

"That pointy mountain on the other side of the valley," Shannon says, "we should try to keep it front and center. Even if we have to detour around lakes or swamps, we should always come back to it. Use it as a reference point."

The thought of climbing out of the valley on the other side and finding a pass through the mountains is too much to consider right now.

Step. Step. Step.

Brooke is hobbling along. She hasn't said much all morning. Maybe she's using her energy just to put one foot in front of the other given the state of her feet.

When we enter the trees, a mosquito buzzes in my ear so I slap the side of my head. One thing we have is mosquito dope. And being in full rain gear, if I can just rub some on my face, hands, and neck, I should be okay.

Did I mention that I freaking hate mosquitoes and that I almost never have to deal with them, because when I'm outside in the summer I'm usually running? But not now. I'm slated to cross a swampy and, so far, windless valley. And I can only go as fast as the slowest person so we can all stay together.

We all stop to put some bug dope on and drink some water. "It'd be good to make it all the way through the valley and up into the mountains on the other side," I say, "so we don't have to stop in the thick of the mosquitoes."

Brooke stares at me. "I'll be lucky if I make it halfway across this swamp." She points at her feet. "Besides, we can just set up the tents to keep the mosquitoes away."

Derrick and Shannon don't say anything. Why is it always me against Brooke when the four of us are together? In the tent the two of us got along fine—we were even laughing and telling jokes and sharing a little bit of personal stuff—but while we're walking we're always on opposite sides.

I consider trying to drag Derrick or Shannon into this—ask them what they think about where we should shoot for today—but decide that the sooner I can get us moving the more likely we'll end up resting somewhere out of the trees instead of in the middle of a mosquito-infested swamp.

The *whop whop whop* of helicopters turns our attention skyward. I pull my binoculars out of my pack and start scanning the sky.

"Anybody see them?" I ask.

"Don't bother," Derrick says, pointing. "They're specks. Way back from where we came from."

I turn and scan up the slope we just came down. And sure enough, there they are. But, like Derrick says, they are way high in the sky. "I think they're Canadian," I say, barely making out the red emblem on the tail of one of the choppers.

"If we were still up high," Brooke says, "maybe they would have seen us."

I almost respond, but then decide that I don't want to have the same broken-record conversation again.

"At least forty birds," I say. "The road system must be screwed for them to be using all this air support."

"Nah," Derrick says. "Pilots like to fly. They'll use any excuse to get up in the air. Trust me. That's the way my dad is."

We keep heading down, and now we're in the thick of the forest. Mosquitoes are buzzing all around. Clouds of them. I want to take off running, but I grit my teeth and keep walking, sweating like a pig in my rain gear. My clothes are tied onto the outside of my pack. I hope they'll be dry enough to wear soon. Another great thing about running is that you can wear less clothes and you create your own breeze when you run. For me, running keeps me cooler than walking, especially since I don't have to wear long clothing to keep the mosquitoes away.

The ground starts to get soggy, so we decide to alter our course. We turn to the right and try to edge our way along the swamp. We can still see the mountaintop Shannon said to keep in sight.

Now I'm happy to have my rain gear on because we've just hit a patch of wild rose.

I put my hands in my pockets to keep them from getting torn up by the thorns, and keep moving. There's a continual scratching noise as the four of us wade through the brush.

"I hope this ends soon," Derrick says.

Brooke has fallen behind by about a hundred yards, so I stop and wait for her.

When she catches up, she says, "Yeah, I know. We need to keep moving."

"I just don't want us to get too spread out." I slap a mosquito off my face. "For bear safety."

I turn and keep walking. We need to at least stay in pairs. I can see Shannon and Derrick up ahead. They've stopped and are standing quietly. Shannon motions for us to keep coming, but she also puts a finger to her lips.

I turn to Brooke and whisper, "Shannon's signaling for us to approach quietly. They must've seen something."

CHAPTER 27

"TWO MOOSE COWS WITH TWO calves each," Shannon whispers as Brooke and I catch up.

One of the mother moose is humongous, and the other is your normal-sized giant. Adult moose are monsters close up. There's no getting around that. The calves are dark brown toys in comparison.

The big mother has a thick scar running down one side of her, like she tangled with a bear or a pack of wolves and is still standing. The moose are spread out before us. A narrow ribbon of dry land passes between the two moose families. On either side, the swamp prevails. The moose with the scar works her way deeper into the water until her belly is partially underwater. Then she sticks her head entirely under for like fifteen seconds and comes back up.

"Is that how a moose drinks?" Derrick whispers. "Weird."

"She's eating," Shannon whispers back. "Aquatic plants. Some type of algae."

Her calves keep to the shallows, sticking their noses underwater. On the other side of the dry land, the other mother and her calves are in the shallows doing the same thing.

It's cool to see this many moose all together. I mean, if I were in Fairbanks or out on a training run, I'd be pulling my phone out and taking a video, but right now these moose are a barrier to where we need to go. We've got to get by them without disturbing them so much that the mothers decide they want to stomp us. More people are injured by moose than bears in Alaska in most years. We've had cross-country races delayed because of moose on the trail. One time we even had a race canceled. There's never been a delay or cancellation because of a bear during all the time I've been running.

"Can we thread the needle?" Derrick whispers, pointing at the narrow strip of dry land running between the two families of moose.

As if the monster moose with the scar can understand English, she lifts her head out of the water and turns toward us. Slimy green strands of algae hang from her mouth.

"It just depends," Shannon whispers. "On what the moose let us do."

We're all waving mosquitoes away from our faces. "We've got to do something," I say softly. "We could try to go around them."

Brooke frowns. "If we do that, we'll get soaked."

"We were soaked yesterday and we survived," I whisper. "Derrick, Shannon. What do you think?"

"Right now, we're outside of their *threat zone*," Shannon says. "That's why they're just eating and not staring us down. Whatever we decide to do, we've got to be able to adjust to how the moose respond."

Derrick holds up his bear spray. "We've got this, too."

Would bear spray work on a moose? I'm not sure, but if I were being charged by one, I'd give it a try.

"We could take a few steps down the middle of the dry area," Shannon says, "and see what the moose do." She points at Derrick's bear spray. "I'd use that as a last resort."

"Can you scare a moose away by yelling at it?" Brooke asks. "Like you can sometimes with a bear?"

"They have babies," Shannon says. "They aren't going to run away from them. They're going to protect them. The question is, will they see us as a threat?"

"And the other question is . . ." I hold up my bear spray. "If they're protecting the calves, will *anything* stop them if they see us as a threat?"

"We'll have to watch their body language," Shannon says. "If they flatten their ears and step toward us, we need to back away. And never turn your back on them. In my Alaska wildlife class, we saw photos of people who'd been attacked by moose. We'll be in serious trouble if any of us get attacked."

We're already in serious trouble. The longer we stand here, the longer it'll take us to hike to Talkeetna. Whether we walk between the two moose families or wade through the swamp to get around them, I just want to keep moving in the right direction. The starvation factor doesn't slow down, unless we can find another food source. All the blueberries we've seen are still green. And these moose in front of us— if we had a gun, we could maybe kill one for food. But we don't have a gun.

We whisper a little more and, in the end, decide to take a few steps forward to *thread the needle*. We go single file with me in front, followed by Shannon, Derrick, and Brooke.

CHAPTER 28

SPINDLY SPRUCE TREES NO WIDER than my forearms dot the narrow strip of land bordered by swamp on both sides. We've all got our canisters of bear spray in our hands with the safety clips off. Under any other circumstance we would've just turned around, but any step backward at this point is a step toward the starvation that's been chasing us since the earthquake.

"Okay," I say softly. "Here goes." I take a step forward, and then another. I can almost feel Shannon's toes on my heels.

The mother moose with the big scar running down her side stops feeding and takes a couple of steps, positioning herself so she's directly between the four of us and her calves.

I can live with that, I think, *as long as she can*. "Just passing through, old girl," I whisper to myself, and keep going.

Now I'm shifting my body sideways to squeeze between two trees and my pack catches on a branch. I stumble from the abrupt stop—but don't fall.

"I got it," Shannon says, and I feel the branch being lifted. "Okay, you're free."

"Thanks," I say, and keep going.

I don't know if it was my stumble or the noise of my pack rubbing against the branches, but now the smaller of the two mother moose— the one off to our right—takes several quick steps in our direction. Her ears are laid back and the hairs on the top side of her neck, right where it merges with her back, are raised.

Like we are one organism, we all move to the left, attempting to put a little more distance between us and the agitated moose. But doing so causes the monstrous moose with the scar to flatten her ears and move toward us.

My heart is beating a hole through my raincoat, and my throat constricts, making it hard to breathe.

"Just keep moving," Derrick says.

I take another few steps forward, and now I'm shifting to the right to get around another tree. The smaller moose off to our right walks toward us. Now, besides her ears being flat and the hair raised on the topside of her neck, she licks her lips.

Maybe twenty feet separates us. The canister of bear spray in my hand feels incredibly small compared to the monster staring me down.

I hear splashes off to my left. I turn my head and see the giant moose closing the distance.

I hope we can just make it beyond the angle where, instead of appearing to move toward their moose calves, we'll be moving away from them. But the two defenders of their young seem intent on stopping our progress. They're like the ends of a giant pair of vise grips intent on squeezing us. Only in this case, squeezing means stomping.

The way we're lined up now, I'll definitely get stomped first if either moose decides to attack.

I can feel my leg tremble as I take another step forward, trying to move straight so I don't favor one side or the other.

"It's okay, ladies," Shannon says softly. "We don't want to hurt your babies."

I take another step, and then another, and another. I don't glance back but I can feel everyone right behind me, like there is almost no space between where one of us ends and the next starts.

The two moose stand like sentinels, staying right where they are, not coming forward but not backing off. I take in a breath, noticing that my throat has loosened up, and I'm breathing almost normally.

I carefully duck down to work my way under a chest-high branch, not wanting my pack to snag and cause a bunch of noise that might enrage the moose.

I'm clear of the branch and stand up straight. And that's when both mother moose charge me at the same time.

CHAPTER 29

THE MONSTER WITH THE SCAR splashes through the swamp that is separating us. I stumble away from her but hear splashes behind me and know that the other angry moose is closing the distance, too.

Everyone is shouting on top of one another so I can't understand a single word.

I'm down on one knee and swing my arm toward the monster moose, who looks even bigger now that I'm not standing up. On dry land she rises up on her hind legs just as I press the trigger on my bear spray. A whooshing noise invades my ears as a wall of dark red fog envelops the moose's head. She comes down with her front hooves on either side of me.

I duck and roll away from her, knowing that another angry moose is behind me. And then a red fog takes over and I feel my throat constricting. My nose burns on the inside, like someone just lit it on fire. I jam my eyes closed just as they begin to get fried. The last image I see is Shannon standing, her arm outstretched with her bear spray pointed in my direction.

CHAPTER 30

I'M COUGHING BUT I'M NOT coughing. I mean, I'm trying to cough. Or my lungs are trying to cough and I'm not in control of them at all.

"Just breathe," Shannon says.

"We gotta wash that stuff off his face," Derrick adds.

"He's going to die," Brooke says softly.

"Brooke," Derrick says.

"Sorry," Brooke says.

I try to talk, but can't. My throat is too constricted. If it closes any more, I probably will die. Anything to keep from feeling the burn engulfing my head. My eyes are jammed shut, but the image of the red fog is etched into my brain.

"Josh," Shannon says. "We're going to dump some water onto your face."

Hands unbuckle my waist strap on my pack and more hands work the pack off my back, and I just curl up in the fetal position like I'm a baby, wishing right now that I'd never been born. I'd trade my life to be free of this inferno.

Water splashes onto my cheek and the top of my head.

"Brooke, you keep refilling the bottles and I'll keep pouring," Derrick says.

The cold water dulls the burn on contact, but as soon as it runs off, the burn comes back.

"You're going to be okay," Shannon says.

But I can hear the hesitancy in her voice. The fear. She's trying to convince herself that what she's saying is true.

And then I realize, *If I can think this thought, I must be getting enough oxygen to my brain. So even though my lungs are on fire and I can't talk, I'm still sucking in enough oxygen to keep myself going.*

"We'll need to stay here," Shannon says, "until Josh can see again."

In response, I try to open my eyes, but can't. Some part of me is blocking that from happening. Maybe some part of my brain knows better than the part where I make conscious decisions and it's stopping me from opening them.

Water keeps running down my cheek.

"I'm going to roll you over to your other side so we can wash your other cheek," Shannon says.

I let them roll me over, and then there's more water washing down on me.

"Can he drink any yet?" Brooke asks. "He's probably got clean water in his pack."

"We're all going to be drinking the swamp water soon enough," Derrick says.

"Yeah," Brooke answers, "but we'll purify it with the pills."

This conversation is happening, and it's about me, but I can't take part in it. I can't say, *Yeah, give me some water to drink.* Or, *No, I can't swallow anything.*

I push up with my arms so I'm in a sitting position, and I hear this weak groan come out of my mouth. More water splashes on top of my head and runs down my face.

"Josh," Shannon asks, "are you feeling any better? Is it burning less? Don't try to talk; just nod yes or no or something."

I hold up one hand and rotate my wrist so it twists side to side, making the universal *more-or-less* sign.

"Do you want to try drinking some water?"

I nod.

I hear a pack being opened, and then there's a water bottle brushing against my hand. I grab it and slowly lift it to my mouth and take a small sip and swallow. Then I cough. I hold the bottle out and someone takes it.

The heat on my face is growing in intensity, and I realize that no one has poured water over my face in a few minutes.

Then an idea pops into my head about how to treat this accident. I try to talk but still can't get my vocal cords to create intelligible speech, so I try to show Shannon, Derrick, and Brooke what I want.

CHAPTER 31

"WAAAAA," I SAY, TRYING TO get the word out of my mouth. Except I don't want to drink it. I reach out with my hands and move my arms side to side until I feel someone. I use their shoulder to stand up.

"Josh, man," Derrick says. "Take it easy. You're going to be okay. But we can't go anywhere right now. Not until you can see."

I let go of whoever's shoulder I've used to help me stand up. I force my eyes open for an instant, and see Brooke, Shannon, and Derrick standing in front of me, but the burning forces them closed again.

Now my entire head is on fire. If I had a cooler full of ice, I would stick my head into it and leave it there forever. Anything to dull the heat waging war on my face.

"Swamp," I try to say. I raise an arm and point and take a step in the direction I think the swamp is in. And since it's on two sides of us, I've got a fifty-fifty chance that I'm right. Two directions out of four.

I swing one leg forward and take a small, blind step in the direction I've pointed, hoping that they'll get the idea. I know there are small spruce trees dotting the dry land we're standing on. And that the ground is bumpy. And there's brush. Lots of things to trip on and bump into if you're walking blind, but I need to get to the water.

Now.

Before my head totally burns up.

I force my eyes open again, and then blink and blink and blink.

"Head." But that's all I can manage to get out of my mouth before my throat constricts in rebellion.

I think about running with Theo. When we would jog, we could just talk, but as we increased the pace, our conversation would become a series of single words or short phrases uttered between the constant sucking in of air we needed to keep the pace up. *One word at a time,* I think, *that's how I'll communicate.*

"Under." My voice sounds alien. Or like an old person on their deathbed saying their last words. I don't know if any of them have understood what I've said because they haven't responded.

"Water," I manage to get out before wheezing. Then I take another blind step in the direction of the swamp. My arms are still outstretched. I don't want to fall, but I need to get there.

"He wants to put his head in the water," Brooke says. I feel a hand take my arm. "We'll get you there. Shannon, grab his other arm."

I feel another hand on my other arm.

"Keep walking," Brooke says. "Small steps."

"And lift your feet high," Derrick adds, "to keep from getting snagged on the brush. Thirty or forty feet and you're there. For a runner like you, that's nothing."

In my brain, I smile.

"Come my way a couple of feet." Shannon gently tugs on my right arm as I continue to walk.

"We're going to turn you sideways now to squeeze through some trees," Brooke says as they shift my body around.

I feel spruce branches brushing up against my back. One grazes the top of my head.

Then they turn me back the way I was, and the three of us are walking in unison. They tell me it's a straight shot now, and I even feel the pace pick up slightly.

We stop.

Derrick says, "Kneel down."

"We'll help you." Brooke increases the pressure on my left arm. "On the count of three."

On *three* I feel the downward pressure on my arms as Shannon and Brooke start pulling, and I follow the movement, going down first on my right knee and then my left.

"Okay," Shannon says. "Now we're going to scoot you forward on your knees."

Brooke explains, "It's like you're walking, only on your knees."

I feel forward movement and scoot one knee forward and then the next.

"A couple more knee-steps," Brooke says.

My head is still a raging firestorm, but now my knees can feel a coolness through my rain pants, so I know I'm on the edge of the swamp. I picture my knees in shallow water.

"You'll want your arms free," Shannon says. "You're going to lean forward. Just pretend you're a baby and you're getting into crawling position."

I pretty much am a baby right now. I'm helpless and communicating mostly with single syllables.

Shannon and Brooke guide my arms forward until I feel the water on my hands.

"While you two dunk him," I hear Derrick say, "I'll set up a couple of tents. I think we're going to be here a while."

My hands hit the grassy bottom, and I'm into the water up to my elbows in a crawling position.

"Just keep moving your head forward and down," Brooke says. "We aren't going anywhere. We'll be right here if you need help."

I do what she says and feel my chin touch the water. Then my nose and mouth are under. I keep going and my ears are submerged, and the only thing left above the water is the back of my head. I lean forward until that's submerged, too.

There's a slight pressure in my ears, and I wasn't able to take a deep breath before going under, so my first dunking is maybe for only five or six seconds, but the relief is immediate. If I could just live underwater, if I could just be a swamp creature, I'd be fine.

I push up with my arms, and now my head is hovering above the water, and I can hear drips as water runs off my head and drops back into the swamp. I take a few short breaths because that's all my lungs will allow right now.

Then I put my head back under.

CHAPTER 32

"ABOUT THREE HOURS, I THINK," Brooke says.

I'm lying down in a tent and Brooke is sitting next to me. I'm on my back, thankful that I can see the blue nylon of the roof above me.

"It felt a lot longer," I say. "I mean, when you all of a sudden can't see, you lose all perspective of time. At least, I did." My face still burns a bunch. And my eyes still sting. And my throat still feels like it's recovering from a fire that was lit inside it. But I can take almost-normal breaths.

"It would have been worse if Shannon hadn't sprayed that moose. When you stumbled away from the one on the left, you must've triggered something with the one on the right." Brooke shakes her head. "It would've stomped you before you could've gotten up. Because of where you fell, she couldn't spray the moose without also spraying you."

I think about how I kept pushing us forward, not wanting to stop and waste time while we grew weaker from having almost no food, and now I'm the one holding us back. "I should be able to keep going soon," I say. But really, I'm dead tired.

Brooke leans toward me, and I see some red puffy areas on both of her cheeks.

Before she can speak, I say, "Did you get sprayed, too? Your cheeks, they're red."

"Mosquitoes," Brooke says. "That pepper spray. They didn't want anything to do with you. But the rest of us got munched on. I'm just happy we have the tents. It's pretty brutal out there if you aren't walking at a good pace."

"So when you were pouring water over me, and guiding me to the swamp, and helping me dunk my head, the mosquitoes—"

"You got it," Brooke says. "Even with bug dope, they were relentless."

I close my eyes and say, "I hope I don't slow us down too much."

"We're going to try to leave tomorrow," Brooke explains. "Just relax if you can. We're still in the middle of a swamp, and it's going to suck until we get out of here." I hear her laugh quietly.

I open my eyes. "What's so funny?"

"I was just thinking about Simon Lake and how picture-postcard perfect it was. About how I was going to show my sisters photos of this amazing place I got to go to. About how I *roughed it* for a whole month—even though, secretly, I couldn't wait to get home so I could take a hot shower, sink into the couch, and just be lazy."

"And that's funny?" I ask.

"Josh." Brooke puts her hand on my arm. "This might be it. We might not ever see our families again. We might be the last people we ever see. What I thought was important—me having a cool experience my sisters couldn't say they'd had—was so stupid." She takes her hand off my arm.

I close my eyes because they're starting to burn. "I hear you," I say. "Running cross-country was so important to me. Even during the quake when my calf smashed into a rock and got bruised, my first thought was about whether the injury would hurt my running performance this fall. Stupid. I didn't even think about my parents until later. I wonder if they're even alive. No one came for us. That has to mean the quake killed a lot of people. Maybe none of our parents are alive."

I reach down and pull the sleeping bag that's draped over my legs up to my chest because I'm starting to get chilled. I realize my pants are damp, but there's nothing I can do about that right now.

I feel the bag being tucked around my chin and know that Brooke is doing that. "Thanks," I say, keeping my eyes closed.

"I'm just glad you didn't die," she says. "When you couldn't talk, I thought your throat was starting to swell shut."

I ask Brooke to tell me everything she remembers about what happened from the moment I got sprayed until they got me into the tent.

She recounts it to me, and I realize that I remember pretty much everything, except for the planes that flew over when I had my head underwater.

"They were big military transport planes," Brooke says. "That's what Derrick called them. They were flying way too high to see us."

"How many?" I say.

"Twenty. Maybe twenty-five," Brooke says. "Canadian was Derrick's guess."

My mind flashes back to the earthquake and how much destruction it must've caused. I hope the tiny town we're trying to get to still exists.

CHAPTER 33

"THANKS FOR WASHING MY RAINCOAT," I say.

"I'd be careful with it," Shannon says. "It could still have some pepper residue on it, so if you touch it with your hands and then rub your eyes, they could start burning."

"I'll try to remember," I say.

A tiny breeze blowing keeps most of the mosquitoes away. And the clouds on the horizon are threatening to erase the blue skies that are above us. I take a deep breath and pretty much fill my lungs without coughing. My eyes are mostly back to normal, but I feel like they're in a permanent squint.

I notice that Brooke's pack is full like the rest of ours and realize that she's back to carrying her own stuff. "Your feet," I say to her. "They're okay."

"They'll have to do," she says. "And yeah, they're healing. And it's a good thing because I'm almost out of Band-Aids."

The tiny solar panel that keeps her phone charged is clipped to the top of her pack. I point at it, and before I can ask, she says, "Still just the red screen."

"Red seems to be the theme," Derrick says. "Cell phone screen. Canadian maple leaf on the birds." He points to the sky. "Welts from mosquito bites. And, let's not forget the bear spray."

I let out a small laugh.

Shannon smiles.

Brooke shakes her head and then laughs, too.

"That's something I'll never forget," I say.

"Me too," Shannon says. "I'm just glad I didn't kill you." She looks down at the ground. "First, I forget my bear spray and get cut off from camp by the wolves, and now this." She raises her head and looks at me. "I'm sorry."

"What are you talking about?" I clear my throat because it's still itchy from the spray. "You were spraying a moose that was going to stomp me, and I stumbled into the attack. And," I add, "I was the one pushing us to try to pass by the moose. If anything, the whole deal is on me. It's my fault. I—"

"Dudes," Derrick breaks in. "We're here and we need to get over there." He points to the mountain that is still in our sights. "Can we like walk *and* talk?"

We all shoulder our packs and start picking our way through the trees with the swamp on both sides of us. We go single file with Derrick leading, followed by Shannon, Brooke, and then me.

The corners of my eyes itch. It feels like there are tiny grains of sand in them even though I know there aren't. I blink a few times to try to get some tears flowing but don't feel any improvement. At least I can see.

Brooke seems to be walking normally, but I bet her feet are hurting. She's gone from being a complaint factory to just sucking it up.

That thing she said last night. That this might be it. That maybe we'll just starve out here. Now that we're walking again, I don't feel so doomed. Like I feel like we'll probably make it to Talkeetna if we can keep moving. But still, we just as easily could walk and walk and walk and never get where we're going because really, we don't know exactly how to get to where we are going. We don't have a map or a GPS or even an old-school compass. So starving still isn't out of the picture. It just feels like less of a possibility when we're moving.

The trees get thicker, and now we're bashing our way through spindly spruce over uneven ground, which is getting squishier and squishier.

"Cranberries." Shannon stops and points downward. Derrick turns around and comes back to join her as Brooke and I catch up.

"They're last year's," Shannon explains, "but they're still edible." She squats and pulls some berries off the plants that grow just an inch or two above the ground. "Try one." She puts a couple of berries in my hand and does the same for Brooke and Derrick.

They are a rusty brownish color and small, about as big as an eraser on the end of a pencil. I pop them in my mouth and chew. They're kind of mealy and tart, but food is food.

Now we're all on the ground, devouring every old berry in the patch.

"We'll have to keep an eye out for more patches," Derrick says. "Maybe we can eat our way to Talkeetna."

"It'll take a lot of berries to do that." I stand up. "I've cleaned this area out."

"There's plenty over here," Brooke says. Then she motions me over with her arm.

I walk over to where Brooke is kneeling, squat next to her, and pick a few more berries. "Thanks," I say.

"They're not mine," she says. "They're for everyone."

Is this the same Brooke who didn't want to dig Theo out and then wanted to leave him as bear bait while he was trapped and still alive? Now I'm liking her, like I did when I first met her and wanted to get to know her better. Truth is, I am getting to know her better. We're all getting to know one another better. I want to tell her everything. About how I felt when I first met her and then how I felt after the earthquake and how I feel now. Next time we stop for a real rest, I think, if we've got some privacy, like if we're sharing a tent again, I'll tell her. When I think of doing this my heart races a little. Yeah, I like her.

We keep walking single file with about five feet separating each of us. The ground stays squishy and the trees stay spindly. We don't see any more of last year's berry patches. The clouds are starting to block out the sun, and I'm glad we've all got rain gear because pretty soon we'll probably need it again.

Derrick puts his arm up and we all stop behind him.

What does he see now?

Another moose?

A bear?

A wolverine?

A pack of wolves?

We all crowd in behind him and then we see it.

Water. And it's everywhere.

CHAPTER 34

"HOW FAR ACROSS DO YOU think it is?" I point to the narrowest spot. "Can we just wade, or will we have to swim?"

The strip of soggy forest we were hoping to take to dry ground ends in the water, surrounding us by swamp on three sides.

"We could go back," Brooke suggests, "and look for another way."

The mosquitoes are starting to gather around us and it seems like the bear spray flavor has worn off enough that they're now as interested in me as they are in everyone else.

We're all waving our hands in front of our faces as we talk to keep the bloodsucking insects from landing. Even with our bug dope on, they're still harassing us.

"This whole valley could be a sponge," Shannon says. "We could retrace our steps, however many miles that would be, and then still have to cross a quagmire."

"Quagmire?" Derrick says. "Give it to me in English."

"It means swamp," Brooke cuts in. "Even I know that."

"And," Shannon adds, "it also describes our situation in general since the earthquake. That we're in a messy and kind of hazardous spot in our lives."

Like my parents, I think. Their marriage is a quagmire, that is, if they are still alive. "Okay," I say, "so we've got two quagmires. One right in front of us"—I point to the water—"and the other that basically goes with us wherever we go until we find help."

"I say we cross." Derrick points toward the mountain we're aiming for. "At least we'll eliminate one quagmire straightaway." He stretches out the *quag* when he says it, and for some reason we all laugh.

I'm not sure why we're standing here laughing, but it feels good.

Then Brooke brings us back to reality. "If the water is over our heads, how will we make it? We can't swim with our packs on."

"It might not be that deep," I say. I look across the shortest distance, which is maybe a quarter mile. There's no way to know unless we try.

Derrick takes his pack off and holds it over his head. "We should cross like this, commando style. That way if the water only comes up to our chins, we'll keep the rest of our stuff dry. If you have to swim, just keep your pack in front of you and kick like hell, like there's a shark chasing you, until your feet touch bottom again." He sets his pack on the ground.

"It's better than standing here and starving," I say, "while the mosquitoes suck our blood."

"It's a good plan," Brooke says, "especially if you're tall." She looks at Derrick and frowns.

"What?" Derrick stretches the word out and gives her an exaggerated shrug. "I don't have any freaking control over my height. Do you have a better idea?"

"She's right," Shannon says. "I'll be the first to swim, then Brooke, then Josh, and then you, that is, if you have to swim at all."

"I get what everyone is saying. And basically, everyone is right. Derrick can't control his height. It is a good plan if you are tall. And Shannon has correctly identified the swim order." I hold up my hand to stop anyone from saying anything until I finish. "But how about if we add this to the plan." I slap a mosquito that's drilling into my cheek and continue. "The taller people cross first, and if the water is deep enough that the shorter people will need to swim, then the taller people will cross back and carry their packs and keep their stuff dry."

"So, me and you head across," Derrick says, "and if we don't have to swim but it's obvious that they do"—he points at Shannon and Brooke—"then we hoof it back and assist?"

I nod, and Derrick says, "I'm game for that, Moose Man."

"It's a pretty good idea," Shannon says. "I'll just add that some of us shorter people might not need help all the way across, but just over places where it's too deep to walk."

"Brooke?" I say.

"Do I even have a choice?" She huffs. "You three are all for it. I'm in whether I want to be or not." She takes her pack off, unzips the top pocket, and pulls out her small waterproof bag that she keeps her cell phone and solar charger in.

She unclips the solar charger from the top of her pack, carefully pulling out her cell phone and detaching the cord running between it and the solar panel.

"That's weird," she says, staring at her phone. "I was sure I turned this thing off. Maybe the button got pressed from all the jostling around." She squints. "But what's on the screen is different than it was before."

We all gather around Brooke, trying to make sense of what we're seeing.

CHAPTER 35

"IT'S NOT THAT DIFFERENT," DERRICK says. "Maybe the bear was there the whole time, and we're just now noticing it."

"No." Brooke shakes her head. "I've been staring at this screen every time I check to see if my apps will come back up, and it's only been red."

On Brooke's phone screen, there is a faint outline of a bear in the center of the still-red screen.

"Maybe it's Canada's state animal," Derrick says. "And some code person thought it'd be cute to have it in the system."

"Canada's national animal is a beaver," Shannon says.

"How do you know this crap?" Derrick asks.

"That same ole Alaska wildlife class," Shannon says.

"Maybe it's military," Derrick says. "Maybe this rescue operation has been named Project Bear or something. My dad is always throwing around these weird names for the stuff he's doing."

"At least we know someone is doing something," I say. "I mean, the screen has changed, so that means people are actively doing something. Maybe once we get across the swamp and back up high, they'll spot us."

Brooke powers her phone down, puts it in the waterproof bag, and zips it into the top pocket of her pack. She says, "How can they just leave us out here? We left a note. There were twenty of us. We all have parents. I just don't understand."

"That's exactly why we couldn't just stay at the lake." I start to rub my eye and then stop because I don't want it to start burning more. "This quake must be an all-time record breaker. We're just not a priority."

"Okay. I get it," Brooke says. "But that doesn't mean I have to like it."

Derrick laughs. "That's what I think almost every time my dad explains why he's making me do something I don't want to do. Like going to that stupid Simon Lake camp. I didn't want to go. And now look where I am. I hope my dad is thinking about that. About the fact that he sent me when I didn't want to go, and now I'm missing. Maybe he'll change his tune when I get back."

I look across the swamp and then to the mountains beyond. *If we get back*, I think but don't say. "How about if me and Derrick get started? Tallest first, remember?"

"We're the tallest?" Derrick says.

"You're the giant," I say. "I'm just a distant second."

"That's more like it," Derrick says, and he laughs.

And I've got to admit, I envy how easygoing Derrick is. How he can make a joke one second and be ready to do something crazy serious like crossing a swamp the next.

He's already hoisting his pack above his head. "Come on, Josh. Let's get this over with."

I was just feeling almost dried off after my last dip in the swamp. I hoist my pack above my head and follow Derrick.

"Don't drown," Brooke says from behind me.

I turn around. "Keep your bear spray handy. You never know what might happen while you're waiting." Then I join Derrick, who's already got his feet in the water.

"It looks longer now that we're actually going to cross," he says.

"Just don't think about the whole thing at once. One step at a time," I say.

"And then one kick at a time if we have to swim." Derrick smiles. "It sucks being the tallest one. Maybe up in the mountains"—Derrick points to where we're hoping to get—"we'll run into some obstacle where it makes sense for the shortest person to go first." He laughs.

We walk into the water side by side. The first several steps are knee-deep and the cold water soaks my lower legs and chills them. Feathery plants that feel like tall grass brush against my shins. My arms are getting a little tired from holding my pack up, but I want to keep my stuff dry, so I rest the pack on my head, which takes a little pressure off my arms, and I keep walking.

Now we're about a hundred yards from where we began, and the water is just starting to touch my crotch.

Derrick hasn't said anything since we started wading but now he breaks the silence. "Do you think there're leeches in this cesspool?"

"If there are," I say, "they've got to get through our clothes to find any skin. I hope we're not in here long enough to find out."

"Me too," Derrick says. "I hate murky water. When we lived in Texas, there was this pond my friends liked to swim in. I hated it. They used to hound me until I'd relent and go in. And then they'd play tricks on me. Touch my legs with branches underwater and I'd think it was snakes. Stuff like that."

I've only ever lived in Alaska and have only traveled out of state a few times to visit relatives or compete in cross-country races. The only scary things up here are big. Bears, wolves, moose. And the cold. Any month of the year and you can freeze to death. No snakes or creepy crawlies. Unless there're leeches.

"Shannon probably knows if there are leeches," I say. "She freaking knows everything."

"She's got it going on," Derrick says, "in a good way."

We keep walking, and now the water is touching the bottom of my rib cage.

Then the surface changes from grassy to muddy, my feet start sticking to the bottom, and I'm in water up to my armpits. "I need to swim," I say, "before I get stuck."

I kick my feet hard and try to push off the bottom, and my right foot comes free. I pull the left one up as hard as I can, and it comes free, too. But my left foot feels colder than my right, and then I know what happened.

Down there.

In the murk.

Somewhere.

Is my shoe.

CHAPTER 36

I'M TREADING WATER TO KEEP my feet off the bottom, but my arms are starting to feel the burn from holding my pack over my head.

"My shoe," I say. "I lost it. The mud sucked it off my foot. I have to search for it." I don't want to move from the spot directly above where I lost it, or I'll never be able to find it.

Derrick turns toward me. The water is chest-deep on him. He's still standing. "I'll take your pack, but I probably won't be able to hold it for long. I'm sinking a little bit now, too." Derrick takes a step toward me. "Hand it to me, and I'll keep walking so I don't get stuck."

He takes another step and reaches for my pack, and I thrust it toward him. Now he's got both packs. He's holding one in each hand with his arms stretching toward the sky.

I stick my head underwater and reach for the bottom. Cold mud oozes between my fingers. I've got my eyes jammed shut. Not that I could see anything if they were open in the murky water. I dig and dig with my hands, searching for my shoe. I feel something solid and pull.

But it turns out to be a stick. I let go of it and move to the right just a little bit. I thrust my hands down again and submerge them into the mud. Leeches or no leeches, I need to find my shoe. I spread my fingers and search side to side. I'm up to my forearms in mud, and now my lungs are starting to scream for air.

I pull my arms toward me and then reach for the surface, popping my head above the water. Derrick is about fifty feet away, still walking in the same pose.

I suck in a deep breath, go back under, and keep searching. I pull up another stick. And then a rock. Am I off by a few feet? Am I not digging deep enough?

I go to the surface and then submerge three more times, but each time I come up shoeless.

Now Derrick is standing still, maybe one hundred yards away, but the water is only thigh-deep where he is. Somehow, he's managed to put one pack on his back and is holding the other close to his chest. He's looking in my direction. I start kicking toward him. I swim the breast-stroke, keeping my head above the water.

"The bottom's solid here," Derrick yells.

I let my feet touch bottom, and now I'm wading in waist-deep water, closing the distance.

"I'm screwed," I say as I reach out to take my pack from Derrick.

"We'll deal," Derrick says. "Let's just get the hell out of this swamp."

We keep walking, and I'm favoring my right foot—the one with the shoe. I'm doing more of a hop-walk than a true walk, not wanting to plant my left foot down too hard in case something sharp is sticking up from the bottom.

The water depth keeps decreasing until we're slogging through shin-deep and then ankle-deep water. "Let's get to that tree." I point to a spindly spruce standing by itself. "We can leave our packs there. It'll be a good landmark to shoot for on our second trip."

"At least our packs are mostly dry," Derrick says. "And we've got three shoes between us. We could still compete in a three-legged race." He grins.

I crack a smile even though there is basically nothing to smile about. Then I say, "Did you sink at all back there, like I did?"

"I sunk in a little bit. But my gigantic feet kept me afloat," Derrick says. "They're like snowshoes. For once, they've paid off." He looks down and says, "Monster Feet, you're finally paying for yourselves."

At the tree we take our packs off and set them down. Then we look across the swamp.

I put my hand to my forehead and scan the narrow point of land from where we started. Derrick does the same.

At the same time, we both say, "Where are they?"

CHAPTER 37

WE LEAVE OUR PACKS BY the tree and wade back into the swamp. Derrick has his canister of bear spray, which he says he can keep above the water, no problem. Mine is mostly empty from the moose encounter. Plus, I'm not confident I can keep it above the water if I carry it in my hand, and if there's any left, I want to be able to use it later if I need to. I don't know if submerging it in water would wreck it, and I don't want to find out.

As we wade, we yell for Brooke and Shannon. I just don't understand where they could've gone. I mean, the dry land ended, surrounded by swamp, so unless they turned around and started heading back the way we came, they'd get soaked.

Besides turning around once at the beginning, I kept myself focused forward when we crossed the swamp, so I didn't see what happened to them, and I don't remember hearing their voices either. Wouldn't they have called out to us if something was wrong?

The trees are pretty thick just beyond the edge of the water, so maybe they're just inside the trees. But if they are, why aren't they coming out when we call for them?

We hit the deep, soggy section where I lost my shoe. I start swimming, but Derrick keeps walking, so I pull ahead of him. I'm starting to get chilled from being soaked from head to toe.

My feet bump the bottom, and I stand up in knee-deep water and start jogging toward shore. I hear Derrick splashing behind me and know he's running, too.

I'm still favoring my right foot, setting it down harder and trying to run in a way that my left foot barely touches the bottom of the swamp. I hit dry ground, stop, and turn around and wait for Derrick to catch up.

Together we head toward the trees, shouting the girls' names. Sticks poke into my sock, but there's nothing I can do about that. I just hope I don't get a puncture wound.

Just inside the trees, we find a light green backpack. "It's Shannon's," Derrick says.

The pack is open, and her stuff is spilled out across the forest floor. Like someone, or some animal, pulled stuff out and tossed it wherever. Like a hurricane tore through it. Her food canister, tent, her blue stuff sack. A purple stuff sack with a bunch of tampons is lying next to it.

"Shit," Derrick says. He unclips the safety from his bear spray.

"Be careful with that," I say.

"I got this," he says.

"Shannon!" he shouts. "Shannon!"

I shout, "Shannon!"

"Over here." Brooke's voice cuts through the silence.

Derrick and I look at each other, and I point off to the left.

Derrick sprints ahead of me, and I follow with my one-foot hop, relieved that we've heard Brooke's voice, but still confused.

Brooke keeps shouting, and we keep following her voice.

"They're here," Derrick yells.

I crash through some spruce trees. My sock catches on a snag from a fallen tree. I stumble and fall down on one knee. I push myself up and snake my way around a couple more trees, and there, in a little clearing, I see Derrick and Brooke squatting, facing away from me.

And between them, on the ground, are two legs sticking straight out. As I approach I see that the legs are Shannon's. She's lying on top of a sleeping pad.

Now I'm hovering over Brooke, peering down at Shannon. Her eyes are closed and she's not moving. I scan her chest and stomach, looking for them to rise and fall, but can't even tell if she's breathing.

CHAPTER 38

"I GAVE IT TO HER right in the thigh," Brooke says, "just like she told me. Then she got dizzy and said she needed to lie down."

Brooke tells us about Shannon wandering off to pee and then getting stung by a yellow jacket, which she's allergic to.

"The side of her face was swelling up by the time I got to her, and only a minute or two had gone by. She pointed in the direction where she'd left her pack and I found it, dumped it out, and got the EpiPen. The swelling has gone down some."

I keep staring at Shannon's chest and stomach, and finally I see the rise and fall that tells me she's breathing.

"I didn't know she was allergic," Derrick says, his hand on Shannon's arm.

"I don't think anyone did," Brooke adds. "Or, if the leaders at Simon Lake knew, they kept it a secret. Her throat could've swollen shut."

Brooke strokes the side of Shannon's head, and Shannon moves a little in response and whispers, "I'm okay. In a minute, I'll try to sit up."

"The monster speaks our language," Derrick says.

"Just shut up," Shannon whispers. "And keep the mosquitoes off my face."

Derrick laughs quietly. I see Brooke crack a small smile and feel myself smiling, too.

But now I'm starting to really cool off from being soaked. The clouds have blocked out the sun. I know I'm going to get wetter before I get drier since we have to cross the swamp one more time.

And my shoe—my freaking shoe—is somewhere in the murky

mud out in the middle of the swamp. How will I climb mountains with just one shoe?

Now I'm the one hoping like crazy that we'll get buzzed by more helicopters and one will actually see us. Or that we'll get some bars on Brooke's phone and be able to call for help or send a text despite the red screen. I took for granted that I could just cover any distance I needed to. Like if I needed to leave everyone behind at an easy-to-find spot and run for help. But that idea that I've kept as a backup plan has evaporated with my lost shoe.

Shannon opens her eyes. "Sorry for the delay." She touches the side of her face and winces. Then she looks at Brooke. "I wasn't sure if I'd need the EpiPen, but thanks for administering it. You're supposed to err on the side of needing it; otherwise, it could be too late."

Brooke says, "I was so scared of being left out here alone, I jammed that thing in your thigh with no hesitation." She smiles. "I'm glad you're okay. We all are."

"There can be rebound effects," Shannon says. "It's been years since I've had an EpiPen shot, but I recovered well last time. You're supposed to seek medical attention after you use one, but I guess I'll have to settle for you three."

"Doctor D. at your service," Derrick says. "I specialize in, well . . . I specialize in not specializing."

Shannon sits up. She touches Derrick's arm and smiles. "Perfect. The last thing I want is special treatment."

"Did anyone at camp know?" I ask. "About you being allergic?"

Shannon shakes her head. "I kept it a secret. Lied on my medical form. I didn't know if they'd let me come if I told them. Hid my EpiPen inside a spare pair of socks."

Derrick says, "Is there anything else we need to know?" He's smiling, but I can tell it's a serious question.

"Is that question just for me?" Shannon says.

"You inspired it," Derrick responds. "But no." He glances at me, then at Brooke, and then puts his hand on his chest, indicating it's for all of us.

After we all fess up to having no other medical conditions to fess up about, I say, "How long until you think you'll be able to cross the swamp, Shannon?"

"I don't feel dizzy, but I'll know more after I stand up." Shannon touches her face again. "That yellow jacket came out of nowhere." She stands up on her own, and we all stand up, too. Then she says, "I should be able to walk."

"How about swimming?" Derrick says. He makes the breaststroke motion with his arms.

"It's that deep?" Brooke frowns. "This is going to suck."

"It's already sucked for me and Old Tenderfoot, twice now." Derrick gestures toward me with his thumb, pointing downward.

Shannon and Brooke look at my feet.

I explain to them how the water won't be exactly over their heads, but if they walk through the mucky part like I tried to do they might end up shoeless, too. "Unless you've got skis for feet"—I point down at Derrick's feet—"I'd swim."

Shannon and Brooke look at each other and then back at me.

I go on. "Me and Derrick will carry your packs. Maybe at some point we'll be able to build a fire and dry our clothes. I don't think I've been dry since the bear spray incident."

Brooke points at my foot. "What are you going to do with just one shoe?" She shakes her head. "How are you going to hike?"

I raise my stocking foot in the air. "I'm just going to have to do it. Somehow. I don't know how, but I will. I can do it." I try to sound confident, but truth be told, I'm pretty nervous about the whole thing. The enormity of my situation is settling in. Will I die in the wilderness because I lost my shoe in a swamp? Putting one foot in front of the other just got way more complicated.

"Dudes," Derrick says. "Let's—"

"I just want to make it clear," Shannon says, "about this *dude* lingo you keep using."

"Dude," Derrick says, looking at Shannon, "go on." He grins.

Shannon cracks a smile. "Historically speaking, a dude is a fashionably dressed man."

Derrick raises his eyebrows and smiles. "Dudes, I'm using the word in a more modern way. I know that I've taken some liberties with the term, but to me, dudes are friends I can rely on. Male, female. Young. Old. My pet dog—if I had one. Makes no difference to me. Now, let's all get across the swamp and then deal with this Tenderfoot shoe issue on the other side, and anything else that comes up, like needing a fire so we don't freeze to death."

"That makes sense," I say. "After we're all across, we'll have one less problem to solve."

CHAPTER 39

THE FIRE CRACKLES AND THROWS some sparks while the four of us sit around it, soaking wet from the swamp crossing. The clouds are breaking up, so at least we won't get drenched from above.

The knee-high flames are giving off enough heat that steam is rising from our clothes.

Through the trees, I look toward the swamp, wishing that my shoe would magically rise from the mud and float to me.

Shannon stands up and stretches her arms over her head. The side of her face where she was stung is still swollen, but other than that she seems to be okay.

"I could sleep for a week," Brooke says.

"I'm too hungry to sleep." Derrick stands up and tosses a giant handful of sticks onto the fire. "I'm going to go collect some more wood. We're going to need it if we want to finish this dry-cleaning job."

I want to help him collect wood but don't want to trash my one sock. I rinsed it and wrung it out in the shallows at the edge of the swamp and then carefully walked up here with one bare foot. Now my sock is propped on a branch close to the fire.

It makes sense to dry off, especially since we'll be climbing the next mountain range to keep going. If we're dry, we'll be less likely to get cold. But all the delays are slowing us down.

The bear spray incident.

The yellow jacket.

The swamp.

And now, my shoe.

I might turn into a continual delay for the group. We could starve before we get anywhere because of me. I might have to tell the group to keep going and I'll follow if I'm moving a lot slower than they are. I can't have everyone die because of me. The last thing I imagined was that I'd be the weight dragging us down. I thought most of my challenges would be about getting the others to keep moving.

I stand up and hop closer to the fire. I look carefully before setting my bare foot down, but I feel a prick and quickly lift my foot off the ground. Without my sock on, it's even more impossible to move around. I think about how much I take for granted when I've got a shoe on each foot. How I run with abandon on trails, on roads—everywhere. Theo and I never talked about how great it was that we were wearing shoes on our daily runs. It was just something we took for a given.

I sit back down, bend my leg, and pull my foot toward me. I examine my heel and see several small rose thorns, some as thin as strands of hair, sticking out of it. There must've been a tiny branch on the ground that I didn't see. With the sock on, it would have been better, but eventually those thorns would have worked their way through my sock and into my foot.

Shannon sits down next to me. "Do you need any help?"

"Maybe," I say. Then I focus in on my heel and try to pull the tiny thorns out with my thumb and index finger, but they keep slipping through my grasp.

I try and try and can feel Shannon's eyes on me. Finally, she says, "Can I try?"

"Sure," I say. "I was about to just cut the whole thing off and be done with it."

"Dude," Shannon says, sounding just like Derrick, "we don't have the bandages to deal with a severed foot, so you may need to keep it for our sake." She smiles.

"Yeah," Derrick says, coming in behind me with a pile of firewood.

"You're gonna need to keep it at least until Talkeetna. If you're still feeling the need after that, I'll cut it off for you."

I crack a small smile, but I'm still feeling lousy about the situation. I don't want to be a drag on the group.

"Flex your foot," Shannon says.

"Which way?" I say, moving my foot back and forth at the ankle.

"Pull your toes toward your shin." Shannon demonstrates with her own foot. "It'll tighten the skin and make the extractions easier."

"So scientific sounding," Derrick says as he sits down next to Shannon. "Let me know if you want me to assist in the *extractions*."

"I'm keeping my distance," Brooke says from the other side of the fire. "Josh, I know your foot's been washed, but you washed it in a swamp." She scrunches her nose up and sniffs like she's catching a whiff of something nasty.

Derrick laughs, and for a few seconds it feels like everything is normal. Like we're just hanging out somewhere and later we'll all go home for the night.

"I'm waiting," Shannon says.

I flex my foot, and Shannon leans forward and puts one hand on the ball of my foot. "Okay, I see a few tiny rose thorns." She touches one, and I wince. "Sorry," she says. "They're pretty flimsy, more like hairs than thorns."

"Yeah," Derrick says. "Too bad he didn't step on something big, like a rusty nail; then any of us could've yanked it out easily."

"I'm going to try to pull them out, but they're so small." She reaches with her thumb and index finger, but when she connects with my heel I pull back.

"Sorry," I say. "That kind of tickled."

"Just try to keep it steady," Shannon says.

She tries again. I resist the urge to pull back, and it feels like a couple of the needles are being pushed into my heel.

"I can't quite get them." But Shannon keeps trying, and I keep feeling like I'm getting stuck with needles. I just grit my teeth and let her try because I know if they don't come out, I'll be in pain every step of the way, and that's not even counting what else I might step on that will cause me problems.

Shannon lets go of my foot and sits up straight. "If only I had some tweezers."

Brooke says from across the fire, "I know something to try. It's kind of gross, but it might work."

CHAPTER 40

"I'M THINKING, IF THERE EVER was a surefire way to spread hoof-and-mouth disease, this is it," Derrick says.

"Are you serious?" Brooke asks.

"If I was planning on doing what you're planning on doing." Derrick's voice trails off, "I don't know . . ."

"I do know," Shannon says. "Hoof-and-mouth is a cow disease. It has nothing to do with humans. There is something called hand, foot, and mouth disease, but that's mostly about little kids putting their hands in their mouths and getting a viral infection because they have germs on them. It's most common in daycare settings."

"How do you know all this stuff? And don't say that ol' Alaska wild-life class . . . Are you one of those new, realistic-looking AI robots?" Derrick asks. "Seriously, how do you know this stuff?"

"School? My mom being a nurse?" Shannon pauses and shrugs. "I don't know. My mom says I have a good memory. And, I guess I just like learning."

The fire is still burning with knee-high flames, and the heat and smoke seem to be keeping the mosquitoes away. If we weren't starving, hanging out around the fire would actually be fun.

"My sister taught me this method to pull out splinters," Brooke says. "I've only ever used it on myself, and never on my feet. Mostly on the palm of my hand." She continues, "Josh fixed up my feet and basically taught me how to wear my boots. I don't think I'd be sitting here if it weren't for him, so if I can help, I want to." She smiles at me, and I smile back.

"Above and beyond," Derrick says. "Above and beyond." The second time he says it he slows it down and drags out each syllable for emphasis and we all laugh.

"More like below and beyond." Brooke points at my foot.

"Let's get this over with," I say. Truth is, I just hope it works.

"Okay, Josh," Brooke says. "Kneel down on your hands and knees, then flex your foot. Everyone else, stand back so you don't block my light."

I do as Brooke says.

"Okay," Brooke continues. "First, I'm going to touch your heel to see if I can feel the tiny rose thorns with my finger."

I feel Brooke's finger on my arch. She slowly runs it toward my heel, and it's starting to tickle until she hits one of the thorns and I reflexively move my foot.

"Keep it still," Brooke says. I feel her other hand press down on the base of my calf.

She must've scooted her face closer to my foot because now I can feel her breath on my heel and arch and my heart races. Yeah, I'm a little aroused by this. Under different circumstances, if she had her mouth that close to my bare foot and wasn't recoiling in horror, I'd be pretty much melting.

"Okay," Brooke says. "I'm almost ready. Stay absolutely still. I don't want to get kicked." My foot has totally heated up from her breath.

I feel her lips brush my heel and then her teeth scraping against the skin.

I close my eyes and concentrate on staying still. I feel a little stinging.

Brooke presses harder on my calf. "I got one," she says. Then I hear her spitting. "There's like three or four more."

Brooke repeats the process like ten or twelve times because she isn't successful on every try, but in the end she gets them all.

I rise so I'm on my knees and turn to Brooke, who is still on her knees. "Thanks." I smile.

"Sure thing." She smiles back at me. Then she stands up.

"You've just proved it." Derrick points at Brooke. "Truth is stranger than fiction."

Even though he's just making a joke and we all laugh, when I think about all we've been through since the earthquake, I totally agree with him. You can't make this stuff up.

And now I'm back to thinking about what to do about my shoe situation. As much as I might like it, I can't be asking Brooke to pull sharp objects out of my feet with her mouth all the time.

Plus, right now my foot is clean. I doubt she would have offered to do that if it were filthy. And hiking without a shoe, you can bet my foot will be filthy. Dirt and grime I can handle, I just don't want to hurt it. I need to be able to walk on it—for miles and miles and miles.

Derrick throws more small sticks and branches on the fire. It flares up, and we all step back because of the heat. If we can keep the fire this hot, our clothes will be dry in no time.

Maybe Shannon can tell I've been thinking about my missing shoe because she says, "I think I know how to protect Josh's foot when he's hiking, but it's going to require each of us giving something up."

CHAPTER 41

I TAKE A STEP, TESTING my new shoe. "I think this will work."

The wind picked up a little bit while we were building the shoe. When I hold my foot up after taking my first step, the wind presses the blue stuff sack that makes up the outer layer of the shoe against the top of my foot and ankle.

"You'll probably have to make some adjustments," Shannon says.

I look at my foot, wrapped in a blue stuff sack that's tied on with the drawstring from the top of my sleeping bag. "This will be a million times better than just wearing a sock," I say.

It took some trial and error to get it to where it is right now.

My sock is on just like I always wear it—that's layer number one.

For layer number two, there's a blue stuff sack, thanks to Derrick donating his.

For layer number three there's a piece of blue foam from Brooke's sleeping pad, roughly cut to the size and shape of my foot. We accomplished this by using a sharp rock as a knife.

For layer number four, there's another blue stuff sack, thanks to Shannon.

The whole contraption is tied together with the drawstring from my sleeping bag. The drawstring—which is basically a small rope—circles my foot three times and is tied snug on top with a square knot. The idea is that the rope will keep the blue foam—the only cushioning I have for my foot—from sliding all over the place.

From the bottom up, something would have to puncture four layers to make contact with my foot. The biggest danger is having something pummel my foot or ankle from the side, where there's less protection.

The other danger is that the stuff sack is kind of slippery. The rope wrapping around it provides some traction, but nothing like a real shoe.

"Thanks, everyone," I say. "With any luck, I won't slow us down too much." My heel is still a little sore where Brooke used her teeth to extract the thorns, but it's way less painful than when the thorns were in my skin.

"I'm going to eat my ramen," Shannon says. "And just pretend we're on a camping trip and are sitting by a campfire."

We all decide that now is as good a time as any for dinner and each break out our second-to-last packs of ramen. When I swallow the first mouthful of crunchy noodles, it awakens my hunger, and I know I'll feel even hungrier after I've finished them.

"The rest by the fire has been good for me," Shannon says. "Coming down off the EpiPen has me feeling kind of sleepy. I can walk, but it sure feels good to just sit here."

"We can all relax at least a little longer." Derrick dumps the last of the wood he's collected onto the fire. "At least until this load burns up."

My clothes are still pretty damp, but maybe a little more time by the fire will do the trick.

A gust of wind whooshes down from the mountains. Maybe this time the breeze is stronger, or maybe it's blowing closer to the ground, or maybe both of those things are happening, because the thick bed of glowing red-hot coals that's built up over the last few hours doesn't exactly scatter, but some of it becomes airborne. Derrick and I are sitting on the uphill side of the fire so it doesn't bother us, but Brooke and Shannon are sitting on the downhill side. They both dive out of the way to avoid being burned by the flying embers. Some tiny coals land right where they were sitting, and some of them sail over their heads, riding the wind. I watch the coals that land on the ground close by to make sure they don't burst into flame.

Shannon and Brooke move to the uphill side and sit between Derrick and me. The sun has come back out, so that will speed up the last of the drying process.

"How does everyone feel about continuing to walk once the fire burns down?" I ask. "I know we've had an exhausting day, but now that the sun is out we might want to take advantage of it."

Brooke sighs. "As much as I want to just set up my tent and crawl in, I think you're right. We should walk, that is, if Shannon's recovered from the EpiPen."

"I'll be okay." Shannon smiles. "Slow miles are better than no miles."

"I like that." Derrick repeats Shannon's rhyme. "I'm going to use that phrase on my dad next time he gets on me to hurry up."

I crack a smile, but I'm thinking, *Yeah, I hope you see your dad again. I hope we all get to see our parents.* On top of not knowing if we'll find our way out of the wilderness before we starve, we don't even know if any of our parents survived the quake. When I left on this trip, my main concern with my parents was figuring out how to keep them from getting a divorce. Now I don't care if they never speak to each other again—I just want them to be alive.

We all keep rotating our bodies, trying to dry off completely. My new shoe feels okay, but it's not the same height as my other shoe, so even walking around the campfire feels kind of awkward, like one of my legs is longer than the other, which I guess it is right now.

I take ten steps away from the fire toward the mountains, and Derrick says, "You leaving already?"

I turn and walk back to the fire. "I'm just trying out my new shoe," I say, "to work the kinks out now, if there are any."

I walk back and forth a few more times. I can feel the blue foam starting to slip, so I untie the drawstring and retie it tighter, hoping that will do the trick.

I'm about thirty steps up from the fire when Derrick shouts, "We might have company."

I start walking back toward him. Shannon and Brooke are both standing up, looking where Derrick is pointing.

"That's got to be someone's fire," Brooke says.

"Maybe they crossed the swamp, too," Derrick says. "And now they're drying out—like us."

"They've got to have a way to call for help," Brooke says. "I just know they do."

As I get back to the group, Shannon says, "That's from us. Our blowing coals have started a forest fire."

CHAPTER 42

"COALS CAN BLOW THAT FAR?" Derrick asks.

"They're pretty light," Shannon responds.

"Look." I point to the left of the first smoke plume. "More smoke."

"I think I can see the flames from the first spot," Brooke says.

"There's another plume off to the right." Derrick points.

The spruce is pretty thick, running in both directions from the swamp. It's only above us, where the wind that blew the coals in the first place is coming from, that the trees thin out and eventually disappear.

"We should try to put them out," I say, "before they spread."

"That's a nice thought." Shannon shakes her head. "But we don't have the equipment."

"Three fires." Derrick slaps his hands against his sides. "Four if you count ours, which will also be a bear to put out. Originally, I thought I'd be able to take a leak on it to put it out, but it's way bigger than that now."

"If the wind switches," I say, "those fires will come our way. As it is, they might come our way anyway. I mean, spruce trees burn, especially with all the needles on the ground."

"We need to go," Shannon says. "Now." She points up toward the mountain we've been aiming for.

We quickly pack up and start heading for higher ground, leaving our original fire burning, because if we tried to put it out now, flames might overtake us.

We tromp through the trees. The rope around my homemade shoe quickly loosens, and soon the blue foam is flopping all around inside the stuff sacks. Every time my foot hits the ground without the blue foam under it, I cringe, waiting for something sharp to stab through the stuff sacks and my sock.

"You all keep going," I say, stopping. "I just need to retie this."

I stoop down, reposition the blue foam, and then cinch down the rope. I haven't done anything different, so I'm expecting it to come loose again pretty quickly. At some point, I'll need to solve this problem, but not while we're making tracks from a fire.

I stand up and almost bump right into Brooke.

"You shouldn't be here," I say. "You—"

"Buddy system." She smiles. "Let's go."

Is this the same Brooke who abandoned the trapped Theo to a bear? She's done some nice things lately, but I still expect her to behave like a selfish child, so when she doesn't, I'm surprised. I just hope she keeps surprising me.

I'm sort of sliding my foot along, hoping that the blue foam will stay in place longer if I don't lift my foot up so much.

Brooke and I walk without talking, and when we break out of the trees and are wading through brush—mostly blueberry and willow—we spot Shannon and Derrick ahead of us. They're on a little rock outcropping, staring back the way we came.

We catch up to them, and Derrick points. "Look."

Down below we can see orange flames consuming trees and black smoke billowing.

"And smell," Shannon says.

I inhale through my nose and take in some smoke.

"The wind direction is starting to change." Derrick coughs. "It's blowing at us. I don't like this."

"Maybe this fire will attract some attention," Brooke says. "Maybe it'll get noticed, and if we're not too far from it, we'll be rescued. This could be a good thing for us."

"Either way," Shannon explains, "we need to be farther away than we are right now. Fire can travel fast when conditions are right. It can scream up a hill if the wind is behind it. This brush will burn. Easily. And quickly."

We keep heading up. Aiming for that same mountain we've been looking at for the last couple of days now.

I have to retie the rope four or five more times, but it sure beats walking with just a sock on for protection. Now that we're in steep country, I'm pretty much keeping up with everyone. If I were out of shape, no way would I be keeping this pace with the number of stops I'm making. The shoe situation is just kind of leveling the playing field. Instead of me stopping and waiting, I'm just maintaining the slower pace that these three naturally walk and then jogging to catch up after I've stopped and retied.

The brush thins out, and now we're walking on low tundra plants interspersed with rocks. When I turn around to check the wildfire's progress, I see that it's reached our campfire spot and is spreading out, consuming trees to the left and right, and marching up the hill.

Everyone else is stopped, too, watching.

"We want to stay out of gullies and ravines." Shannon's voice sounds strained. "Anywhere that could funnel wind is a potential death trap."

"Let me guess," Derrick says, "you took a wildfire class?"

"Not exactly," Shannon says. "My mom's old boyfriend was a fire-fighter. I learned this just by talking to him."

"What I don't get is how you remember everything you hear," Derrick says. "If I had half your memory capacity, my dad would be through-the-roof happy."

Shannon cracks a smile. "Dude, we've all got our strengths."

I look at the blue stuff sack surrounding my foot and think about how my main strength, being able to cover distance at high speed, has been cut down. Derrick's got physical strength and a sense of humor. Shannon's got brains. Brooke is becoming more giving and resilient. It's just me who's diminished, but I'll do everything I can to not let anyone down.

The breeze is blowing smoke toward the mountains. I taste it with every breath. "We should keep moving," I say. That's one strength I have: I'm a relentless pain in the ass when it comes to staying still for too long.

"Look at the gray smoke." Brooke points downhill and to the left.

The fire has reached the brush we've just crashed through, and it's not slowing down.

CHAPTER 43

"THE SCREE SLOPE HAS THE least amount of vegetation," I say. "It should offer the most protection from the fire, right?"

Shannon nods.

We've walked maybe a half mile since the brush started burning, and now gray soupy smoke is cutting our visibility down.

I hear Brooke coughing. We were going to fill our water bottles from the swamp and use our tablets to purify it, but since we had to leave in a hurry, no one has any water.

I take a step from the tundra onto the scree and immediately wish I had real shoes on both feet. The brown rocks covering the slope are pointy, and lie on top of one another every which way, making for sharp angles. Most are the size of loaves of bread but some are bigger.

I turn around. "I'm going to try to angle up one way and then switch back so we can zigzag up." I want to stay as far from the edge as possible because that's where the vegetation is.

No one argues with my zigzag idea, so I keep going. The blue foam provides a lot more protection from the rocks than a sock would, but I can feel their hardness poking through with every step. *Don't try to go any faster than you reasonably can*, I tell myself.

I'm planting my next step when a thunderous roar almost knocks me down. I step sideways and lean into the steep mountainside, supporting myself with one hand. Ear-splitting roars continue for several seconds and then they're gone.

"Sonic booms," Derrick says. "From fighter planes."

"Maybe they had to get somewhere in a hurry," I suggest. "I mean, if you had to get somewhere to help with the earthquake, that'd be the fastest way, right?"

"I guess," Derrick says. "Or maybe they're assessing damage or taking pictures or something. It's not like they can just land anywhere like a helicopter can."

"Not very likely they saw us through the smoke," Brooke says.

"No," I agree. "But they'll probably report the fire, and that might get someone else out here."

Shannon hasn't said a word. She's just staring back the way we came. Now she turns forward but still doesn't say anything.

I keep moving upward at an angle. I glance over my shoulder. We're spread about ten feet apart, all climbing at the same slant.

The gray smoke is a constant, and I can only see a couple hundred feet in any direction, but that's far enough to see that we need to make a turn to stay in the middle of the slope, so I pivot and head in the opposite direction, starting our first switchback.

The scree slope isn't the route we would have taken if the fire weren't chasing us. We'd be below and to the left, climbing through a vegetated saddle—a low pass in the mountains.

As I keep going up, I'm not sure there'll be a way off this slope without retracing our steps back down.

Everyone has made the turn, and we keep walking in silence. I make a second switchback, then a third, and then a fourth. Now the rocks are bigger, like flat slabs the size of school desktops. But I've got a rhythm going, and the angle I'm tackling the slope with isn't so steep that we have to use our hands. And now that the rocks are big enough, I can plant my foot down in the center of some of them and not subject my improvised shoe to all the sharp edges.

As I work my way up the scree, I think about all the groups of planes and helicopters we've seen, and the fact that none of the sightings resulted in a rescue. I think about the note we left at Simon Lake and wonder if anyone has been there, and if they have, whether they figured out there was a note in the canister surrounded by flags. And just how long has it been since the actual earthquake? We stayed at the lake for six days, and now we've been walking for at least three, maybe four days.

I want to believe someone is searching for us, but when I try to convince myself that it's true, I get this sick burning feeling in my stomach.

I turn to start another switchback, and the rock I step on starts sliding beneath my foot. I scramble forward, and the blue foam padding in my shoe contraption shifts sideways.

"Rock!" I yell to warn the others as the rock tumbles downslope.

The sliding rock sets off a chain reaction, and the rock above it skates forward, coming to rest on my ankle, and then the rock above that one tumbles on top of it, and now my leg is pinned from the knee down, and I can't move.

CHAPTER 44

I TWIST MY UPPER BODY around, look over my shoulder, and see Shannon and Brooke standing below me. Derrick is down on his knees with both hands pressed to his forehead.

"I'm trapped," I yell.

Shannon looks toward me, then down at Derrick, and says, "Brooke, go help Josh while I deal with this."

"Be careful coming up," I say. "There's loose rocks everywhere you step."

Brooke takes her pack off, sets it down, and then slowly works her way toward me.

Shannon's pulled out her sleeping pad and has it oriented so that when she guides Derrick to lie down his head is on the uphill side.

"Just keep pressure on the wound," I hear Shannon say. "Foreheads tend to bleed a lot no matter how deep or shallow the cut is."

Brooke scrambles over the last of the rocks that are separating me from her.

She looks down at my leg. "Does it hurt?"

"Not exactly," I say. "I mean, it hurt when it slammed into me, but I'm hoping I'm just trapped and not injured too badly."

Brooke nods and then looks downslope where Shannon and Derrick are. "When we move this rock, we've got to make sure we don't send any more strays down that way."

"What happened to Derrick?" I ask.

"That rock you tried to warn us about," Brooke says, "it clipped him in the forehead. He's bleeding." Brooke coughs a couple of times. "Nasty smoke."

"I didn't know it was coming loose until it came loose. Everything had been so stable, I think I let my guard down." I grit my teeth. I hope Derrick will be okay. His injury—it's on me and I feel awful about that. More than awful. Guilty.

Brooke's voice breaks into my thoughts and zaps me back to the present. "We should move the rock to the left." Brooke points. "That way, it won't be directly over where Derrick is recovering."

I glance back at Derrick's position and nod. "Okay."

Brooke grabs the rock with both hands. "I can pull while you push."

We do that, and the rock moves to the left.

"One more time," I say.

We do it again, and now I can see the rock that's pinning my ankle.

"My knee feels okay," I say. I press on the side where the rock hit, and it hurts a little bit. "It might be bruised, but if that's all the damage, I'll be happy."

Brooke looks down past my knee. "Where's your foot?"

"It's down there." I point. "Under that rock."

The rock pinning my foot just above the ankle is smaller than the one that slammed into my knee, but it's also wedged in more firmly.

"I think we'll need to move a couple of rocks before we can move the one that's pinning me down," I say.

Brooke glances down the slope to where Shannon and Derrick are, and I follow her gaze. Derrick is still lying on his back with both hands pressed to his forehead. Shannon is sitting with him.

"Same plan?" Brooke says. "We'll move rocks to the left to avoid our friends."

She lifts the topmost rock on the downhill side and places it a few feet to the left. I want to help lift the rocks, but I can't reach where we need to put them because I can't move.

"One more," Brooke says, "and then we'll work on the one pinning your foot."

She lifts another rock and moves it just far enough away that the rock pinning my foot is now totally exposed. I try to slide my foot out from under it, but it won't budge.

"We'll have to lift this last one," I say, "or at least tip it up."

"I can pull up on the lip of it." Brooke points to the downhill side of the rock. "And you can try to slide your foot out."

Brooke positions herself on the uphill side and grabs the lip of the rock.

On the count of three she lifts and I slide my foot, which comes free partway and then stops. I can see the edge of the blue stuff sack. "I'm caught on something."

"Okay," Brooke says.

She pulls the rock toward her, and at the same time, I move my foot away from the rock and then take a step back.

"I'm free," I say. I rotate my ankle and bend my knee, and everything seems to be working. I look for blood seeping through the blue stuff sacks but don't see any.

I turn to Brooke. "Thanks. That was close. I could've just as easily broken my foot. Especially with this soft shoe." I point at my foot.

Brooke just nods and looks downslope. I follow her eyes. Shannon is still sitting next to Derrick. She's leaning over him and talking softly so I can't hear what she's saying. But one thing is for certain. Derrick hasn't moved the whole time Brooke's been helping me.

CHAPTER 45

"I'M SORRY," I SAY. "THAT rock coming loose took me by surprise."

Derrick gives me a tiny nod. His hands are still on his forehead applying pressure to the wound.

"About four more minutes," Shannon says. "Then we'll take a look."

Shannon goes back to counting quietly to herself so she'll know when approximately fifteen minutes are up.

The smoke is skidding up the scree slope. Down below, we can see where it's burned the brush up to the start of the scree. The fire is working its way up the tundra bordering the left side of the scree. We're safe from it though—for now.

I wonder how Shannon decided on fifteen minutes but don't want to ask her and screw up her counting.

Brooke takes her phone out of her pack, turns it on, and shows me the screen. Still red with an outline of a bear. She turns it off and puts it away.

Now that we're just sitting, I'm starting to cool off a little bit. The sweat that I didn't realize I'd worked up is starting to dry.

"Okay," Shannon says to Derrick. "I want you to slowly take your hands away from your forehead, but don't sit up."

Derrick peels his blood-soaked hands away from his forehead. Blood has run down his face in streaks. "What—"

"Don't talk," Shannon says. "I don't want your skin stretching any-where near the gash. We need the blood to keep clotting to slow the bleeding." She leans in close. "It looks pretty good."

A zigzag gash about two inches long runs across Derrick's

forehead. A little blood is leaking out of it at one end, and I wonder if the cut is deeper in that spot.

Shannon looks at me and Brooke. "Can one of you get out a sleeping bag?"

I pull out mine and help Shannon cover Derrick.

"We should probably sit tight for another half hour or so," Shannon says. "If we can get the bleeding to completely stop, that'd be ideal."

Shannon tells us that the fifteen-minute rule for head gashes is something she learned from her mom. "There are lots of capillaries in the head so wounds tend to bleed a lot whether they're shallow or deep. My guess is that Derrick has a pretty shallow wound since the bleeding has slowed way down."

"How big is the cut?" Derrick says softly, barely moving his lips. "What's it like?"

"About two inches long. It sort of zigzags up as it goes from right to left," I say.

"Just call me Frank," Derrick whispers.

"Frank?" Shannon says. "Why?"

"Tall guy. Big scar across his forehead. Short for Frankenstein." The corners of Derrick's mouth curve up into a smile.

"Just be quiet for now," Shannon says. "You don't want your sense of humor to end up killing you."

"I can think of worse ways to go," Derrick mumbles, and then he's quiet, following Shannon's instructions.

I turn my attention to my improvised shoe. I dismantle the whole thing and study the parts. And then I get an idea.

I put the foam piece inside my sock and try to put my sock back on, but my foot and the foam won't fit inside it together.

I lay the piece of foam flat on a rock, then I pick up a small sharp rock and go to work cutting it down to make it narrower and just a little shorter.

Brooke watches me put the modified blue foam into my sock. "Good idea," she says.

"We'll see," I reply. Then I pull my sock on. I have to push the blue foam down because it wants to ride up on my heel, but once I get it set on the bottom of my sock it stays in place pretty well. I put one stuff sack inside the other and pull them over my foot. Then I take the string and wrap it around my foot a few times and tie it off.

I stand up and shake my foot, and the contraption stays on. I want to test it out by walking, but I don't want to dislodge more rocks. I glance over at Derrick. I caused that. Accident or no accident, I feel terrible about it.

I sit back down and take a breath.

Shannon says, "Okay, Frank, I want you to sit up slowly."

Derrick props himself up on his elbows. Then he pushes with his hands so he's sitting all the way up.

"How do you feel?" Brooke asks.

"I'll live," Derrick says. He looks at me. "It'll take a bigger rock than that to keep me down."

"Man," I say, "I'm sorry."

"I know," Derrick says. "You already told me once. You think I've got brain damage from this?" He smirks.

I know he's joking around to try to make me feel better, and it kind of works. But I still feel lousy.

"We'll have to come up with a new way to go up the slope," I say. "Walking below someone else is too risky."

"Now you tell me," Derrick says.

"We could spread out a little," Brooke suggests. "And each climb the slope in a different spot."

"That would work," Shannon says. "Good idea."

Derrick slowly stands up. "What are we waiting for? Let's go."

CHAPTER 46

TWO DAYS LATER WE'RE STARING down at another valley. We hiked high ridges after dodging the fire we started, but now we have no choice but to go down again.

"I think we should expect there to be a swamp," Derrick says. "That way we won't be bummed if there is one." His forehead wound has scabbed over and looks like a dark red lightning bolt.

My improvised shoe has held out, but one of the stuff sacks is starting to wear thin. I'm not feeling the effects of the bear spray anymore, and Shannon says she's fully recovered from her EpiPen experience. And Brooke's feet—she hasn't mentioned them and she's keeping up with everyone, so they must be okay, too. Her cell phone is still red, with an outline of a bear.

Our biggest problem at the moment is food. We don't have any.

Walking on well-drained tundra when you're starving is barely manageable. Bashing through brush and bushwhacking through a mosquito-infested black spruce forest is something entirely different. It takes way more physical energy and mental concentration. Plus, my homemade shoe could get caught or snagged on downed branches and tree roots.

"It's hard to tell from here," Shannon says, "but this valley looks bigger than the one with the swamp."

"Could be a river snaking through those trees," I say. "Or at least a creek."

The sun is poking in and out behind big white cumulus clouds.

"Empty country," Derrick says. "We haven't seen one scrap of anything that would suggest people have been through here."

I wish we had some topo maps so we could try to match the valley in front of us with one on a map. At Simon Lake, we learned how to read them so we could figure out where we were and what we were seeing.

We're probably not taking the most efficient route to Talkeetna. We don't even know how far off we are. But if we keep walking west, we'll at least eventually hit the highway, even if we miss Talkeetna. That is, if we don't starve to death first.

We start heading down and Derrick says, "Josh, try not to draw the moose toward you this time. We've only got so much bear spray."

"I'll do my best," I say. I have sort of become the point guard when we're walking. I like route finding, and everyone seems to be happy with me taking on that role once we've decided on a direction.

The first part of the descent is gradual. We're walking on a well-drained tundra ridge sloping gently downward. I keep us on the spine of the ridge that I think will penetrate the valley the deepest. That way, we'll have more tundra walking and less forest walking. At least, that's the idea.

My pants are fitting more loosely than they were at the start of the hike. None of us had much weight we could lose, but we're all looking thinner, even Derrick, who was already pretty thin to begin with.

Gaunt is how Shannon described us when we broke camp this morning. And then Derrick chimed in, saying, "We're the gaunt, out for a jaunt."

After a couple of hours, I reach the absolute edge of the spine we're walking on.

I stop and wait for everyone so we can discuss where we want to go from here. Will we pick a mountain to aim for on the opposite side of the valley like we did the last time? Will we decide to follow the valley? Maybe this drainage will lead to Talkeetna?

Brooke pulls up next to me. Then Derrick and Shannon.

"Hmmmmm," Derrick says. "So many great choices."

"I don't know how much farther I can go today," Brooke says. "I'm feeling kind of weak."

"How about if we rest here for a while?" I ask. "It's breezy so there are fewer mosquitoes."

Everyone agrees, and we take our packs off and drink some water. We all ran out of purification tablets yesterday. Up high on the ridge, it was easy to find snowmelt water, but down where we're going, we'll just have to risk drinking what we can find.

We talk for a while about which direction to head. The spine here splits into two smaller spines. Both of them end in the forest pretty quickly. We decide to take the right spine because it points farther up the valley and it looks like we'll have less spruce to crash through before climbing out the other side.

"We can always set up the tents in the trees and take another break before we climb out the other side," I say, hoping that will ease the stress I know Brooke is feeling.

We slowly stand up and put our packs on. I start heading down the right spine. I hit a patch of big rocks and slow my pace, taking care each time I set my shoeless foot down.

I'm working my way through a spot with jagged gray rocks when Derrick calls out, "Hold up, people. I just saw something."

We all turn toward Derrick, and he's pointing to the left and across the valley.

"In those trees on the far side," he says. "It was something human-made."

CHAPTER 47

"IT WAS GREEN," HE SAYS as he pulls his binoculars out of his pack and scans the area he was pointing to.

Now it's my turn to make a joke. "That's really helpful in a sea of green spruce trees. Maybe that knock to the head did have an impact."

Derrick ignores my jab, keeps looking through his binoculars, and says, "It was long and narrow, and I didn't see it until it started moving. When it was still, it blended in with the trees." Derrick pauses and lets his binoculars rest on his chest, hanging from the strap. He puts one arm in the air. "When it moved"—he pulls his arm down—"it came straight down."

"Could it have been a falling branch?" Shannon asks.

"Branches grow out from tree trunks, and when they fall, you can really see them tumble," Derrick says.

I think about what Derrick says, and it makes sense to me. "So, how did this thing move again? And how big was it? I mean, you saw it from way over here."

"It was long, and it was moving vertically. But it was narrow and smooth-looking. And green." Derrick makes a tight circle with his hands. "Like a small diameter pipe. I wouldn't have picked it out of the trees if it hadn't moved. It was just as tall or taller than the trees, and then it disappeared straight down into the trees, like someone was lowering it."

We all keep staring into the spruce trees on the far side of the valley and down to the left. I'm trying to pick out anything unnatural down there. Anything that would make me want to change our course, because if we go that way we're going to be bashing through at least twice as much forest and brush. I pull my binoculars out and scan the area but turn up nothing out of the ordinary.

"Could it be some scientific research station that's operating automatically?" Shannon asks. "Like whatever you saw was programmed to do what you observed, but no people are actually there?"

Derrick cocks his head sideways. "Raining on my parade again." But he's smiling. "I'll bet you . . . hmmmm . . . nothing much to bet . . . that it's more than just some automated thing."

"Why do you think that?" Shannon asks.

"Because I want to believe it," Derrick says. "If there's a minute chance that there's a person over there doing whatever they're doing, we'd be idiots to walk in a different direction. We've done some idiotic things, but we're not true idiots. Not unless we ignore this." He turns and starts scanning with his binoculars again. "It could be our *Get Out of the Wilderness Free Card*. Right over there. Hidden in those trees."

I want to believe Derrick. To believe that what he saw wasn't just a branch falling straight down. Or a play on the sunlight hitting the trees. I wish more than one of us had seen it. I wish I could have seen it. Truth is, I am very concerned about how, without any food, every mile will just get harder and harder. If we hike over there and find something, that's great. But if it's nothing, we've just wasted limited, precious energy we could have used to keep us moving toward our goal.

Brooke, who hasn't said a word since we stopped, says, "I'm in. I want to see what's over there. Even if it is some automated science station, we could break it and then maybe someone would come out to fix it."

Shannon responds, "Sometimes stations are set up and data is collected on-site, and periodically someone visits the station to get the data. So, if that's what it is, it's not necessarily sending information back, so someone might not realize it's broken for quite a while."

"Whatever," Brooke says. "I still want to know what it is that Derrick saw. I'd have a hard time just walking away from it."

"We've got nothing," I say. "If we expend our energy with extra bushwhacking, that'll just exhaust us sooner."

"But think about it," Derrick says. "We've got to cross this valley anyway. So, we go down the valley a ways instead of up a ways. The forest will be harder to navigate. I can see from here that the trees are thick down there. But we're not adding that much distance."

"I'm thinking about every step." I point to my un-shoe. "I don't want to be a burden on the group if this thing falls apart."

"We've got plenty of blue foam pads to cut from, and two more stuff sacks to use." Derrick sets his binoculars on top of his pack and crosses his arms.

I take a breath. "Okay," I say. "I'm in." I want to believe what Derrick believes. I want to trust his vision and his interpretation of what he saw. I want to believe that it'll be worth the expended energy, but right now I don't have that 100 percent belief. But what I do have, I realize, is hope. I can't control what is and is not over there, but I can control my decision to put forth the energy to check it out.

"Derrick makes a good point," Shannon says. "If there's nothing there, we've walked maybe a day or two out of our way. But if we don't check it out, it will haunt us."

"We're the gaunt out for a jaunt," Derrick says, "and we can't take no haunt."

And with that, we study the new route. When we agree on the general direction to take, I start leading my starving friends down toward the thickest, most inhospitable-looking vegetation in the valley.

CHAPTER 48

BELOW THE TUNDRA, WE HIT chest-high willows growing so close together you can't tell where one plant stops and another starts.

"Keep your eyes open for bear sign," I say. The last thing I want is to surprise a grizzly. But with the four of us crashing through the brush, we're making so much noise that hopefully any bears in the area already know we're here.

I catch my un-shoe on a sharp branch, and I hear the unmistakable rip of nylon. The tear is on the outside of my ankle and is only through one stuff sack. I tuck the torn parts under the string and keep going.

The willows seem to go on forever. Like we're adrift in a willow ocean and the shore keeps getting farther away. We work our way slowly because that is the only way to swim through willows this thick.

I'm bending a branch and there's this explosion of vegetation right in front of me, and I leap back and fall as I let out a scream. My feet are sticking straight up in the air, and I'm waiting for the bear to pounce, but it doesn't. Then I notice a medium-sized roundish bird, perched on a stout willow branch, moving its head up and down.

Then I hear Derrick's voice. "Always grousing around."

I kick my legs forward and sit up. "Thought it was bear." I point at the bird. "A grouse." I shake my head.

"More specifically," Shannon says, "that's a ptarmigan—our state bird."

"Ptarmigan sharmigan," Derrick says. "It acts like a grouse."

"Yeah," I agree, "and I was the birdbrain."

"How much farther?" Brooke asks, not laughing at my joke.

I stand up and look back where we came from and then to where we're going. "We have to crash through at least as many willows as we have so far to get to the spruce forest, and then we've got to cross most of the spruce to get to Derrick's mystery spot."

Brooke sighs. "I wish this were easier."

"Don't we all," Derrick says.

The sun is low in the sky. Soon it'll be setting. It won't get super dark, but it might be a good time to take a break.

"How about when we get to the edge of the willows"—I point in the direction we are heading—"we find a spot to set up a couple of tents. We can sleep for a few hours and then continue our search."

"That makes sense," Shannon says. "Whatever we're looking for, it'll probably be easier to spot in the daylight."

"And," Derrick adds, "we wouldn't want to surprise someone who's sleeping. Judging by how this guy"—he points at me—"reacted to a bird, whoever is there may think we're a bear and just start shooting."

It takes a couple more hours to reach the edge of the willows. The sun has sunk behind the horizon and the mosquitoes are getting thicker. We decide to set up two tents because there's not much open ground, and—while I can't speak for everyone—I like having a person next to me when I rest, even if it is kind of crowded. There's some kind of support or energy you get from doing things together. When we got to do our solo experiences at Simon Lake, I was way into that. I was itching for a new experience, for a new way to push myself. I was going to be all by myself in the wilderness. That was cool and intense, and I was hungry for it. But now, maybe because we're so alone out here, being truly alone in a place like this would feel overwhelming—like if I woke up and Shannon, Brooke, and Derrick were gone without a trace. I don't really want to be in a tent by myself. I don't want to be anywhere by myself.

And I like Brooke. If circumstances were different, I don't know what would happen between us. I mean, we haven't talked about any of this stuff. I don't know if she feels even remotely how I feel. Maybe someday, if life gets back to normal—if we do survive—we'll find out just how much we like each other. I like her enough that I want to know if being together would work for us. I wonder if she wonders about this very same thing.

But in the tent right now, I'm content to lie head to toe with her to get a few hours of sleep before resuming our foodless search for something green in a spruce forest.

"Josh," Brooke says softly. "If there's nothing where Derrick thinks there's something, we should write something in our journals. All of us should. Just in case, you know, if things keep getting worse and we keep getting weaker, we may not have the energy to write anything."

"What kind of writing?" I say. Then I sit up. "You mean like what we're doing?"

"Not just that. More like what we think of our families and what we think of each other. Something to kind of honor the journey we're on. Something to let people into our hearts who may read our entries if . . . we don't make it."

I have to ask myself again, is this the same Brooke who abandoned trapped Theo to an approaching bear, and who unwillingly, grudgingly dug for survivors?

I take a deep breath and let it out. "Brooke," I say, "tell me who you are. I mean, I formed one opinion those first few days after the quake, but slowly you're breaking that opinion apart with your actions."

"Something changed for me when you took care of my feet," she says.

I sit there waiting for her to go on.

"All I did leading up to you helping me was oppose you in almost every little thing you did." Brooke sits up. "I know I was so selfish about Theo when he was dying. But I was also scared of dying. I guess I was trying to preserve my own life at all costs. Basically, I just wanted to survive." Brooke scoots forward so her face is closer to mine. "All my life, I've competed with my older sisters. In a way, they taught me to be selfish, but they also taught me self-preservation." She puts her hand on my knee. "You taught me. No, you showed me, that I can keep the self-preservation instinct alive and still help other people. I'm not saying I've totally got that down all of a sudden, but I'm thinking of others way more than I used to since you fixed my feet."

"I don't know what to say," I say. "I mean, I was feeling like a tyrant for the first several days of this *jaunt*." In the dim light, I look Brooke in the eye. "You're not the only one to learn some things about themselves." I pause. "The bear spray. Losing my shoe. I was so used to being number one that I was comfortable in the leader role. In the role where I didn't need help from others. But now, there's no way I wouldn't want help. There's no way that I don't need help.

"When I was running cross-country, I wanted to do my part to the fullest. My teammates could do what they wanted, but I was going to do extra practices because I was driven to have a shot at number one. That created some distance between me and the rest of the team, but that was a price I was willing to pay to pursue my goal. But out here, that same approach didn't work. All I created was distance between me and the three of you. Slowly, I've been bridging that distance. At least that's what I'm trying to do."

"It's kind of strange that we spent a month at a leadership camp," Brooke says, "but then when the quake forced us to put those skills to work, it was like we were starting from scratch."

"I guess when you're given hypothetical situations to learn from, like we were given at Simon Lake, the learning can only go so far. Like running can only teach me so much about racing, when really the best way to learn about racing is to race."

Brooke still has her hand on my knee, and right now that's by far the warmest part of my body. Will the friendship we're building now hold up back in civilization? Will it turn into something more? The drive to find out compels me all the more to survive.

CHAPTER 49

"WE NEED TO BE THOROUGH," Derrick says as he stuffs one of the tents into a stuff sack. "It's not going to be easy to just pick out the spot where I saw that green thing get lowered from the trees."

We're getting ready to head into the spruce forest. The sun is a pale orb in the sky, covered by a thin veil of clouds. The land is still sloping downward, so there's no guarantee we won't hit a swamp before the land slopes up on the other side, which is where Derrick saw whatever it was.

"If we get all the way out of the spruce forest and don't find it," I say as I shoulder my pack, "maybe we'll be able to see it from above on that side of the valley."

"I hope we find it soon, and that it helps somehow," Brooke says. "I'm starving."

"I'm still full from last night's imaginary meal." Derrick pats his stomach and then glances at Shannon. "Right, Chef Shannon?"

"It was a stroke of luck that we found that feather to induce vomiting." Shannon opens her mouth, pretends to stick a feather down her throat, and then fakes throwing up. "I ate so much."

I think about the serious conversation Brooke and I had in our tent, while these two were playacting. The important thing is we all had a short rest, and now we're ready to keep going no matter how exhausted we each feel. I wonder if Derrick likes Shannon, and if Shannon likes Derrick, the way I'm starting to like Brooke. And yeah, of course I wonder what Brooke thinks about me.

"What do you all think about me leading today?" Derrick asks.

"Not that Josh hasn't been giving Daniel Boone, Davy Crockett, and Natty Bumppo a run for their money on route finding." He cracks a smile. "It's just, I know what I saw, and I'm the only one who saw it, so I'd kind of like to be out front."

"Fine by me," I say.

Shannon and Brooke both say it's fine with them, too.

Derrick suggests the general direction he wants to go, pointing in a way that makes it so we'll angle our way down the next part of the slope, and then, when we get to the bottom, we'll reevaluate based on whatever we find—a swamp, a stream, or just dry land. Who knows?

We've all got our bear spray in our hands—even me and Shannon, who probably have next to none left because of the moose incident—as Derrick leads us into the trees.

Unlike the spruce forest we were in when we emerged from the swamp—the one we set on fire and burned down—this one seems to have way more underbrush. Thorny wild rose plants and blueberry bushes without blueberries grow thick, overlapping one another. According to Shannon, it's too early in the summer for blueberries. Some of the bushes have tiny green unripe berries, but that's it.

At first, Derrick leads us around the thickest clumps of brush, but then when the growth gets even thicker, he stops and says, "Let's put our rain gear on so we can just crash through this worthless stuff without getting scratched up, and without our clothes getting full of rose thorns. I want us to stay on track."

"The roses aren't worthless," Shannon says. "A few weeks ago we could have eaten the flowers that were on them. And at the end of the summer we can eat the fruit they'll produce—rose hips."

"Point taken." Derrick smiles. "I just hope we're not still out here to see them ripen up."

It's kind of warm out to put our rain gear on over our pants and pile jackets, so we all strip down and quickly change into our rain gear before the mosquitoes can turn the scene into a bloodbath. Rain gear with nothing on under it is a sticky way to travel, but at least our clothes won't be all wet and sweaty later.

I take the time to retie my un-shoe since we're going to crash through brush intentionally, and then we keep going.

The spruce trees start out small and sickly but grow bigger the farther down the slope we get, and the brush is getting thicker and thicker, too.

I hate putting my foot down through the brush when I can't see what's there, which is almost every step through some stretches.

You take so much for granted when you have real shoes on. You can slam your foot through the brush and use it to stomp down rose bushes to get the thorns out of the way. But two stuff sacks, a sock, and a piece of blue foam as a shoe substitute, all tied together with a small string, makes you careful. You have to think and worry and wonder about every step in an overgrown forest like this. When you add in starvation and how your mind doesn't work great when it's deprived of energy, you open yourself up to making even more mistakes.

We get to a spot where the brush totally disappears and there's just spruce trees, but up ahead, in about forty yards, the brush begins again.

Derrick stops and puts his hands on his hips. I decide this is a great place to retie my un-shoe, so I stop a few yards behind him, and as I tie, I say, "Too bad the rest of the forest isn't like this spot."

Derrick says, "And just why is that? Why is this spot like this at all?"

Shannon and Brooke enter the clearing and join us. They must've heard Derrick because Shannon says, "It's highly likely that someone cleared the brush out of this spot. It's so different. It's been cleared, and it *hasn't* grown back. Why?"

Brooke takes her pack off, sits down, and leans against a tree. "This is paradise. Pure paradise compared to that." She points to where we've come from. "Not counting the fact that we're starving, of course."

I don't know if she's seen where we are headed, which is just as bad, but I don't say anything because she'll find out soon enough.

"Clearing this would take some work." Derrick gestures with his arm, sweeping it in a circle. "Why here?"

"Why couldn't it be natural?" Brooke asks.

"Look at the border on all sides," Shannon says. "It is so definitive. Things like this don't happen very often in nature. Usually natural boundaries are more crooked."

I finish tying my un-shoe. "Whatever it is, no matter how it got here, I hope there's more of it beyond that jungle of brush." I point in the direction we're heading.

We leave paradise and keep crashing through the brush. Derrick is so focused on keeping his direction true that he bashes right by the second clue that this area might have been visited by humans.

CHAPTER 50

"HOW OLD DO YOU THINK it is?" I say, pointing.

Shannon picks it up and crinkles it a little bit. "It's not disintegrating in my hand so it can't be super old, I think."

The piece of black plastic sheeting is about four feet long and a foot wide.

"I was so focused on moving forward," Derrick says. "I'd picked my next tree and was heading toward it. Leapfrogging from the last one. I blew right by it."

"Isn't it odd that there's just one piece?" Brooke asks.

"Yes," Shannon says, nodding. "Just like it was odd that there was that one small clearing."

"We could've missed other clearings," I say. "We hit that clearing because it was in our path, but we had no idea it was there. It wasn't like we saw it and headed for it."

"True." Derrick stretches his arms over his head. "We could be missing a lot of stuff made invisible by the brush."

"Let's just keep going." I point forward. "And let's all keep a close eye out for anything out of the ordinary. Anything at all."

The wind picks up and is blowing at our backs. My un-shoe is staying on my foot. The top of my shin is still sore from when the big rock slid into it but doesn't seem to be getting worse. Yeah, hunger is our number one problem. It's hard to get un-hungry when you don't have any food. I'm feeling light-headed from pushing my body without resupplying my muscles.

The land levels out but we're not at the bottom of the valley yet because I can see where it starts going down again. In this level area, we start to see small birch trees mixed in with the spruce, and the brush seems to have thinned a little bit.

Up ahead, Derrick stops and says, "Everyone, check this out." He motions us forward with his arm.

Where he's standing looks just like where I'm standing. I keep walking toward him, lifting my un-shoe high with every step to lessen the chances of snagging it on rose thorns and sharp branches.

I can hear Shannon and Brooke behind me.

They catch up with me just as I catch up to Derrick.

"What gives?" I say.

Derrick points down and in front of him.

At first, I don't see anything different from what we've just bashed our way through, but as I look more closely, I see two straight lines running parallel to each other and just a few feet off the ground. They're about ten feet apart, surrounded by brush.

"Old cabin walls," Shannon says.

"Who would build something out here?" Brooke asks.

"Maybe it was part of a trap line," Shannon responds. "A place where a trapper could take shelter in the winter when checking traps."

I take a few steps beyond Derrick and bend down for a closer look. "Where are the other logs? I mean, if the walls fell apart, wouldn't the ground be bumpy around here from the logs falling and lying all over the place?"

"Maybe this is as far as the person got," Brooke offers. "After getting the walls this high, maybe he or she abandoned the project. I know I would have." She lets out a breath.

"True. It could be just another failed Alaskan dream," Shannon says. "The whole state is littered with them. My mom says people in general used to be tougher than they are today. Her people—my people—used to live seasonally based on where the resources were."

"Kind of like nomads?" Derrick asks.

"Yes," Shannon responds. "Except they would go to the same places year after year, traveling by foot in Interior Alaska. Like we are, except they had established routes."

I say, "At least these remains show that someone was here at least once. Maybe when we get to the bottom and go up the other side, the walking will be easier. I have a hard time believing whoever started to build this place got here by the same route we did. It's just got to get easier."

"It better," Brooke says.

"Whatever," Derrick responds. "It's obvious that this place has nothing to do with what I saw, especially now that you've pointed out that maybe the place didn't even get built."

"Let's get down to the bottom." I cough a dry cough. "I'm hoping there's some water we can drink."

"This is taking way longer than I thought it would," Brooke says as we all start walking, following Derrick's lead.

At the edge of the flat area, the brush thickens, and as we start down I think I see something snaking its way through the trees. A tiny ribbon of water running down the center of the valley. Even if Derrick's sighting turns out to be nothing, at least we'll be able to drink some water soon and fool our bellies into thinking they're full for a while.

CHAPTER 51

"IT DIDN'T LOOK THIS BIG from above." I stare at the sluggish but wide creek in front of us.

"We're going to get soaked again?" Brooke sighs. "Do we have to cross?"

I look up and down the creek. "It's brushy in both directions," I say. "Looking for a different place to cross would be a real pain. I—"

"And it'd get us off track," Derrick says, pointing in the direction he thinks we need to go, which is pretty much across the creek and then up to the left.

Shannon has her water bottle out of her pack and is filling it up. I get mine out to copy her.

Derrick and Brooke take their packs off and get their bottles out, too.

I fill mine, drink the entire thing, and then fill it again. The water is cold and tastes pretty good, but I'm still nervous about it having bacteria in it that could get us sick. But since I don't have any way of purifying it, I just drink, knowing that dehydration can cause headaches and basically make you feel sleepy.

"Make sure you all drink a lot," I say. "At least a bottleful right now."

"How many times are you going to tell us to drink?" Derrick asks. "Do you think we all have short-term memory problems?"

"It's just that it's important—"

"To stay hydrated," Shannon, Brooke, and Derrick say, finishing my sentence.

"Okay," I say. "Point noted." Sometimes words come out of my mouth before I've thought about what I'm saying. I take a few more glugs out of my bottle and then top it off in the creek. *Just drink*, I think, *and let the others drink, too.*

"If we can keep our packs dry," Shannon says, "we can keep our clothes dry since we're only wearing rain gear."

"What do you all think about taking our shoes and socks off?" Derrick asks. "We could keep those dry, too."

"We could keep everything dry," Brooke adds, "even our rain gear, if we crossed naked."

"The only bummer would be if it were so deep that if our packs went under, everything would get wet anyway," I say. "Other than that, I like the idea."

"I'm in," Derrick says. "It'll be like taking a quick swim."

"We don't want to injure our feet," Shannon says. "I'll do it. I'm taking my socks off, but I'm keeping my boots on."

Derrick looks at me. "What do you think, *Ole One Shoe?*"

"Socks off. Shoes on," I say. "For the crossing, I'll use one stuff sack and the piece of blue foam cinched down tightly with the string."

"Maybe I should go first," Derrick says. "In case it's super deep, I can help with everyone's pack."

"Frankenstein to the rescue again," Shannon says.

"We could do a bucket line, except it'd be a pack line," I say. "With Derrick in the deepest water." I point to the creek. "It does look kind of deep in the middle."

We talk a little more and decide to get the pack line set up and organized. Brooke will wade in and hand packs to me. I'll transfer them to Derrick, and he'll get them across the deep part and give them to Shannon, who will take them to the opposite shore.

The mosquitoes, like they can sense something good is about to happen, start hovering around us in larger and larger numbers as we make our plan.

We all strip and put our shoes back on, and I do a pretty good job of keeping my eyes to myself.

Shannon wades in and manages to walk across the deepest part with her mouth and nose just above the water. Derrick goes next and stops when the water is up to his armpits. Then I go in and stop about ten feet from Derrick, the water topping out just below my chest. I turn around and Brooke is right there with the first pack, holding it out to me. I grab the pack, hold it over my head, and wade to Derrick and hand it to him. I return to my spot, where Brooke is already waiting with the second pack.

We repeat the process for all the packs, and I hear Brooke splashing behind me as I give Derrick the last pack. My whole body is feeling fresh from the cold-water submersion, but I'm starting to get chilled, too. Brooke's hand brushes my hip underwater, but I resist the urge to turn around. I'm pretty sure she wasn't trying to get my attention— that it was just an accidental touch—but it still sends a zing through my body.

Shannon has the last pack in her hands and is carrying it toward shore, and Derrick is walking out of the water right behind her. I keep moving forward and soon am standing next to my pack.

Brooke splashes out of the water, and I turn my face away as she walks toward her pack, wanting to give her the privacy we're all entitled to. The mosquitoes find us almost instantly, and now we're racing to put our rain gear back on. I decide to leave my underwear, which is still dry, in my pack. I don't know what everyone else is doing, but I'm not into making this a discussion.

"That worked," Shannon says. She's the first one finished with redressing.

"How'd you do that so fast?" Derrick says.

"I pulled my rain gear on right over my boots," Shannon says. She points at Derrick's monstrous feet. "You don't have that option."

"Us tall guys," Derrick says, "we're always getting screwed."

I'm retying my un-shoe, and I can already feel my sock getting wet from the soaked blue foam and stuff sack. Shannon must've kept her socks in her pack and is wearing her boots barefoot. I don't have that option since my sock is what holds the blue foam in place.

I glance over at Brooke. She's tying her boots, and I can see the skin of her ankles, so she's not wearing her socks either. She finishes up, looks over at me, and then stands up.

Derrick says, "Okay, now, let's go find that green thing."

I slap at some mosquitoes trying to make a meal out of my neck, and shoulder my pack. My stomach is still full of water, but hunger is starting to pour in around the edges.

Brooke groans as she picks up her pack. She looks in the direction Derrick is starting to head and says, "Oh no. Not uphill again."

She sounds genuinely surprised, which surprises me, since we've been staring at our route all day now. I say, "It's the only way to go from here unless you follow the creek downstream."

"I get it," Brooke says. "It's just that I'm so tired."

"We all are," Shannon responds.

"How come I'm always the only one saying it?" Brooke asks.

"I'm just trying to put my energy into what we have to do," Shannon says, "and not use it up by focusing on things I can't change."

"When things get hard," Brooke explains, "sometimes I just need to vent. Getting it all out actually gives me more energy because I'm not trying to hold it all in."

Shannon nods. "We've all got our ways of dealing with difficulties. Your way is kind of like my mom's." She smiles and then starts walking in Derrick's direction, and Brooke falls in behind her.

I follow Brooke. My first few steps with my un-shoe go okay, but then the stuff sack snags in a particularly nasty clump of wild rose. I set my bear spray aside, reach down with both hands, and try to pry the branches away without getting totally scratched up by the thousands of tiny thorns.

I twist my foot around so I'm facing the creek, thinking maybe I'll have better luck with a different angle, and that's when I hear Derrick shout, "Yo. People. I think I found something."

CHAPTER 52

"WE CAN'T CARRY IT WITH us," Brooke says. "And even if we could, what good would it do?"

"Don't you see? Someone packed this up and tried to conceal it." Derrick points down at the waterproof gray bag the size of a washing machine. It holds a parachute and had been mostly covered with spruce boughs someone had cut to camouflage it. "They'll be coming back for it."

"It is the best sign we've had so far," Shannon says, "even if it's nothing conclusive. The boughs aren't green. Either they cut up a dead tree to cover the parachute, or they were cut green and have since dried up."

"What do you mean, not conclusive?" Derrick says. "We still haven't even gotten to the spot where I saw that green thing." He huffs. "They have to be related."

"It could be a low priority now," I say, "with the quake and all."

"Why is this bag even here?" Brooke asks.

"That's what we're going to find out," Derrick says, "up there." He points. "Where I saw the—"

"I know, I know," Brooke says, "where you saw the green thing." She says 'green thing' in this high-pitched, singsong voice.

It's still hard to believe the green thing wasn't just a tree, I think but don't say. Instead, I say, "Let's leave the chute and keep going. If nothing else, the sooner we get out of the trees and brush and back on the tundra, the easier the walking will be, and the easier it'll be to get spotted by a plane or a helicopter."

Shannon takes off her pack and pulls out her journal. "I'll leave a note on the parachute saying who we are, where we're from, and where we are going, on the outside chance that after we walk away from this thing the owner will come along."

We all wave our arms to keep the mosquitoes away as Shannon writes. When she's finished, she reads us what she's written, and then she tucks the note just inside the gray bag.

She looks at Derrick. "Okay, Frank. Lead on."

Derrick smirks at her. "You can thank me later."

The uphill climb through the spruce forest would be hard enough given our lack of energy, but when you add in the thick brush, it brings us to a much higher level of punishment.

In some spots, the brush is so tall that it hangs down the slope, so instead of just having to step through it, we now have to deal with it being at eye level. In these places I use my arms, swimming the breaststroke uphill to keep the thorns off my face. I start to sweat, which makes my rain gear stick to me, and any cleanliness I felt after being submerged in the creek is replaced with the same old stink I've been exuding since the earthquake.

We hit a level spot and stop to rest. I pull out my water bottle and take a long drink.

"If we find another clearing," Brooke says, "like the one we discovered earlier, can we stop for a rest?"

"You mean, can we set up the tents?" I ask, looking at her.

Before she can answer, Derrick says, "Brooke, I'd really like to see this thing through. To find whatever it was I saw. What if there're people there now, but we set up our tents and miss them by a day?"

"We can always take a vote if we need to," Shannon offers. "That is, if we find a clearing."

Brooke sighs. "Whatever. I'll just try to keep up. I got this."

The old Brooke, the just-after-the-earthquake Brooke, would have fought like a cornered cat to get her way. It's like the old Brooke asked for the break and the new Brooke accepted the answer.

Derrick leads on through the level area, and then we start our next uphill climb. Even though I'm used to beating my way through brush, that doesn't make it any easier, especially with a stuff sack for one shoe.

We hit a spot where the trees are markedly taller and wider. Derrick stops and turns a complete circle, quietly searching. The three of us just stand there, waiting.

Finally, Derrick says, "Anyone want to volunteer to climb one of these trees and have a look around? I get the feeling that we're close."

CHAPTER 53

"SCARED OF HEIGHTS?" I ASK. "Really?"

Derrick nods. "It's just one of those things. I deal with it when I have to. Like if no one volunteers to climb I'd give it a try for sure, but I probably wouldn't make it as high as anyone else here."

"I'll do it," I say.

"How are you going to climb with one shoe?" Brooke asks.

"Actually," Shannon says, "it might be easier to climb barefoot. Shoes with rigid soles aren't that great for climbing."

"Ms. Rhodes Scholar, how do you know all this?" Derrick makes a fake microphone out of his hand and thrusts it toward Shannon.

Shannon shrugs. "I watched a tree-climbing documentary with my mom and her now ex-boyfriend."

"Do you want to give it a try?" Derrick asks, pointing up a tall spruce tree.

"I think Josh is a good candidate," Shannon says. "With all the running he does he's easily got the strongest legs out of all of us. You need strong legs to climb. Plus, because of my height, my reach would be a limiting factor. So would Brooke's."

"I don't think I should go barefoot since I've got to be able to walk once I come down," I say. "If I injure one of my feet, I'm screwed."

"See if you can squeeze into my boots for the climb," Brooke says.

She sits on her pack, unties her boots, and takes them off.

I put my pack next to hers, sit on it, and take my shoe and my un-shoe off. Next, I take the laces out of Brooke's boots and hand them to her, knowing that the only chance I have of getting my feet into her boots is to have the openings be as big as possible.

I stick my right foot into her boot, move it side to side, and at the same time keep working my foot forward, and finally, it's jammed in there. I do the same with the other boot and stand up. "Definitely only for climbing," I say. "If I were walking, I'd have blisters after ten steps."

We pick out the tallest spruce tree in the grove. Derrick puts two hands together to give me a leg up. I put my foot in his hands, and he lifts. At the same time, I feel Shannon's and Brooke's hands on my butt and thighs pushing me upward, and soon I'm reaching for a branch that's at least nine or ten feet off the ground.

I grab it with both hands and wrap my legs around the tree.

"Now what?" I say through gritted teeth.

Shannon responds, "Try to work yourself onto a branch with your hands and then work your feet up to it. Then you can reach for another branch with one arm while keeping the other one wrapped around the trunk. Ideally, you want three different points of contact at all times." She pauses. "That won't always be possible, but that's what you want to shoot for."

I take in what she's just said, scoot my legs up the trunk, and then shift my torso upward, and that gives me the leverage to get one elbow over the tree branch I was hanging on to.

"That's the way," Derrick shouts.

I repeat the process two more times, and now I'm straddling the branch and hugging the trunk.

"Once you stand on that branch," Shannon yells, "you'll be able to keep going."

"Okay," I say, "I've got this." But I can feel my legs and arms shaking. Derrick may not be the only one scared of heights.

I reach as high as I can with both arms, wrap them around the trunk, and then carefully swing one of my legs up so my knee is resting on the branch. My heart is beating a hole in my raincoat, and I'm only getting started.

I press my hips into the trunk of the tree and get up on one knee, which hurts like hell pressed against the branch. Then I pull myself higher with my arms and put my other knee on the branch. I quickly get one foot and then the other under me, and I stand up.

I'm hugging the trunk like I've just found my true love. I take a breath. The next part of the climb is relatively easy because there are several branches staircasing upward that are spaced in such a way that I don't have to fully extend myself to get from one to the other. Now I'm about as high as I can go because the trunk is narrowing, and just above me it splits in two.

I glance down and feel my stomach press up against my Adam's apple. I immediately jam my eyes closed while hugging the tree trunk closer.

"See anything?" Derrick yells.

I've been so busy being scared out of my mind climbing that I forgot to even look. I open my eyes, take a breath, and then twist myself around to search.

I start with what's right in front of me and slowly move my eyes up the forested land. The trees are uniform big spruce trees like the one I'm perched in, and the land is like a giant staircase. Big flat forested areas alternating with steep slopes. I think about the hike to get here from the creek, and that's how it was.

Steep and then level.

Steep and then level.

Repeating itself.

When my eyes hit the fourth leveled area, I pause. The land there, although still forested, seems a little sparser, like there are fewer trees growing so close together, like there could be a few cleared areas. And above the leveled area, a quarter way up the fourth slope—the slope that leads to the ridgetop—I see the green thing.

CHAPTER 54

"WE'VE STILL GOT SOME SERIOUS brush to bash through," I say, "and some steep hills to climb. But I saw it, and it's definitely not natural." I squeeze my feet out of Brooke's boots and hand them to her. "Thanks."

She smiles. "Sure thing."

"The other thing I noticed," I say as I work the sock with the blue foam onto my foot while Brooke laces up her boots, "is that there might be a clearing just below the hillside where the green thing is. It seemed like maybe the trees weren't as thick right there. And it was a flat spot."

"Maybe there's a little camp for the scientists for whatever they're studying," Derrick suggests.

Everyone seems to have more energy now that there's actually something we're walking toward. Not that we didn't all want to believe Derrick when he saw the green thing the first time. But he saw it disappear and then he couldn't find it again. No one could. I'm guessing where I saw it is where it stays until they raise it for whatever reason. Maybe it takes air samples or something. I don't really care what it does. I'm just happy that we might be on the verge of getting some help.

The group lets me take the lead since I'm the one who last saw the green thing. I tell everyone that right now we're in a flat area, and the next climb will be the first of four before we get to the level area below the green thing.

"Four climbs," I repeat, "remember that."

My mind drifts back to the parachute we found. I still can't figure out what that was doing there and how anyone would be able to find it again. Unless whoever left it marked the coordinates on a GPS.

We hit the first of four slopes, but I just push forward, maintaining my pace. I keep waiting for Brooke to ask to stop and rest but she doesn't. When we reach the next flat area, I stop. I pull out my water bottle and take a drink, and everyone does the same.

"Do you think they'll have a clean water source up there?" Brooke points in the direction we're heading.

Shannon says, "If anyone's there, they probably do." She takes a drink and then says, "I'm just having a hard time picturing a field camp in the middle of all this. How would anyone access it? Josh didn't see a landing strip or a big lake to land a floatplane on, or a cleared area to land a helicopter—just a green pipe-shaped object flush with the trees."

"Someone went through some trouble to put the green thing there," Derrick says. "And we found that parachute down below."

"But it was in a heavy-duty waterproof bag," Shannon says. "It could've spent a couple of winters there, or more."

Regardless of what Shannon thinks, she still can't explain away the green thing. And we did walk through what looked like a human-made clearing on the other side of the creek. And we did find a large piece of black plastic. So, however inhospitable this endless brush country is, someone took some energy to do something here, and maybe they're still around.

A few hours later we're climbing through the brush on the fourth steep slope. I'm a wet rat, marinating in my own sweat beneath my rain gear. My un-shoe is cooperating as long as I retie it as soon as I feel it starting to loosen. If I wait too long, the whole thing gets twisted and I have to take the stuff sacks off, straighten the sock and blue foam, and then put it all back together.

The land starts to level out, and I stop and wait for everyone to catch up. Then I say, "This is the flat spot below the green thing. There might be a clearing somewhere on this level."

The woods look just as thick here as they have all day, but I remember what I saw from up in the trees—a hint of an opening. A possible break in the trees.

We talk a little more and decide to keep going single file. It's the same old story—thick brush, tall trees. But at least we've come this far. And even if the green thing is all on its own, I know from my tree climb that the forest will turn to tundra if we keep going up, and the walking will be easier if we need to keep going.

The ground starts to get bumpy, and the trees get smaller and are growing closer together, almost forming a wall. I turn us to the left, and we work our way along the line of small trees for a couple hundred yards until they give way to bigger trees.

I angle us back through the big trees, trying to pick up from where I turned us when we hit the small trees. The more I angle us back, the more the brush thins. And then up ahead the land rises in a big mound, maybe forty feet long and eight feet tall at its highest point. Small trees grow all over the mound. Instead of walking up on the mound, I decide to go around it where the brush looks thinner.

I'm on the far side of the mound, nearing the spot where the land starts rising. I know that slope in front of me has the green thing on it somewhere. In my mind, I picture what I saw from the tree, and I think that maybe the place where I'm now standing is the clearing I spotted. That the short trees growing close together on this mound are what caused the appearance of a break in the landscape.

Brush grows thick right up against the back side of the mound, which is steeper than the front side—so steep it's like the wall of a building that's made of brush. Then right in the middle of the wall the brush starts to move, but it's moving in a very unnatural way, like a small section of the backside is detaching and swinging open.

"Hey," I say as I watch a person emerge from what turns out to be a real doorway.

He freezes, like he's surprised, and then he walks toward us.

"We're from Simon Lake," I say. "No one came to get us after the earthquake."

He tells us his name is Sam.

We are all talking at once, asking Sam about the roads, the buildings, and what kind of damage there is. We all can't wait to get back to Fairbanks to see if our parents are okay, to see how they weathered the earthquake.

But when Sam finally responds, what he tells us changes everything.

CHAPTER 55

SAM SCRATCHES HIS BEARD WITH one hand. "Canadian helicopters?" He shakes his head. "That can't be. They would've been fired upon the second they crossed into enemy airspace."

"I know my birds," Derrick says. "They had a red emblem on the side. A maple leaf."

"They were flying high, right?" Sam asks as he shifts his weight from one leg to another. "Is it possible that the red emblem you saw was a star?"

I replay it in my mind and say, "Yeah. It could have been a star."

Derrick nods. "It's a possibility."

Brooke pulls out her cell phone and powers it up. "What about this?"

The red screen pops up with the bear outlined faintly in brown.

"Turn that off now," Sam says calmly. "It's one of the ways the Russians are monitoring people. They're blocking all normal cell and web-based communication, but they have tracking capabilities."

Brooke turns her phone off.

Sam reaches toward Brooke, his palm open. "Please give me the phone."

"Why?" Brooke asks.

"It's still a potential security risk," Sam responds.

"Will I get it back?" Brooke asks.

Sam shakes his head. "That phone could get us all killed. I will take it from you if I have to, but I'd prefer that you just give it to me."

Brooke hands Sam the phone. He sets it on the ground, picks up a fist-sized rock, and smashes it several times. "Hopefully they haven't pinpointed our location."

Brooke's face is scrunched up and I see one tear escape her eye.

"It's okay," I say. "I mean, we had no clue that your phone could be putting us in danger."

"I know," Brooke says. "It's just that my dad gave it to me and I don't know if he's alive or dead. If you had something from your dad right now, wouldn't you want to keep it?"

I nod and so do Shannon and Derrick.

Sam says, "I'm sorry I had to do that, but now we need to move on. You all look hungry. Why don't you come inside, and I'll explain a little more in detail what we're up against and what you missed." He starts walking, and we all follow. At the camouflaged doorway, he turns and says, "I can understand why you're confused. You saw things—like helicopters and jets—and your brains made connections that made sense to you." He gestures for us to go inside.

At the doorway, Derrick says, "So . . . the Russians invaded Alaska while we were at camp?" He shakes his head. "I hope my dad is okay. He flies helicopters for the army."

Once we're all inside, Sam closes the door and turns on a lantern that's hanging from the ceiling.

"What is this place?" Shannon asks.

"There are things I definitely want to tell you," Sam says. "And there are things I can't tell you because you'd put a lot of people in danger if you told anyone else. Say, if you were captured and questioned by the Russians." He raises his eyebrows. "You weren't the company I was expecting."

Brooke and Derrick start talking at the same time, and then they both stop and wait for each other, and I say, "Let's let Sam tell us what he can. Then we can ask questions. What do people think?"

"That's a good place to start," Shannon says.

Brooke nods her approval.

Derrick looks at Sam and says, "Can we have something to eat while you talk? Last time we ate was two days ago. And it wasn't much. We've been on starvation rations for about a week."

"One thing I've got out here is plenty of food," Sam says. He hands out packages of crackers and cheese. "This will get you started."

Derrick says, "I was expecting military rations."

"I'm not exactly military," Sam says. "At least not in the way most people think of the military."

I rip open the package of crackers and cheese, take one of each, and put them into my mouth. I chew and swallow. And before I know it I've inhaled the whole package and Sam motions for me to grab another.

We all eat as Sam talks.

"I'm going to paint with a broad brush," Sam says. "I'm in a part of the government that deals with all types of extreme emergencies. We've planned for a Russian invasion of Alaska for a long time but didn't plan on some of the particulars encompassing this one." Sam takes a breath. "We've got a vast defensive missile system at Fort Greely. Secretly, we converted a number of those missiles to be offensive with nuclear capabilities. In a combination of actual physical infiltration and hacking, the Russians have gained control of our nuclear missiles at Fort Greely and have them locked and loaded on targets in the Lower Forty-Eight—New York, Los Angeles, Boston, Denver, Atlanta, Chicago . . . You get the idea?"

I feel my stomach go raw, like someone is dripping battery acid down my throat.

Shannon says, "So what's the extent of the invasion in Alaska?"

"There's a large and growing military presence. Many people are still living in their houses, but more and more homes are being appropriated for Russian troop housing—especially around Fairbanks and Anchorage. There's evidence of people being rounded up and held captive. And from the limited intelligence we've gathered, more round-ups will occur as the Russians bring more of their forces into the state." Sam opens a bottle of apple juice. "You all don't mind drinking from the bottle, do you?"

Derrick takes the bottle and glugs some juice, then passes it to Brooke. Then he asks, "So, what is your job?"

Sam looks at each one of us, then folds his hands in his lap. "I'm in charge of getting the missiles back under United States control. If we can do that, we can retake the rest of Alaska."

I almost spit out the juice in my mouth but manage to swallow it, and then say, "This is nuts." I remember Theo's words during one of our runs when he was talking about a new coach who acted like he was an expert but later was fired for having falsified his resume: Never blindly follow anyone. "How do we know you're legit?" I ask.

Before Sam can answer, Shannon adds, "You must have some type of ID."

"We'll need more than that," Derrick says. "IDs can be faked. And how would we know if it was a fake? We're not experts on that kind of stuff."

"Just because you've got some high-tech camp," Brooke adds, "doesn't mean anything. I just want to get out of here and see if my parents are okay."

"Please don't try to go anywhere right now," Sam responds. "If it'll help, I can show you proof of what's happening. Some of the images are classified so I'll need your word to keep what you see to yourselves."

Before anyone replies, Sam opens a drawer and pulls out a tablet.

"Is that an iPad?" Derrick asks.

"It looks like one," Sam says, "but it's much more sophisticated." Sam spreads his palm and puts it on the screen. "It will only open with full hand recognition."

The screen lights up. Sam taps on an icon and an image fills the screen. "This is a magnified satellite image. Recognize this place?" Sam holds the screen face-out toward the four of us.

I see a large green space with people scattered throughout.

"Those are soccer fields in Fairbanks," Shannon responds. "I live a few blocks from them."

Sam taps another icon. "Here's what they look like now."

I swallow once and take in the new image. In the center of the green space there are large gray tents, and surrounding the tents are lots of people. On the perimeter of the field soldiers dressed in gray complete the picture.

"That looks like the real deal," Derrick says.

"I used to watch my older sisters play there," Brooke says.

"Who are all those people?" I ask.

"The Russians are using large, fenced spaces as detention areas," Sam replies. He taps his screen and an image of my high school football field appears.

"That's my school," I say. The image has the same basic setup as the soccer fields, with tents in the center and soldiers on the perimeter.

"That's all I can show you," Sam says as he puts his palm on the tablet and it goes blank. "Now, I need to ask you some questions about how you all got here."

We tell Sam about our wait at Simon Lake after the earthquake that killed everyone but us. And how we walked in this direction, hoping to get to Talkeetna.

He stands and walks a few steps to a wall with a huge map of Alaska. He finds Simon Lake and Talkeetna and then points out our current location. "You were doing a good job. You'd covered about ninety miles and still had about seventy-five to go. The epicenter of that quake must've been close to Simon Lake, which is very remote. But it was a strong enough quake that there was some highway damage. Although it didn't cause major damage in heavily populated areas, it provided a distraction that the Russians took advantage of while our government was focused on assessing impacts and preparing for aftershocks."

When Derrick tells Sam about seeing the *green thing* getting lowered in the trees, Sam says, "You could see it? That's not good. Of course, we never expected people to approach this location from the direction you all did. We deliberately picked the most inhospitable, brush-and-swamp-infested country to keep people from stumbling into our installation."

"Josh even lost his shoe." Brooke points down at the stuff sack surrounding my foot.

"You walked in that?" Sam shakes his head.

We tell Sam about the bear spray, the EpiPen, the tiny amount of food we had to cover the distance we did, and the bear, moose, and wolf encounters we survived. We also tell him about the parachute we found and he informs us it was probably from a supply drop a couple of years ago.

Sam says, "Like I said earlier, you weren't the company I was expecting. One of my key crews experienced difficulties and has been rounded up by the Russians just outside of Fairbanks. But I'm wondering . . . I mean, after seeing what you all went through and how you beat the odds to get here." Sam pauses. "We're down to the wire." Sam grips one hand in the other. "I'm wondering if you'd be willing to help me out, for the sake of taking back our country?"

CHAPTER 56

SAM'S SHELTER IS PRETTY INGENIOUS. I mean, it looks like an earth shelter, but it's not. It's blanketed with a thick layer of soil. Thick enough that there are trees growing out of it, covering it. And the front side, where the door is, is all brush. But really, it's this totally sturdy metal structure that's about forty feet long and ten to twelve feet wide. The ceiling curves and slopes down at either end on the back side, so it's like being inside a half dome.

The gear is packed in plastic totes. Plus, there's this long counter and a bunch of communication equipment. Along the back wall, there are bunks that fold down.

The green thing, we learn, is how he sends and receives information. That's how he found out one of his crews got nabbed by the Russians. He raises the antenna to send and receive. Otherwise, he keeps it retracted. And some of the spruce trees surrounding it aren't really trees but structures composed of hundreds of mini solar panels. Years ago, lots of sling loads delivered by helicopter—under the guise of a fake mining company doing some exploration—established this place.

"If that antenna of yours wasn't moving," Derrick says, "we wouldn't have come this way, because we wouldn't have seen it."

"So you came out here *after* the invasion?" Brooke asks.

"I was ordered to this station when it was happening," Sam says. "But the fewer specifics you know, the better. I'm focused on regaining control of the missiles, and to carry out your part of the mission, if you choose to help me, I'll tell you everything you need to know."

Brooke asks about getting back to Fairbanks.

"In general," Sam says, "the past few years, as the United States has backed off from cooperating on international issues, our allies have formed stronger alliances with each other. Now we're pretty much on our own. Russia has ordered the speedy and peaceful withdrawal of our troops from all places in the world where they're stationed, the docking of our nuclear submarines, and the grounding of fighter jets from our aircraft carriers. At the same time, they have our nukes in Alaska pointed at the Lower Forty-Eight, and they are slowly assuming control of the entire state. I—"

"But what about Fairbanks?" Brooke cuts in. "That's where our families are. That's where we want to be."

Sam holds up one hand. "I'm getting to that. Local militias have started organizing, which the Russians basically love because it gives them the excuse to use force. And these militias, while they may give state troopers or local police a run for their money, are no match for sophisticated military weaponry. At the same time, Russia has said that actual military retaliation will result in a nuclear response on the Lower Forty-Eight." Sam takes a drink of water. "If you showed up in Fairbanks, you'd be detained. They'd intensely interrogate you at a minimum. They don't take kindly to people showing up outside of the boundaries they've set up. If they find you somewhere else, they may shoot first and ask questions later. Like if you made it to Talkeetna or the highway. You're quite lucky that you ended up here, given that you had no clue about what's happening."

Shannon asks, "What has the Native response been?"

Sam says, "You're Athabascan?"

"My mother is Athabascan. My father is white, but I haven't seen or heard from him in a long time."

"The public response from leaders in the Native community, at least from what I've gotten via my limited communication, goes something like this: Alaska Natives of all tribes were here the first time the Russians invaded. They were here when the Americans invaded. They are still here this time around with the Russians. And will still be here after they leave."

"That sounds about right," Shannon says.

"I can understand it," Sam says. "I would hope, however, that individuals, whether Native or non-Native, would see the urgency in defusing the current nuclear situation. If nuclear weapons are launched, everyone loses." Sam looks at his watch. "Time for me to raise the antenna and grab whatever information is coming my way today."

"Won't the Russians detect your presence when you do that?" Derrick asks.

"The technology we use prevents *most* attempts at detection from being successful," Sam says as he gets up, goes over to the counter, and sits in a chair in front of some type of control panel. We gather around him as he puts headphones on and flips up a switch. A panel with several green lights glows, then blinks, then glows. Sam toggles another switch and messes with a dial. After a minute or two he flips the first switch down, toggles the other switch back to where it was, and takes his headphones off.

Sam swivels around in his chair to face us. "The other teams are continuing their preparations. We're getting closer to executing the plan. I know you all are tough, just given the fact that you survived the hike from Simon Lake. In order to maintain the integrity of the mission I'm hoping you'll help me with, I may not tell you everything, but I won't lie to you. It will be dangerous. You'll be pushed to do things you've never done before. But the skills aren't so technical that I can't teach them to you over the next few days before we would move out."

"How much walking would be involved?" Brooke asks.

"If all goes as planned," Sam says, "not much. About seventeen miles."

"You haven't exactly said what we would be doing," Derrick says.

Sam lets out a breath. He looks at each one of us and says, "I need a commitment from you first. As an agent of the US government, I have the authority in emergency situations to deputize you all as agents of the US government as well. Your identity will be protected. Nothing will be put down in writing and the government will probably deny any of this ever happened. And you will never be able to talk about it once your job is completed."

"I get that," I say. "It's just normal to want to know what you're agreeing to before you agree to it."

"True," Sam says, "but these are about as far from normal times as you can get. If I tell you the whole plan and then you decline and are captured and tortured, you'll have vital information that would compromise the mission." He rubs his beard with one hand. "I'm going to step outside and use the outhouse. Then I'm going to take a short walk to do a little maintenance on my antenna. You four talk it over and give me an answer. I'll be back in a half hour."

CHAPTER 57

"CAN WE TRUST THIS GUY?" Brooke asks.

"He's got to be the real deal," Derrick says. "Look at this setup. You can't make this stuff up."

"I think he's legit," Shannon says. "Those satellite images don't lie."

"Me too," I say.

"I just want to get home," Brooke says, "not blindly agree to some dangerous plan. Look what we've been through already."

"We might not have homes if things stay as they are," I say. "I don't like the idea of agreeing to some plan before we know what it is either. But if those are the choices, then those are the choices."

"What's he going to do with us if we don't agree to help?" Derrick asks. "Do you think he'd even let us walk out of here? We stumbled onto some top-secret camp that has more authority than the United States Military. These are the people who they call when the military fails."

"How can we not agree to help with the plan?" Shannon says. "You heard him. The Russians are holding our entire country hostage, and the key lies a couple hundred miles away at Fort Greely. If we can get those missiles back under our control, they lose all their power."

"True," Derrick says. "Then our military can ask them to leave, and if they don't, wage war on them."

"Look what we've been through already," Brooke says. "I thought when we actually found this place, our struggle with death was over. And now we're going to intentionally put ourselves at risk." She shakes her head. "I just—"

"Brooke," Shannon says, "you've impressed me by how much you've come through." She pauses. "Honestly, out of all of us, you've pushed yourself the most. This next thing. This thing that none of us knew was coming. This thing that might save the world political system as we know it. This thing"—she puts her hand on Brooke's shoulder—"whatever it is, you can do it."

"But what if we die trying?" Brooke asks. "I just—"

"Is that really worse than not trying to save our country?" I cut in. "If we do nothing and the plan fails, then what?"

Derrick says, "Which side of history do we want to be on? Do we want to be the people who shied away in a time of need or the people who stepped up to the plate?"

Brooke says, "It's obvious where the three of you stand. I'm not saying I won't do it, I'm just saying how I feel. Everything seems so easy for you three. Hike up mountains and through swamps. Go without food for days."

"Don't forget, Brooke," Shannon says, "it was you who gave me the EpiPen."

"And it was you," I add, "who walked for miles with the worst blisters I've ever seen."

Derrick puts his hands on his hips. "I'm with these two. Don't underestimate what you've accomplished. And don't underestimate what you're capable of." Derrick puts his hands on the top of his head. "Yikes, that last thing sounds like something my dad would say—even if it is true."

"Okay," Brooke says. "If all of you are in, then I'm in, too."

CHAPTER 58

THE NEXT DAY, AFTER A breakfast of oatmeal and coffee, we start our training.

"Basically," Sam says, "we've got to create some distractions and cut off road access to Fort Greely simultaneously." He points to the map spread out on the counter. "We need to blow three bridges—one on each road leading toward Fort Greely. If we do it right, we'll cut off transportation into the fort, and hopefully we'll draw significant numbers of soldiers away from the fort to deal with the disturbances."

"Do you think simultaneous really is best?" Shannon asks. "I think an initial explosion would tend to draw a large response. Then when another one follows, say, fifteen minutes later, that creates another response. And the third one fifteen minutes later would create another response. It might result in more soldiers being drawn away."

"Very perceptive thinking." Sam smiles at Shannon. "What you say is true. If we come out of this alive and you want a job, we'll talk."

Derrick says, "You'd be lucky to have her. We'd basically be dead if it weren't for Shannon. She's the only one of us who didn't mistake marmots for people."

Sam tilts his head sideways. "Let's get back to business. We considered staggering the explosions for the very reason Shannon stated. However, we can't guarantee that we can block their communications, so the patrols at the other two bridges would likely be put on high alert because of the first explosion. If that happens, it would make it harder for our other teams to blow the other bridges, and, as a result, more difficult to take control of the missiles. Your job will be to blow one of the bridges."

Derrick asks, "Which one?"

"This one." Sam points to the bridge spanning the Tanana River just north of Delta Junction.

"What if there're people on it when it goes?" I say.

"The Russians are controlling the traffic over all three of the bridges. The majority of the traffic is troop-and-weapons related. The other traffic is supply delivery. No Americans are allowed to drive their cars around. Everyone is basically confined to their communities, so there's very little chance of civilian casualties."

"But there's a chance we might end up killing some people?" Brooke asks.

Sam takes a breath and exhales. "We're trying to prevent a nuclear catastrophe. Not just from the Russians launching toward the Lower Forty-Eight but from our own president trying to strike first. So far, he's complied with the worldwide withdrawal of our troops and the takeover of Alaska, but his actions could change. He hasn't scuttled the submarines yet. So, yes, some soldiers may die. Or a person driving a delivery truck. Although supply delivery for civilians has been sporadic. They're living pretty close to the edge."

"Dudes," Derrick says. "This is war, and we've agreed to help. People could die. I just hope it's not us."

"More people could die if we don't do this," Shannon says. "Winter will come. If the supply shortage worsens, people could starve or freeze to death, and not just in Fairbanks. Villages depend on food and fuel deliveries in the fall to make it through the winter. If those don't happen, we could lose a lot of Alaska Natives."

"The way to have the best chance at success is to totally give yourself over to the mission. One hundred percent," Sam says.

Just like running cross-country, I think. *You give it your all if you want a shot at coming in first.*

"I'll give you every tool you need to succeed," Sam says. "And I'll show you how to use the more complicated ones. It'll take concentration, effort, and a certain amount of risk. I'm totally invested in you succeeding because if you don't, it greatly lessens the chance that I will."

"So," Shannon says, "you won't be with us when we blow up the bridge?"

"You're just going to kick back here," Derrick says, "eat crackers and cheese and monitor the whole thing?"

Sam shakes his head. "I'm the one who knows how to bypass the Russian hack job that unlocked and pointed our missiles at the Lower Forty-Eight. Hopefully I'll be breaching the security systems they've set up, but I need to do it from inside the fort. There's a secret control panel that needs to be physically accessed and activated. And I helped design it."

CHAPTER 59

"LET'S WORK BACKWARD," SAM SAYS. "I want to start with how to blow the bridge, because those are the skills you're probably least familiar with."

We follow Sam away from the shelter and toward the hillside with the antenna. At the base of the hill, Sam stops and says, "After this is over, you'll need to keep mum about this site as well as the mission in general. We'll make something up about where you hiked to after the earthquake. We've got stations like this all over the United States, and we can't have people intentionally looking for them. I'm still baffled that you stumbled upon this one."

We all agree that we won't talk about this place.

Sam parts some brush at the base of the hill and reveals a metal storage unit. "This whole hillside, at least the front side of it, has storage capacity. Units like this are hidden by the brush."

I think about the effort that went into making this place what it is. About the sheer volume of supplies. About how it had to be developed carefully so as to not disturb the landscape too much; otherwise, it'd be easy to spot from the air.

Sam unlatches the door, and we can see that it is basically a wide locker with deep shelves. He pulls out a dark cylindrical object about as big around as a coffee can and twice as long. "On this end, there's a heavy-duty drill with a fully charged battery. The middle is packed with explosives." Sam runs his hand along the cylinder. "There are also two handles that pull up." He pulls them up and they click into place. Then, holding the device by the handles, he shows us the part opposite the drill. "This end has two buttons. The gray one operates the drill. Once you've got the device situated, you press it and the drill will engage. It will stop automatically when it reaches its predetermined depth. The drill is powerful. Designed to penetrate metal, concrete, wood. It's multipurpose."

"Do we keep hanging on to the handles once the drill has penetrated and is drilling?" Shannon asks.

"At the start, yes," Sam says, "so you can do some initial guiding, but it's not essential to hang on the whole time. The red button arms the device and activates the timer. If you drill but don't press the red button, or if the red button malfunctions, then it self-activates after fifteen minutes. Either way, once the explosive is activated, it will go off in twenty minutes."

"How is this synchronized?" Derrick asks. "If we press the timing devices independent of the other teams blowing the other bridges, what makes them all go off at the same time?"

"Good question," Sam says.

Derrick glances at Shannon. "Maybe I'll get a job offer, too." He smirks.

"You'll have a communication device," Sam says. "It's simple." Sam hands Derrick the explosive and roots around in the storage locker, emerging with a small black rectangle. "You'll have one of these. You press the green button when you're in position and ready to place your explosives. When you see the red light illuminate, then you place your explosive devices"—he points to the device Derrick is holding—"and activate them."

Brooke says, "What if you're not ready when the red light lights up?"

"That shouldn't be an issue," Sam says, "because you've communicated via the green button that you're ready. I won't activate your red light until all teams are in position."

"How much time could elapse between when we press the green button and when the red light goes on?" Shannon asks.

"That depends on how long it takes you to get to your spot," Sam replies. "There are three teams. The first team to press their button will obviously have to wait the longest, the last team the shortest." Sam pauses. "The other variable is when my team will be in position to penetrate the fort. Be prepared to act immediately after you press the button. Also be prepared to wait up to a day or two."

Sam has us each hold the explosive device by the handles. He tells us it weighs about twelve pounds, and although the drill makes noise when it's on, the sound from the rush of the river should cover it up.

"You'll have three devices to place," Sam says. "I understand that you haven't been trained to work in cold, swift-moving water, but you'll all be wearing dry suits."

"What if we can't place all the devices?" Brooke asks. "Will this still work if we only get one or two drilled into the bridge?"

"Obviously the goal is to place all the devices," Sam answers. "Just do your best. The bigger the distractions from the explosions, and the more access we can cut off to the fort, the more likely I'll succeed with my part."

Sam has us repeat back to him everything we've learned so far. He makes us each recite the information twice and I go over it in my head one more time: We get into position and hit the green button on our communicator. Once the red light goes on, we drill our explosive devices into the bridge and arm them with the red buttons. If we don't arm them, they'll arm themselves after fifteen minutes. After they're armed, they'll blow up twenty minutes later.

"Okay," Sam says, "you're done with the first part of the training. After we have some chow, we'll talk about how you'll be getting to the bridge, which is about two hundred miles from here."

CHAPTER 60

INSIDE THE SHELTER, SAM STANDS at a built-in counter and heats some kind of dehydrated stew he's added water to. I notice he's shorter than Derrick but taller than me.

"What I don't get," I say, "is why the Russians are doing this. Would they really want to start a nuclear war?"

Sam says, "Although we have a president who says America has never been stronger, the reality is that we've never been weaker in modern history."

"But our military is the strongest in the world," Derrick says.

"True," Sam replies, "but it's being held hostage by the threat of a nuclear strike on basically all major American cities by American missiles in Alaska. Maybe if we hadn't snubbed our nose at our allies and insulted them repeatedly the last couple of years and pulled out of long-standing defense agreements, they'd be more willing to take a risk to help us out."

"Even if they did," Shannon says, "what could they do? I mean, wouldn't Russia just launch a nuke from Alaska if our allies initiated a military response?"

Sam continues to stir the stew. "It's likely that they would. The other piece to the puzzle is that our digital defenses have weakened over the past few years. We've never been more vulnerable to cyberattacks."

"How many people are involved in this operation to take back the missiles?" I ask.

"I don't mind talking some politics," Sam says, "but specifics about the mission I'll need to limit to what you need to know, in case you're captured. I've probably already told you too much, but under the circumstances . . ."

Sam spoons the stew into five bowls and says, "Enjoy the hot food while you're here because it'll be all cold, dry rations during the mission."

The chunks of solid food in the stew are kind of chewy, and the liquid part has a salty beef taste to it. We all eat in silence for a few minutes.

"One thing about this mission bothers me," I say. Everyone stops eating and looks at me. "If Russia has threatened to use the nukes if anyone retaliates, aren't they going to use them when we blow the bridges?"

We all turn toward Sam. He swallows a mouthful of stew and says, "Our government is going to say some local militias must be acting independently to sabotage the bridges, and that this wasn't a retaliatory response from the United States."

"Will they believe that?" Shannon asks.

"The Russian government would rather hold the nuclear threat over us as a means of control than actually use it," Sam says. "My guess is that, at the most, they might do a limited launch to show they're serious. The more likely response is some embarrassment that a local militia caused a ton of damage right under their noses, with some wrath from the Kremlin. The Russian soldiers stationed here will be more worried about being punished than about the enemy."

Brooke says, "Will they lash out at random civilians? Like our parents in Fairbanks?"

My stomach burns. "Our parents, if they're even alive, have it bad enough. I don't want to make it worse for them."

Sam sets his bowl on the counter. "The Russians will probably respond locally around Delta Junction by searching houses and detaining people, if they're still in charge after the operation, which they will be if we fail. And any militia activity across the state will most likely be dealt with swiftly and harshly."

"How long will it take," I say, "if the mission is successful, for the United States to resume control of Alaska?"

"The Russians definitely have the advantage in the short term," Sam says. "But as our military gets up and running, their advantage will disappear. I think they would eventually lose a conventional war. They didn't take Alaska because they wanted Alaska. They took it for the missiles, and the main reason they were able to take it was because they initially gained control of the missiles remotely." Sam puts his hands on his head. "They may have had a little help from the inside, too. That's something we don't know."

"What are we going to do after we do our part?" Shannon says. "Provided we even survive."

"I'll show you on a map where you should go after you've finished," Sam says. "Right now, it's time for dessert." He rustles around to the left of where he was cooking and comes back with a package of chocolate cookies. "Eat as many as you want," he says. "After I'm done—"

Something beeps three times, and we all turn toward the communication panel.

Sam says softly, "That means that something is flying overhead." He quickly walks to the panel, sits in the swivel chair, and puts his headphones on.

CHAPTER 61

"HEAT SEEKING?" DERRICK SAYS.

"That's one way to detect our presence," Sam replies. He points to the ceiling. "This shelter is pretty well insulated, so it's less likely to show up as significant on a heat detector. But we've just increased the number of humans from one to five, so we've increased our heat output four hundred percent."

"You think the Russians are onto us?" I ask.

"Not necessarily," Sam says. "But we need to be cautious. If the number of flyovers increases, I'll be more concerned. But if we stay on schedule, we'll be out of here in two days anyway."

Brooke stands up and stretches. "I wish we could just stay here." She yawns.

"That's a natural desire," Sam says. "Who wants to be in a situation where their life is at risk? And hopefully when we're through, you and your families will be at less risk. Hopefully everyone will. That's the goal of the mission."

Brooke just nods and then sits back down.

And I realize I feel the same way that Brooke does; I just wasn't saying it out loud and wouldn't have tapped into it if Brooke hadn't spoken up. We've all got to be feeling that way. No one wants to do this. Sam acknowledged it. And now that I've acknowledged it in myself, thanks to Brooke, I can put all my energy into moving forward.

"We've got more equipment to look at," Sam says. "Follow me."

Outside, in front of another camouflaged storage unit, Sam pulls out four gray waterproof bags. "Each of these inflatable kayaks weighs about ten pounds. They come with a foot pump. Anybody ever paddle a kayak?"

"I've been in a canoe," Shannon says, "with my mom on the Chena River in Fairbanks."

"I've been rafting a couple of times around Denali," I say. "But I didn't have to do anything. There was a guide."

"My dad has a sailboat that he keeps in Valdez," Brooke says. "We usually go out on it at least once every summer."

"When we lived in Texas," Derrick chimes in, "I floated down some river in an inner tube for the day."

Sam says, "These inflatables are very forgiving." He pulls one out of the bag and instructs us to inflate it so we learn how to use the foot pump.

When we're finished, he says, "This is basically a lightweight river kayak. It's self-bailing, which means when water pours in over the top there are holes between the sides and the floor that allow it to drain. And there are walls within the inflated compartments, so if you spring a leak, the whole kayak won't deflate. The walls respond to pressure changes and seal off compartments during a pressure loss."

"But we only pumped it up through one valve," Shannon remarks. "I haven't seen anything like this."

"Good observation," Sam replies. "It's single valve so you can inflate it quickly. The smart-wall technology inside the kayak, combined with the single valve, isn't commercially available."

I study the boat. It's basically a tube that's been shaped into the form of a kayak. It tapers to points in the front and back and is a couple of feet wide in the middle.

"It looks kind of small," Derrick says.

"It's the smallest boat we could get away with for the job that needs to be done." Sam faces Derrick. "You'll have to bend your knees more than the others to fit in the boat. But it's doable."

"You sure you don't have something bigger for me?" Derrick asks.

Sam shakes his head. "You're each going to be carrying these boats, and all your other supplies, about seventeen miles before you get to the place where you'll put them in the river, so the smallest, lightest boats to get the job done are essential."

"Seventeen miles?" Brooke says. "Why?"

"It has to do with where the Russians do their patrols," Sam says. "I'd take you all the way to the river if I could, but that'd be too risky."

"What do you mean, *take us*?" Shannon asks.

"We never did finish looking at the maps," Sam says. "I got distracted by that flyover. After we finish up with the kayaks, I'll show you where we're going."

Sam instructs us to set up and inflate the other three kayaks to make sure all the parts are there, to ensure there are no leaks, and to give us practice. Each boat comes with a small paddle that breaks into two pieces and fits in the bag.

After we finish and pack up the kayaks, Sam says, "I've got backpacks, lightweight tents, and lightweight sleeping bags for all of you." He looks at Derrick. "You'll be a little cramped. No one on the original team was near your height."

"Us tall guys," Derrick says, "we're always missing out in this tiny world." He cracks a smile and Sam smiles back.

Back inside, Sam spreads a map out on the counter. "Here we are." He points to a spot on the map marked with a red dot. "Here's your bridge." He points to a spot on the map marked with a green dot. "That's us. The bridge is about one hundred fifty miles away. And here's the drop-off spot." He points to a blue dot upriver from the bridge. "After you're dropped off, you'll proceed by foot approximately seventeen miles to this lake." He runs his finger to another blue spot on the map. "You'll assemble your kayaks and paddle along the lakeshore to the outlet and then down this small river—really it's more of a creek—until it merges with the Tanana. Then you'll paddle down the Tanana to the bridge." He traces his finger along the whole route. "Any questions so far?"

Shannon says, "How do we get to the drop-off point?"

Sam takes a breath. "I hope no one gets airsick. I'll be flying you there in my plane."

CHAPTER 62

THE NEXT MORNING AFTER BREAKFAST, Sam says, "I know I've been throwing a lot of new things at all of you since you arrived. My intention is not to overwhelm you, but there's a lot of information you need to know."

"There are four of us," I say, "so hopefully what one person forgets, someone else will remember."

"Ideally," Sam says, "everyone should know every part of the mission and how to perform each skill I've taught you so if one or more of you gets hurt or if you get separated, the mission can continue."

Shannon nods. "That makes sense."

"This next part," Sam goes on, "you can't practice, but at least you can get familiar with the equipment."

We follow Sam outside. He opens another camouflaged storage locker and pulls out several gray bags and a bunch of gray flippers. "The bags have dry suits in them. You'll wear them when you're paddling the boats and when you're attaching the explosives."

Derrick picks up a bag, unclips it, and pulls out a gray dry suit. "What's with all the gray? Is it the unofficial color of whatever secret government agency you work for?"

Before Sam can respond, Shannon says, "The gray probably matches the color of the Tanana River. It's silty because it is primarily fed by glaciers."

Sam points at Shannon. "What she said."

"Got it," Derrick says. Then he looks at Shannon. "You really do suffer constantly from that genius disorder, don't you?"

Shannon flashes him a smile.

I point to the flippers. "I'm guessing we'll be doing some swimming?"

Sam explains that in order to get to the bridge's middle support in the river, we'll need to swim. He pulls out a rope with carabiners attached to each end, and a couple of belts with carabiners. "The idea," he says, "is for two of you to enter the river upstream of the bridge. Each swimmer will carry one end of this rope. Here, let's play it out."

Sam gives Brooke one end of the rope and Shannon the other end and tells them to pretend Derrick is the bridge support. "One person will swim into position on the closer side of the support and the other person will swim to the far side. The goal is to stretch the rope across the bridge support on the upriver side."

Following Sam's direction, Brooke goes to the far side of Derrick, so she and Shannon are stretching the rope out in front of him.

"Then you'll both swim under the bridge, to the downriver side of the support," Sam says, "and then you'll swim toward each other." Brooke and Shannon step behind Derrick and move toward each other. Their rope now wraps around Derrick.

Sam says, "The water should be relatively calm there, with the bridge support—represented here by Derrick—protecting you from the current. It's like being behind a huge rock in the river." He points to the carabiners. "Once you're in this position, click a carabiner from the rope onto the carabiner on your belt. The rope should snug up against the bridge support on the upriver side, and your weights should counterbalance each other, holding you in place in the river. Make sense?"

We all nod.

"I almost forgot." Sam reaches in the storage locker and pulls out a small gray pack made of waterproof material. "One of you two swimmers will be wearing this—with the explosive inside."

"How will we place the explosive and drill it in?" Brooke asks. "I mean, we'll be in the water."

"Your dry suit has a little built-in flotation to help you stay buoyant," Sam says, "but it won't be like wearing a life vest, where you're like a floating cork. One person will lift and support the person who's placing the explosive. After you've drilled it in and activated it, just unclip your carabiner and swim to shore."

"So," I say, "where will the other two people be while these two are placing the explosive?"

Sam says, "They'll each be placing explosives in the supports that can be reached by land on opposite sides of the river. We want to put three explosives on the bridge."

"It'll look like this." Sam picks up a stick off the ground and draws lines in the dirt. "Here's the bridge." He makes two Xs in the dirt. "Here're two people upstream from the bridge, who'll be the swimmers. They'll have the rope and the communication device that tells them when to place the explosives." He draws two more Xs—one on each side of the bridge. "These represent the other two team members."

"Will the swimmers just abandon their kayaks?" Shannon asks.

"Ideally, no," Sam says. "When the four of you get to the upper point where the two swimmers will be, the swimmers will stay behind with the gear they need and the other two team members will each tow a kayak behind the one they're paddling to their spots. When the swimmers finish, they'll each join one of you and reclaim their kayaks. All of you will then reunite at the rendezvous spot downriver."

"What if the Russians spot us?" Derrick says.

"You'll be wearing gray, the same color as the river, and ideally we'll be conducting the mission sometime between sunset and sunrise, so it'll be as dark as it can be. The dry suit flotation is designed to keep you just at the surface, not floating above it. But if you are spotted, just carry on as best you can. At this point, there's no *plan B*. There's no guarantee that you'll be successful, and even if you are, there's no guarantee that I'll be successful."

"So you're sending us on a suicide mission?" Derrick says.

"It's unlikely they'll spot you under the bridge since they'll be on top of it. The most likely time for you to be spotted is after you've placed the explosives, when you paddle your kayaks downriver from the bridge. But you'll all have dry suits and gray neoprene bathing caps on, so if they start firing you can jump in the water and swim. You'll be much smaller targets that way."

"But we've got a lot of distance to cover just to get to the bridge," Brooke says. "A seventeen-mile walk. And then how many miles by kayak?"

"About twenty-two," Sam says, "but you'll be doing all that during the dusky parts of the day, and you'll be lying low during full daylight."

"It's going to be risky," I say, "but we can do it."

"Or," Derrick says, "we'll die trying."

"That's not funny," Brooke says.

"Sorry," Derrick responds. "It's just that it's basically true."

"We should keep going," Sam says. "We've still got a lot to cover."

CHAPTER 63

WHILE WE EAT LUNCH, I think about how we could die.

But to not try is to say to all those Alaskans held captive right now, *your lives aren't worth the risk*. I definitely think it's worth the risk, and I think I'm physically capable of carrying out the plan. But I'm still scared out of my mind.

Sam is over at his swivel chair with his headphones on, gathering information from the antenna.

I'm finishing eating some crackers and cheese when Sam takes his headphones off and says, "Politically—no, geopolitically, things are heating up. North Korea has launched a test missile that reached the Gulf of Alaska. Russia has shifted a significant portion of its air force to the Siberian coast just across the Bering Sea from Alaska. And the president and Congress are at odds about how to respond."

"None of that sounds good," Shannon says.

Sam responds, "A government in active and visible turmoil could embolden our adversaries to step up their game, and that could make the situation much, much worse."

"What if our plan fails?" Brooke asks.

Sam shakes his head. "It's conceivable that our own government may attempt a nuclear first strike on Fort Greely to take out the missiles."

"But what about the rest of Alaska?" I ask.

"Obviously, there would be massive destruction and casualties." Sam pauses. "Both immediate and long-term."

"Wouldn't they give people time to leave?" Brooke asks.

"No," Sam says. "I believe it would be a pretty immediate response if we fail. Otherwise, it would probably fail, too. It's the best-case scenario for Russia: the United States using nuclear weapons on the United States."

I think about what I learned in my United States history class last year, about the radiation from the bombs dropped on Japan in World War II. "So Alaska could be the sacrifice that saves the rest of the United States if we fail?"

"If we fail," Sam says, "and Alaska is sacrificed, I hope it saves not only the United States, but the rest of the world—because with the way things are heating up, we're looking at World War III otherwise."

CHAPTER 64

"I BET YOU'RE SORRY TO be losing that stuff sack," Derrick says, pointing at my foot.

"I'm devastated." I give Derrick my best exaggerated sniffle and he laughs.

"Okay," Sam says, "enough joking around. We're on a tight time schedule." He's holding a pair of rubber boots in his hands. "The hike from the drop-off point to the lake will be muddy and mucky."

"What if mine don't fit?" Brooke asks. "My feet have just healed up. I had major blisters until Josh helped me out."

"These look like regular old rubber boots," Sam says, "but they have an adjustable inner boot. It's like a boot within a boot. So even if they look big on the outside, you can adjust how much your foot will move around on the inside." He sets one boot on the floor and puts his hand inside the other. "There are several settings. You can manipulate the inner boot with your hand."

Brooke nods.

Sam has us each grab a pair of boots, and then he gives us each a new pair of wool socks. We all put our new socks on and work on adjusting the boots to fit our feet.

Sam goes on. "You're going to need to move quickly. You might need to run if you're being pursued. If you can keep your feet in good shape, you'll have a better chance of succeeding. That said"—he looks at Brooke—"if you do get some blisters, you're just going to have to tough it out."

"I got it," Brooke says. "That's what I did to get here." She looks at me. "Josh really helped me out, but I was still in a lot of pain until recently."

Sam opens a gray bag and pulls out more shoes. "These are neoprene booties. You'll wear these when you're swimming. Sizewise, these are pretty forgiving." He tells everyone to take their new boots and socks off and find a pair of booties that fit.

I'm sitting on the floor, pulling a bootie over my foot. There's a lot of resistance, but when I pull on one side, and then the other, the bootie starts to slide on. Then, when it's halfway on, I pull hard from the heel and work it over my ankle.

While we're getting our booties on, Sam goes outside and returns with the flippers. "These will give you more control in the water. Find a pair that fits over your booties. After you put them on, stand up."

"I thought only two of us would be swimming," Shannon says.

"Two of you will be designated to place the explosive on the middle pillar, but everyone should have all the gear in case something happens," Sam says. "Once we've got the gear figured out, we'll discuss specific roles."

We all work on putting flippers on, and when we're all standing, Sam says, "Take a couple of steps backward."

We all do that successfully.

"Easy, right?" Sam says. "If you need to walk in your flippers—say you put them on and have a short distance to cover to get to the river— walk backward. I'd have you try walking forward, but I don't want anyone falling and hurting themselves on the hard floor or the edges of the counters."

Sam has us all sit back down, then says, "You can put your flippers on before entering the river and then walk backward, or you can sit in the shallows and put them on. Just don't walk forward with them."

We all take off our flippers and neoprene booties and put them with our new boots and wool socks.

Then we put our shoes back on. I want to save my rubber boots and new socks for the mission, so I put my sock with the blue foam back on and tie the two stuff sacks around it.

We spend the next hour moving all the gear from the storage lockers into the shelter, except for the explosives, and then we work on packing everything up. Sam gives us each a small bag of food with granola bars, crackers and cheese, chocolate bars, and beef jerky.

I put my sleeping bag, lightweight pad, one of the tents, and my food inside my pack. Then I slide the flippers in and put the neoprene booties inside. On the outside, I use straps on the pack to secure the dry suit and the inflatable kayak, which are each contained in their own bags.

After we finish up, Sam pulls a small rectangular device about half the size of the palm of his hand out of his pocket. "This will help you get from the drop-off point to the lake."

He turns it on, and a green dot lights up on the bottom of the screen, and a red dot lights up on top. "The green dot represents where you are. The red dot represents the lake. There's an arrow that will point in the direction you're walking. The more you keep the arrow pointing at the red dot, the sooner you'll get to the lake. If you have to make a detour because you see people or run into a bear or there's a forest fire, this little device will keep you from getting lost." Sam turns off the device and holds it out toward us.

I take it. "How long will the battery last?"

"Longer than you'll need to make the walk," Sam says. "You'll probably do it in twelve to fourteen hours if you don't run into major obstacles, and the battery will last four or five days."

"What about protection?" Derrick asks. "Will we have guns?"

"To reach your goal, you're going to need to travel light," Sam says. "If you get into a firefight with Russian soldiers, it's unlikely you'll come out of it alive."

"I get that," Derrick says. "I just—"

Sam cuts in. "Who here has ever fired a gun?"

Derrick raises his hand.

"What kind?" Sam asks.

"A twenty-two," Derrick says, "when I went bird hunting with my dad."

"The crew you're replacing," Sam says, "they were bringing limited weapons with them, but they'd been trained in how to use them."

"Still," Derrick says, "you're going to send us out there with nothing? That's a raw deal."

"Derrick has a point," I say. "What if we run into trouble we can handle with a gun but we don't have one?"

Shannon says, "We've still got some bear spray, but I agree, some type of gun would be good to have."

"I think so, too," Brooke says.

"This place has to be loaded with weapons," I say. "It's a worst-case-scenario shelter."

Sam scratches his beard. "Yes, I've got some weapons. And, like I said, the crew you're replacing was bringing weapons they were trained with. Usually people learn how to use them before taking them into the field." Sam sighs. "I'm giving you each a knife in case you encounter someone at close range, or if you need to ambush someone guarding the bridge from below. But I'll give you one pistol, too. Again, use this only if you encounter a problem that can't be solved any other way. That's all."

"Agreed," Derrick says. "Obviously, I hope we don't need to use it."

I think about having to kill someone, and it really starts to sink in. What we're going into is a life-and-death situation. We might encounter enemy soldiers. We might have to quietly *take out* a guard with our knives—or our gun. A chill runs up my spine.

A couple of beeps burst from Sam's control panel. He puts his fingers to his lips, goes over to the swivel chair, and puts his headphones on.

Someone must be flying overhead again.

For several minutes, we sit in silence while Sam has his back to us. He fiddles with a knob or two, but mostly he just sits and listens.

Finally, he takes his headphones off and turns toward us. "They're gone, but they circled around a few times before leaving. They must know something is down here. Hopefully they won't be back until after we've gone. In thirty-six hours, we're out of here."

CHAPTER 65

WHILE SAM WORKS ON HIS own preparations, the four of us keep practicing using the equipment and discussing who's going to do what.

"I think I should be one of the swimmers," Derrick says. "I used to be on a swim team. And since I have long arms, I can lift the person up who does the drilling."

Brooke nods and says, "I don't want to have anything to do with swimming in the river. I'll do it if I have to, but I don't know how good I'd be at it."

"Swimming isn't one of my strong points," Shannon says. "I know how to swim, but when I'm swimming that's all I can do. I can climb things and run, but swimming? Like Brooke, I'll do it if I have to for the mission, but I don't know how successful I'd be."

I feel all eyes on me. "I guess I better make sure my flippers fit."

Brooke and Derrick each crack a smile.

Shannon says, "Thanks."

I nod. "Now we can plan the rest of the mission details. For starters, you two"—I point at Brooke and Shannon—"will take all of my and Derrick's stuff, kayaks included, after you drop us upriver a little ways from the bridge."

"You and Derrick will keep the communication device that lets us know when to place the explosives." Shannon picks up the device off the floor and hands it to me. "It'll take you two longer to do your job since you have to swim, and Brooke and I will already be in position on opposite sides of the river. When we see you start to swim we'll know it's time."

Sam turns around from his desk and says, "One thing to keep in mind: The pipeline crosses the river just upstream from the bridge. There've been a couple of land-based attempts to sabotage it, so it might be guarded. When you get close to the pipeline, but before you get too close, stop and scout so you know what the deal is."

"Thanks," I say.

Sam nods and turns back around.

"So, after me and Derrick set our explosive, one of us will swim to you." I point to Brooke. "And one of us will swim to you." I point to Shannon.

"Let's really pin it down," Shannon says.

"Here's what I think," Derrick says. "From whatever side you drop us on, I'll swim to the opposite side since I have the most swimming experience."

"Sounds good," I say.

"I'll cross the river towing Derrick's kayak," Shannon says, "since I have more boating experience than Brooke."

"That works," Brooke says. "I'll tow Josh's and stay on the same side of the river."

"Does anyone else . . ." I pause. "I mean, does it hit you—what we're doing and why? I keep thinking I'm going to wake up from this intense dream, but I never do."

"From all the way back since the earthquake," Brooke says, nodding. "How is it that we survived the quake, survived a starving ninety-mile hike where we didn't know where we were going, and now we're doing *this*?"

Shannon says, "My mom's people—my people—have lived on this land for thousands of years. Why should they suffer and possibly have their land rendered uninhabitable by a nuclear strike that has absolutely nothing to do with them? What choice do I have but to try to stop this destruction?"

Derrick points to Brooke. "I get what you're saying. We're lined up to do all these things that heroes do." Derrick pauses. "Mostly, I'm a lazy person, if I can afford to be one. My dad's pretty much right about me on that count."

"Yeah," I say, "but you've got good judgment. You know when to be lazy and when not to be."

"True." Derrick smiles. "It used to be that I tried not to look lazy when I knew my dad was watching. But that quake changed me. Seeing that it was only us who survived and then seeing what we needed to do to keep surviving . . ." He shakes his head. "And now this? Like Shannon said, we don't really have a choice."

"If I chose to do nothing," I say, "and I survived, I wouldn't be able to live with myself."

CHAPTER 66

"WE SHOULD TRY TO KEEP the rope in front of us as we swim toward the bridge," Derrick says. "That way, we'll have less of a chance of tangling our legs in it."

"Maybe we should keep it bunched up tight until we're in the middle of the river and approaching the support," I add. "We could swim side by side and then separate when we're close to the support and let the rope spread out from there."

"That should work," Derrick says.

Our packs are all packed up, and we're all wearing gray long-sleeve shirts and pants that are supposedly bug-bite proof. We've got gray rain gear if we need it, and we have the gray dry suits, gray rubber boots, gray bathing caps. Gray everything.

Sam also gave us each a water bottle with a built-in filter. You fill the bottle, put the filter in the top, and screw it into place with the lid, and when you squeeze the bottle to take a drink, water is pushed through the filter before it leaves the bottle, and it's purified.

"Graze on what you want." Sam points to some shelves filled with crackers, cookies, and granola bars.

"What happens to this place after we leave?" I ask.

"It's pretty tightly built," Sam says. "We don't really have any perishable food. And I'll close off the spring water we've got routed through the pipe that gives us drinking water. The solar panels—the ones disguised as trees—will keep the batteries charged so when someone does need to be stationed here, they'll have some juice when they arrive."

"How'd you get into this line of work?" Shannon asks.

"There's a part of the government that's secret," Sam says. "It is, ideally, independent of politics. We go into action during emergencies. What we do goes on in the background. I ended up where I am by being good at what I do. By getting an invitation."

"How many of you are there?" Brooke asks.

Sam says, "I've probably already told you too much. I can't disclose how many people or how many official stations, but I'll tell you this. Sometimes we plan our missions and are ready to act, and then a conventional solution is successful and we abort. That's the preferable alternative almost every time."

"How will we know if that happens with this mission?" Derrick asks.

"If the light doesn't come on instructing you to place your explosives, then don't place them," Sam says.

"How long should we wait?" I ask.

"If your light doesn't come on, someone will make contact with you. Don't move from your position until either your light comes on and you carry out the mission, or someone makes direct contact. Whoever contacts you—*if* someone contacts you—will say *the river is running high*."

"So there's a chance we may not have to go through with blowing up the bridge?" Brooke asks.

Sam looks at Brooke, and then makes eye contact with each one of us. Then he says, "You never want to go into a mission thinking that you may not have to carry it out. Psychologically, you have to be ready."

I'm eating my second pack of cheese and crackers, and I'm thinking about what Sam said. How can I not think about how great it would be to abort this mission? That's what I hope for, and now he's given us a little bit of hope. But I also know what Sam's talking about in terms of being psychologically ready. It's like when the weather turns bad and there's talk about canceling a cross-country race. Our coach drilled it into us to always be prepared to run your best no matter how likely it is the race will be canceled.

Don't lose your edge.

Shannon's voice jolts me back into the present. "Should we take these?" She's holding up her binoculars.

Sam swings around in his swivel chair. "Yes," he says. "They'll be good for scouting, especially once the bridge comes into view."

"Do we just leave the rest of our stuff here?" Derrick asks. "You know. Our old packs and sleeping bags and stuff."

"If you have anything small that's personal that you want to take, that would be okay," Sam says. "But you don't want anything big or heavy that would slow you down. Or anything that would help the enemy if you're captured."

After I get my binoculars, I pull out my blue stuff sack with my journal, which I haven't written in since we left Simon Lake. I glance over at Brooke. She's got the solar charger her dad gave her in her hand. Derrick is rustling through his possessions, and Shannon has her journal in her hands.

Whatever small stuff we all end up bringing, I just hope we come out of this alive.

CHAPTER 67

THE NEXT MORNING, SAM SAYS, "We'll be flying around midnight to take advantage of whatever amount of darkness we have."

Two more flyovers happened yesterday late in the afternoon, and that has Sam on edge.

"It'll take a couple hours to walk to the plane, and then an hour or so to check its systems and clear the runway, so we'll leave here around nine p.m.," Sam says. He turns back to his communication desk.

Twelve hours, I think. Twelve hours, and we'll be starting this crazy mission to save the free world. I think about the other two teams that will be blowing up bridges, and Sam's team, which will try to penetrate the fort and reset the nukes. They've all got to be highly skilled to have been chosen and trained. Like Sam.

And then there's us. Yeah, we're pretty tough, because we survived a crazy earthquake and then a starving hike.

But highly trained we're not.

How will I react if we come under fire? How will I deal with the swift flowing river? I'm not talking just about the swimming part, but also the kayaking. And then there's the drilling while Derrick somehow treads water and holds me in place so I can set the explosives.

Everything is high stakes. And everything is new. Not a good combination.

It's like if, as a freshman at the beginning of cross-country season, I'd been told, *Okay, train for a week and then you'll be racing the top runners in the state, and if you don't win, you die.*

I glance over at Brooke. If I knew this was the last time we'd be together, I'd want to kiss her—that is, if she'd let me. Or at least tell her that I'm attracted to her. But I don't want to dilute the energy and focus it will take to pull off our mission.

But maybe she wants to kiss me, too. If we both wanted to, then what would one kiss hurt? But if I wanted to, and told her, and she didn't, would that create some weird energy that might get in the way when we need to focus so we don't die?

She looks up and catches me staring at her.

I nod and flash her a smile.

She smiles back.

I don't know what to do next, so I pretend to focus on my gear. I open the blue stuff sack and pull out my journal. I turn to the first and only page I wrote on and read the few lines there.

Running. How can I get faster and stronger?

My parents. How can I keep them from splitting up?

Brooke. How can I get to know her better?

Control. What do I really have control over?

I'm basically still searching for answers to all these questions. But the one about control really sticks in my brain. To a certain extent I can control my actions. Or at least try to control them. Or try to act in a way that will move me in the direction I want to go.

The other questions about running and my parents—they don't really matter right now. I just want my parents to be alive. But Brooke . . . I glance up from my journal and look over at her. She's turned a little to the side and looks beautiful silhouetted in the lantern light in this shelter. I've repaired her feet. I've had my head smashed against her hip when we were moving rocks. We've shared some good talks in the tent.

I want to just walk over to her, to tell her that if we do make it out of this mess alive, that I'd like to hang out with her and get to know her better.

I take a step, but the mission stops me. *No*, I tell myself.

Not now.

But if we survive. If we've blown the bridge, or aborted, and are still alive—when our lives aren't in danger—I'll tell her then.

I tuck my journal back into my blue stuff sack and put it in the gray pack Sam has given me.

What is everyone else thinking about? Are they all tossing around questions in their minds? Or are they going over the mission?

I walk to the back wall of the shelter and lie down on one of the bunks. Derrick comes over and lies on another. And then Brooke and Shannon do the same.

"We may as well get some rest now," Shannon says. "I don't think we'll be sleeping much for the next several days."

My stomach and chest feel raw. I take a deep breath and exhale through my nose. Then I hear two sharp pings from Sam's communication panel, alerting us of another flyover.

I lie on my side and watch Sam. He's got his headphones on and is perfectly still. We're all lying quiet, having learned the drill from Sam. After a couple of minutes, he puts his headphones down and walks over to the bunks. "I think it'd be best if we left now. We can hide in the brush by the plane until it gets as dark as it's going to be. Get your boots on."

CHAPTER 68

IT'S MORE OF A HOLLOWED-OUT tunnel through the brush than a trail that snakes its way up the slope behind the shelter. We're walking stooped over to keep our packs from catching on the brush. The new boots feel good on my feet. Hot but good. Way better than a stuff sack. I'm right behind Sam, and he's methodically working his way up through the brush tunnel. It's obvious that someone spent time clearing the lower brush away while letting the willows get tall on either side of our route.

It would be hard for someone to detect anything from the air. Unless of course they're using heat detection devices, like Sam thinks they are doing. *Those flyovers may be plotting coordinates for other aircraft*, Sam whispered before we left the shelter. *Let's hike without talking*, he said. *Just follow me single file.*

Now, as we reach the top of the ridge, Sam stops and whispers, "We'll have about a quarter mile of tundra to cross. This is where we'll be the most exposed. I'm going to jog, and I want you to do the same. Stay in line, because I'm going to take us across the shortest possible way in order to cut down our chances of being seen from the air."

We all agree to follow single file. Sam breaks into a slow run, and I'm right behind him. I feel more in my element than I have since the last time I ran with Theo. The flat ridgetop is rocky, and you've got to place your feet carefully so you don't turn an ankle or catch your toe. My pack is going *thunk* with every step.

We're about halfway across now, and it's like a dance where every foot placement is a new move. It's like being in a trance and having to pay attention at the same time. We keep going with the steady pace Sam has set, and when we get to the other side of the ridgetop the brush tunnel trail continues. Sam stops about fifteen feet into the brush. He doesn't look winded at all, and that's when I realize that not only is he super smart, he's also in top-notch condition. Shannon, Brooke, and Derrick reach the brush, and I can hear some huffing and puffing, and I see sweat on their foreheads.

Sam takes off his pack, gets out his water bottle, takes a drink, and motions for everyone else to do the same. "The plane and runway are still a couple of miles away. When we get close, we'll stay under the cover of the brush until the sun dips behind the ridges to the northwest."

We all put our packs on and keep going, stooping under the brush. My midback tightens up from all the slouched-over walking, but I don't care. I'm just glad that Sam is leading the way. We walk in silence, following the brush tunnel as it goes up and down some hills and winds its way around others.

The land levels out and Sam stops. Once we're all gathered around him, he says, "We'll wait here. We're close."

"How close?" Brooke asks.

"The plane and landing strip are in this area." Sam points across the flats. "There's ample cover by the plane for a couple of people, but not for a group this big."

I peer in the direction he's pointing, trying to pick out where the plane is, but it all just looks like brush and more brush to me.

Sam takes off his pack, sits on the ground, and motions for us to do the same.

Once we're all seated, Sam says, "Let's briefly go over the plan. I want you each to tell it to me."

After we each successfully tell him the plan, Sam says, "You passed. How do you know when and if to abort?"

"If we have a face-to-face interaction with someone who says, *The river is running high*," Brooke says.

"Great," Sam says. "Here's the next part. After you set the explosives, paddle like hell downriver. You're going to cross the mouth of the Delta River. It dumps into the Tanana just below the bridge. Once you're past the mouth of the Delta, you're going to be going around a big bend. At the far end of the bend the river splits into two channels. Take the left channel until you come to the mouth of a creek. Set up camp in the woods on the far side of that creek and wait there. If no one comes after three days, you're on your own."

"What do you mean, *on your own*?" Derrick asks.

Sam tilts his head. "It's possible that you'll blow the bridge, but I won't succeed. Or it's possible that you'll blow the bridge, and I'll succeed but will be killed in the process. At this point, I'm the only one who knows where to look for you."

"Can't you tell someone else?" Brooke asks.

"I'm trying to protect you," Sam says. "The more people who know where you are, the greater the chance that someone who's captured will expose you."

"You mean if they are being tortured?" Shannon asks.

"That's a possibility," Sam says. "I'd rather have you take your chances in the wilderness than have the Russians hunt you down because someone was pressed into disclosing your location." Sam takes a breath, then continues, "If you are captured, try not to talk, but if you *have* to talk, lie. Tell them you're part of the Sons of Alaska Militia. That's a made-up name, but it'll buy the rest of us some time to attempt our parts of the mission. I really shouldn't have told you what I'm doing for my part, but I felt like you needed to know how high the stakes are since you're putting your lives on the line."

Derrick lifts up his hand. "Do you all hear that?"

In the distance, I hear a faint humming sound.

"Nobody move," Sam says. "They won't be able to see us."

The humming grows louder and louder, and then we see a large plane crossing the flats in front of us. It passes over us, keeps going, and disappears over the ridge from the way we came. Seconds later we hear a muffled roar and the ground shakes under us.

I picture the shelter back at Sam's camp, blown to pieces.

"They're onto us," Sam says. "I wonder what that means about what else they know."

CHAPTER 69

WHEN THE SUN GOES BEHIND the ridge, Sam marches us three quarters of the way across the flats.

We talked a little more about the shelter being blown to bits, but Sam said that didn't necessarily mean they know what we're trying to do. He said that's what it *might* mean, but regardless, he didn't receive an abort message, so we were proceeding as planned.

Sam moves some already cut brush aside. He does this in two directions until he's got a short path about twenty feet wide. Then he points in the direction he started clearing and says, "Clear the rest of the cut brush off the strip while I do the preflight checks."

"Did you cut all this brush when you arrived?" I ask.

"A crew landed with a helicopter and cleared the landing strip since it hadn't been used in a few years," Sam says. "When I arrived, I recovered the runway with the brush to camouflage it."

"But—"

"Just clear it," Sam cuts off Derrick. "We're on a tight time schedule now that the sun is behind the ridge." Sam steps in the opposite direction from where he started clearing, moves some more brush, and exposes the wing of a plane.

He looks over at us, and we're all just staring at him. "Haven't you ever seen a plane before?" He points to the landing strip again. "Clear it. All the way to that spruce tree. We've got to move."

The four of us clear the brush, pushing it aside just like Sam did. We work our way down the runway.

"This whole deal is moving pretty fast," Derrick says.

"I think we got used to living in the shelter and just preparing," Shannon says. "That was safe. Or at least it felt safe. But now that we're having to do everything, well, we're kind of in shock."

"The next bomb," Derrick says. "It could be for us." He shakes his head. "I don't want to die."

"None of us do," I say as I'm dragging brush off the runway zone.

"My dad is always lording it over me about how he puts his life on the line for our country while I'm lazing my way through school, doing as little as possible." Derrick pushes more brush off to the side.

Now we've got about five more feet, and we'll be at the spruce tree.

"People who decide to devote their lives to defending the country, people like your dad or like Sam, they're basically selfless," I say to Derrick. I push more brush aside and reach the spruce tree. "Now it's our turn to do our part."

Back at the plane, which Sam has now totally uncovered, Derrick says, "Aren't we going to be detected by the Russians when we're airborne and flying across what is now their airspace?"

"This little plane may look simple and old-fashioned, but it's got some pretty complex radar-blocking and scrambling equipment," Sam explains. "We'll be flying low mostly. Under the radar, so to speak."

"What about the noise?" Brooke asks. "Small planes are loud. That's what I remember from doing a flight-seeing trip with my family."

"This one's got a special engine," Sam explains. "We need the fuel for takeoffs and landings, but once we're airborne we'll run on battery power for most of the flight. It's like a hybrid car. There's a layer of solar cells on the topside of the wings that feed into a battery system." Sam motions to the packs piled on the ground. "Let's load those up and get out of here."

CHAPTER 70

BEFORE WE'RE AIRBORNE, WE DECIDE to stay clear of the smoke rising from where Sam's shelter used to be. As curious as we all are about how direct of a hit it was, we all agree that flying too close to it could expose us.

Not that any of us has any control over what Sam does. He's in charge. Luckily for us, Sam has been a smart and reasonable dictator so far.

After we're airborne, I look down at the land below, hoping the dusk will provide the cover we need.

When Sam switches over to battery power, the plane goes from making a constant roar where you can't hear your own thoughts, to a loud hum.

I'm in the front seat next to Sam, and he's fiddling with knobs and pushing buttons, and I decide to just let him be. I glance over my shoulder and see Derrick pressed against one window, and Shannon in the middle. I can only see part of one of Brooke's legs because she's sitting directly behind me.

The gear is all tied down in the rear of the plane.

Before we took off, Sam showed us the emergency bag with food, a sleeping bag, fuel, a small stove, flares, fire-starting material, and a pistol.

We fly over a stretch of blackened forest that ends at a swamp, and I shout, "That's where we were. That's the fire we started!"

Everyone peers out the windows and nods. Then we fly low, following a tundra ridge, and I'm sure it's one of the ridges we walked when we left Simon Lake. We follow the ridge as it climbs higher and higher, and in my mind I picture us walking it in the opposite direction. Starting high above Simon Lake and then gradually descending, trying to stay above the tree line for as long as we could.

And then, way off to the right, Simon Lake comes into view. I tap Sam on the shoulder to get his attention. "That's Simon Lake," I say.

He nods and makes a slight shift in steering, and the plane dips toward the lake. The big rock slide comes into view, and even in the dim light, I can make out the green flags we planted to direct rescuers to the note we wrote. It's pretty obvious that no one has been there; the flags are undisturbed. I'm glad we left when we did. And then I think about the fact that if the Russians do succeed in taking over, or if everyone's parents are dead, and we die, too, then no one may ever know about the Simon Lake disaster. There would be no one looking for anyone. And then I realize that thousands of things could have happened that no one knows about. Things that go wrong in the wilderness where people disappear seemingly without a trace. Their history erased.

Sam waves his hand to get everyone's attention. "Sorry I don't have headphones for everyone so we can talk more easily." He points down at the lake and then at the controls. "Mileagewise, I think you all walked at least one hundred twenty miles to get to my shelter."

"Great," Derrick shouts. "Now I'm more tired than I thought I was."

I smile. Part of me wishes I could be lighthearted and always joking around like Derrick. I mean, he's strong and competent, and funny, too.

I feel the plane dip and start to turn, and Sam says, "We'll be at the drop site in about an hour and a half."

A shiver runs up my spine. It was scary enough walking through unfamiliar territory when we left Simon Lake. Now we'll be doing the same thing, except we have to worry about running into Russian soldiers who might just shoot us on sight.

How do you go from being a month or two away from starting your senior year in high school to being part of a bridge-bombing operation?

I guess I always took for granted that I lived in a safe place. That our country was stable.

Yeah, I knew things were getting kind of bad in Washington, DC, but people were making lots of jokes about what was happening. Like they couldn't believe the government was so—what was the word my dad kept using—dysfunctional. But I'd always just lived my life despite what was happening in other places. But not anymore.

I don't want Alaska to be sacrificed to save the Lower 48. That's not fair. To pack our state with missiles and then to totally screw up and let some other country take charge of them? Why should we pay for that?

I guess that was my main reason for wanting to succeed—to keep Alaska from being obliterated because of some people in Washington, DC, who couldn't keep the enemies from taking control of our missiles. The missile silos should be some of the most secure places ever.

"Drop site is coming into view," Sam says, jolting me back to the present.

I see a thin, straight line in the trees.

I know as soon as we land, we're on our own.

CHAPTER 71

"WE COULD MAKE SOME PROGRESS before it's too light out," I say, after we've all come back together. We scattered after Sam dropped us off, all having to empty our bladders. I pick up my pack and sling it on, then buckle the thick waist strap.

"I got sleepy on the plane ride," Brooke says, yawning. "Walking is going to suck now."

"I'm just glad I didn't puke," Derrick says. "I was super queasy just before we landed."

Shannon's got her pack on and is looking around, turning in a slow circle. When she's facing the rest of us, she says, "Hiking from dusk to dawn." She shakes her head. "I understand why we have to do it that way. It's just that's also when the animals are most active. We'll have to be on the lookout."

"We've got a gun," Derrick says. "Relax."

"It's not for animals," Shannon responds. "Besides, that pistol would only piss off a grizzly bear unless you hit every shot into its vital organs."

"The gun," I say, "is supposed to be used at close range. I think we should use it as a last resort for anything that's preventing us from carrying out the mission, people or animals."

"I get that," Shannon says, "but we can't just march blindly forward because we have a gun. Firing it will attract attention, so if we can avoid bears, wolves, or moose, that'd be the way to go. Plus, we still have two full canisters of bear spray."

"I'm down with all that." Derrick pats the pistol in the holster that's strapped to his waist. "I don't want to shoot a bear, only to have a bunch of Russian soldiers shoot us. But I still feel more comfortable having the gun. Don't you all agree it kind of takes some pressure off?" When no one says anything in response, Derrick raises his eyebrows. "I don't know. I just feel more secure having the gun."

"Gun or no gun," I say, "we should go."

Derrick gives Shannon his full canister of bear spray since he's carrying the gun, and Brooke has her bear spray in her hands. I still have my canister, but it's mostly empty.

I tuck it into a mesh pocket on the side of my pack and then pull out the route-finding device and turn it on. Everyone crowds in to see the screen.

A little green dot appears toward the bottom of the screen, and a red dot appears at the top, both about the size of a pencil eraser. The arrow stretching out from the green dot points off to the right of the red dot. I slowly swing the device around until the arrow points at the red dot.

"I hope that thing works," Derrick says. "I mean, if it's a little off, we could miss the lake entirely."

"Whatever." Brooke shrugs. "It's all we've got. Let's go before I fall asleep."

Beside the openness of the narrow landing strip, the forest is thick.

"Hopefully the Russians will stick to the roads," I say.

"I would." Derrick points in the direction the arrow is pointing. "That's just as thick as the brush we crashed through to get to Sam's little hideout."

The mosquitoes have finally figured out that we're here, but because of our high-tech clothes and the bug spray Sam had us use that supposedly lasts for several days, they're not really landing and biting.

I take a step in the direction of the arrow and then another and another. We're going single file, and I'm dodging trees and the thicker clumps of brush so my path forward is kind of a zigzag, where I'm constantly correcting to keep the arrow pointed at the red dot. We move through the forest like this for maybe an hour, and then we hit a big obstacle that makes us all lie down on our bellies and try to stay perfectly still.

CHAPTER 72

"SAM SAID TO AVOID EVERYONE," I whisper, "Russian, American, it doesn't matter." We're all lying shoulder to shoulder and peering down with our binoculars on a camp with a bunch of green wall tents in sparsely forested flats.

"How are we going to get around them?" Shannon whispers.

"My dad thinks the people forming these militias are paranoid," Brooke says softly. "They believe everyone is a potential enemy. He interviewed a few of them when he was contracted to do an article about militias."

"They've got way more firepower than us," Derrick whispers. "Maybe they could help us out."

"Um. I don't think so," Shannon says. "I'm with Brooke on this one. These people may be carving out their own little country, like the South tried to do during the Civil War."

"We've got to trust Sam on this." I rest my binoculars on the ground next to the route-finding device. "If he'd wanted us to seek out help, he would've said so."

"Guns are guns," Derrick says. "That bridge might be heavily guarded."

"Guns aren't guns," Shannon counters. "Hunting rifles versus military assault weapons and rocket launchers. Trained assassins versus wannabe Rambos."

Before Derrick can respond, I say, "Sam told us that the Russians basically use these militias as an excuse to attack. Think of it this way.

If we can carry out our mission, maybe the Russians will be forced to leave before they find and kill this group of people. We could save their lives if we can avoid them now and get on with what we're supposed to do."

"I hear all that," Derrick says, "but not everyone in the military is some awesome fighting machine. My dad used to gripe about some of the losers in his squadron. You might be surprised at the lack of competence." Derrick points down to the camp. "Some of these people might be just as good or better than a whole lot of soldiers, Russian or American. How do you think we got into this mess? And now look; we've got four high school students who stumbled into a top-secret operation helping to carry it out."

"The Rambo dudes my dad interviewed," Brooke says, "had an extreme men-are-superior-to-women mentality and whites-are-superior-to-all mentality."

Shannon says, "I hate being around guys like that. Not only are they idiots, they can be dangerous."

"Okay," Derrick says, "I get it. All I'm saying is that at some point we may need to be open to accepting some help despite Sam's instructions not to." He motions toward the militia. "I totally get why it's not a good idea to approach this camp, but I'm asking you all to at least entertain the idea that somewhere between here and the bridge we might need to do something like that."

We talk some more and we outvote Derrick three to one when he suggests we consider approaching people for help in the future. Luckily, all this talk is happening as it's getting lighter, so we don't actually lose that much time since we're supposed to stop and hide during the day. Since the Rambo camp is close by, we decide to keep a continual watch during the day. Two people sleeping and two people up. We back away from the edge of the bluff and quietly set up one tent, figuring that two of us can use it while two of us are on watch, and then we'll switch. Then when dusk hits and it's time to pack up, we'll be out of here quickly.

We're just getting finished setting up the tent when we hear voices coming from somewhere behind us.

Only the voices aren't in English.

CHAPTER 73

ALL FOUR OF US SLINK away from the noises, leaving the tent unattended. We're basically trapped between the Rambo camp and what I'm pretty sure are Russian soldiers. We lie on our bellies, but instead of facing the Rambo camp below we're now facing toward our tent.

None of us know Russian, but what they're speaking isn't English. And it sure doesn't sound like Spanish or French to me.

The voices grow louder, and then all of a sudden they go silent. Through the woods I can make out at least two, maybe three people. They're carrying large brown sacks.

"They're Russians," Shannon whispers, "but not *the Russians*. Delta Junction has a large Russian immigrant population." She motions with her head. "They're collecting mushrooms."

"Still," I say, "don't you think there could be some infiltration into the community? Some spies reporting to the soldiers? Some people loyal to the homeland?"

Brooke whispers, "Even if they aren't spies, we can't trust them. We can't trust anyone."

"Yeah," Derrick says, "I get all that." He pauses. "It's just, what do we do now that those mushroom hunters or spies or whatever they are have discovered one of our *Sam's Special* camouflaged tents?"

"Where the hell are all these people coming from?" I whisper. "I mean, we walk for days from Simon Lake looking for people and don't see any, and now Sam drops us at some secret brush-infested location and we're surrounded?"

"If they aren't communicating with the Russian soldiers," Shannon whispers, "then we'll be okay. But even if they are, we'll be okay. As long as we break Sam's rule and get out of here now, in broad daylight."

We crawl along the edge of the low bluff, not wanting to expose ourselves to the Civil War–era militia below nor to the Russian mushroom hunters who've found our tent.

Sleepiness isn't a problem since, in the new world order, any human we encounter can derail the mission, and we're all wired from feeling surrounded even though we haven't slept in over twenty-four hours. I thought most of our challenges before approaching the bridge would be from the natural world, and now it seems like the natural world is just a stage where our lives are playing out.

At least we've only left behind a tent, and we've got one more. I haven't pulled out the route finder because I figure we can start following the arrow once we get away from this spot.

The mushroom hunters have started talking again, and their voices grow fainter as we move farther away. The Rambo camp is still visible below, but it seems like we're approaching one of its edges.

I stop and turn and face my friends and wait until we're all bunched up. "The land is sloping downward," I whisper. I pull out the route finder and power it up, and the arrow points directly through the center of the Rambo camp. "We'll need to keep going around." I point off to the right of the camp and start down that way. I'm glad we've all got rubber boots because as soon as we hit the flat area to the right of the camp we are in a quagmire of hell.

"They did this on purpose," Shannon says. "For protection. They built their camp on a dry island in the middle of a swamp."

The mud and water are suctioning my lower legs up to my shins, making it feel like I'm walking through wet cement. Except instead of a cement smell, it reeks of sulfur. My rubber boots stay on my feet despite the continual attempts from the swamp to claim them.

The idea that we're going to make it to the lake, inflate the kayaks, paddle down a creek to the river and down the river to the bridge, blow the bridge, and get away with it seems about as remote as the chances of us going to the moon. But I keep putting one muck-sucking foot in front of the other because to stop would pretty much mean to choose to die. And let a lot of Alaskans die.

CHAPTER 74

WHAT SEEMS LIKE HOURS LATER we're out of the swamp and following the arrow again. The forest thins and we enter a meadow where the walking is easy, which has me both psyched and scared out of my mind. I mean, since we had a major detour because of the Rambo camp, we're now coming at the lake from a completely different direction, a direction I'm guessing Sam didn't pick for a reason.

I stop and wait until we're all bunched up. "I don't like the feel of this," I say softly. "It's so open."

"We could backtrack"—Shannon points over her shoulder—"just a couple hundred yards to where the forest is thicker, and rest until dusk."

Derrick nods. "Dusk to dawn activity. Stay dormant during the day. Those were Captain Sam's orders."

Brooke and I both agree, and we all backtrack until the underbrush is thick enough to provide some camouflage.

"We've got one two-person tent for the four of us," I say.

"We'll have to stack ourselves like firewood to fit," Derrick says.

Shannon shakes her head. "Two of us rest while two of us keep watch. Then we switch."

"I'll take—" But then I'm cut off by a high-pitched chattering sound that goes on for at least thirty seconds.

"A squirrel giving a warning call," Shannon whispers, putting into words what I'm already thinking.

We all peer in the direction where the call came from, where the forest opens up into a meadow. My experience with squirrels around my house is that they break into warning calls almost every time I walk out the door.

We're far enough into the thick brush that it'll be hard for someone to see us if we aren't moving, but we're close enough to see a little ways into the meadow. I wonder if there are Russian soldiers on the march or if the Rambo camp people are out on patrol or if there are more mushroom hunters. Whatever it is, we need to remain still or melt farther into the underbrush.

But then what I see materializing on the edge of the meadow makes me pause. I know the smartest thing to do would be to stay still and not be seen, but part of me wants to make contact. To see what they know. To find out what they're doing and where they're going.

I glance at Shannon, Brooke, and Derrick, and whisper, "We need to break Sam's rule."

They all agree and we slowly move toward the edge of the brush.

CHAPTER 75

"CANADA," THE MAN SAYS. "WORD is, they're not turning away anyone who makes it to the border." He strokes his beard, which hangs to just below his collarbone. "Word is, the Russians are rounding people up." He shakes his head. "They're not getting my girls."

The three girls standing in a row next to their father are younger than us. The two oldest ones—obviously twins—are maybe thirteen, and the youngest is nine or ten, I'm guessing.

"The border is over a hundred miles from here," Shannon says, "and that's by road."

"We got food," the man says. "We can hunt and fish if we need to." He's got a rifle slung over one shoulder, and the girls all have fishing poles strapped to the outside of their packs. "As long as we keep to the woods and off the roads, we'll be fine."

I tell them about the Rambo camp, and the man thanks me for the information.

"Did you live in Delta Junction?" Brooke asks.

The man replies, "The people there didn't even have a chance to leave. The Russians came at the town from all sides. It's basically one big refugee camp. Our place is about twenty miles out of town."

I tell him about the Russian mushroom hunters we saw, and he says, "They could've worked out a deal with the soldiers, or they could be working for them now. Who knows?"

The girls haven't said a word the whole time. Maybe they were instructed by their father to keep quiet.

"Are there a lot of people doing what you're doing?" Derrick asks. "I mean, are the woods full of people fleeing the Russians?"

The man shrugs. "I got a tip from a friend. Called me from town before the Russians got to his place. Me and the girls, we packed up, climbed a high ridge, and watched for a few days. Tanks on the highway. Truckloads of soldiers." The man shakes his head. "I love my country. But I love my girls more. My wife—may God bless her soul—I promised her I'd always keep them safe."

None of us ask him what happened to his wife. We don't know if she died three weeks ago or three years ago.

The man asks us what brings us to where we are. We tell him about Simon Lake and the earthquake, but say nothing about Sam and our mission.

"And you're doing what now?" the man asks. "The high-tech clothing and packs. Carrying rafts. All gray. You look like the military, but you're just kids."

"We can't tell you everything," Shannon offers. "All our families are in Fairbanks. We hope what we're going to do will not only help them but all Alaskans."

We don't tell the man that if our plan fails and the United States decides to nuke Alaska, he and his girls will probably die on their way to Canada.

"You're smart to get out of here," I say. "Go as fast as you can."

For a few minutes, we watch the family continue along the edge of the meadow, and then we backtrack into the brush to get some rest until dusk.

Refugees, I think. *Those people are refugees fleeing America, land of the brave and home of the free, because it's unsafe to stay.*

CHAPTER 76

SHANNON AND DERRICK INSIST ON taking the first watch so Brooke and I set up the tent and crawl in. This tent is a little bigger than the one-person tent we shared on our trek from Simon Lake. We've got our sleeping pads and bags spread out, but it's too warm to crawl inside the bags so we're lying on top of them. And since the tent is spacious enough, instead of lying head to toe we're both oriented the same way.

"I wish the world wasn't so screwed up," Brooke says. She's lying on her back but then turns to face me. "That's what put us in this situation."

"People in power created this emergency," I say, "but it's regular people who suffer the most from it."

Brooke puts her hand on my arm and leaves it there. "When that guy and his daughters said they were heading to Canada, I wanted to go with them." She bows her head. "I'm no hero, Josh. I'm scared out of my mind." Then she pulls her hand away, but I can still feel the warmth from it being there.

"Brooke," I say, "I'm scared, too. Who wouldn't be?"

"You sure don't show it," Brooke says.

"I deal with it the way I deal with anything that's stressful," I say. "I do something physical. And there's plenty of physical things to do on this mission."

"Tell me about it." Brooke sighs. "And that's part of my fear. I mean, besides getting shot, I'm worried that I won't be able to do what we need to do."

"Brooke," I say, "you hiked one hundred twenty miles with your feet full of blisters while eating almost nothing." I turn toward her and look her in the eye. "You can do this."

"I need a way to deal with my fear," Brooke says, "so I don't freeze up and cause us all to fail. The three of you would be better off without me."

"Brooke, we need you." I put my hand on her arm. "As it stands, we need all four of us to set the charges on the bridge." I take my hand away. "If any of us gets hurt or caught or drowns, then the ones who are left to do the job will be needed even more."

"You're right, Josh." Brooke licks her lips. "Sometimes I just get overwhelmed, and I don't have a thing I do when I'm scared like you do. I used to complain that all I got to do was tag along with my sisters on things they did. But I never had to do anything on my own. I never had to pick up the slack. I was always *just there*. You know, being passive." She swallows once. "For this, I can't be *just there* or *just here*. Wherever we are, I need to be active, to stay active, to not freeze up in fear. I can't be just *here*."

"Maybe that's it," I say.

"What do you mean?" Brooke asks.

I look her in the eye and say, *"I can't be just here."* I pause. "Make that your mantra to keep yourself present in what's going on. That way your mind won't have the time or space to think about whatever it does to get in the way of you doing what you need to do. Just don't give your mind a chance to psyche yourself out."

"I guess I could try that," Brooke says. *"I can't be just here. I can't be just here."*

I nod and then say, "We better get some rest because it'll be our turn for watch before we know it."

"Thanks, Josh," Brooke says.

I tell her no problem and turn on my side facing away from her. She's beautiful and there's no way I'd get to sleep if I kept facing toward her.

I close my eyes and think about what Brooke said about being scared. It takes guts to just plain admit it and then ask for help. Brooke didn't know how I'd react when she told me. I'm glad she trusted me enough to say something. And I feel better now that I've told her that I'm scared, too. It's good for me to remember that we all must be scared out of our minds—not just me. I think about Derrick. He deals with most things by making jokes. I think about Shannon. She analyzes things. We've all got our ways of dealing with tough stuff—with fear. I hope the suggestion I gave Brooke will work for her because without everyone 100 percent on board, we could all die.

CHAPTER 77

DERRICK AND SHANNON WAKE US up, and we trade places so they can get some rest. And now Brooke and I are sitting at the edge of the forest, hidden by some brush, looking out across the meadow toward the forest that starts up on the other side.

"I changed my mantra," Brooke says softly, "to *just be here*. It's more positive, and it's more accurate. I have to put my energy into what's right in front of me and not try to escape by wishing I were somewhere else."

"That sounds good," I reply. "It makes way more sense than what I came up with earlier."

"I know it won't be easy." Brooke looks me in the eye. "I mean, just since we've traded places with Shannon and Derrick, I've already wished I were somewhere else like five times."

"But just the fact that you're aware of it," I say, "makes all the difference. We're all going to fantasize about being other places, but your mantra is what brings you back to the present moment." I pause. "At least that's how I use my mantra in cross-country races to keep my mind from straying."

"What is it?" Brooke asks.

"Step," I say.

"Step?" Brooke says. "That's it? Why?"

"Because," I say, "that's the action I have to perform over and over from the start of the race to the finish." I look at the sky. "When the sun touches those treetops"—I point—"I think we should get moving."

"Do you have a mantra now?" Brooke asks.

"Not really." I turn and face her. "My mind is filled with all the stuff we're supposed to remember. I'm pretty good at focusing on a task, so I tell myself to just focus on what I'm doing if my mind starts running. Like right now, we're talking softly, but I'm scanning the clearing with my eyes, searching for movement because we're on watch."

"I hate this," Brooke says, "but I know how important it is. I thought what happened at Simon Lake was horrendous. So horrendous that I couldn't deal with it. But this is potentially a million times worse if we fail."

"Or," I say, "we might succeed, but the mission might fail. If that happens, we're so close to Fort Greely that we'll probably be vaporized if the United States nukes it."

"That's the part of the plan I don't like," Brooke says. "I think after we set the explosives, instead of heading downriver and stopping at the spot Sam described, we should just keep on going toward Fairbanks. Maybe we'll be far enough away that if the fort gets nuked we'll survive. Why sit around and wait to see if we're going to die?"

"I think I agree with you on that one," I say. "We can see what Derrick and Shannon think and then make a decision." I take a breath. "The only reason I hesitate is because maybe Sam knows something about what's downriver that we don't. Maybe there's some Russian presence that he wants us to avoid."

"He didn't say anything like that," Brooke says.

"Maybe he knows that if the mission fails," I say, "the nukes will get launched so quickly that no matter how fast we paddle there's no way we'll get out of the death zone. Maybe there's—"

"Josh." Brooke points. "I see movement on the far side of the meadow."

I follow Brooke's finger and sure enough, I see people pouring out of the woods, coming this way.

CHAPTER 78

"WORD MUST BE GETTING AROUND that this is the route to take," I whisper to Brooke as we watch about thirty people making their way along the far edge of the meadow, traveling in the same direction as the man and his three daughters did earlier.

We sit in silence, blending in with the brush, as the refugees pass by a couple hundred feet away. People of all ages, size, and shapes. Most of them have backpacks. A few carry duffel bags slung over their shoulders, and some have rifles. I wonder if these people have come from the same area as the man and his daughters or if they've escaped from Delta Junction. Or maybe they've come from somewhere farther away. Somewhere closer to Fairbanks.

And that makes me think of my mom and dad. Are they being detained in Fairbanks, or did they slip off into the woods like these people did? I don't care if they stay married or not, I just want them to be alive.

"What makes different people do the things they do?" Brooke asks. "I mean, our case was kind of unique because we stumbled upon Sam and learned about the invasion, but other people, how did they decide what to do after the invasion?"

I think about the militia we saw, and then the refugees fleeing. "I don't know what I would've done. Part of it would depend on what was happening where I was. Sounds like some people were just plain captured and had no choice."

"I see the people leaving, and I want to go, too," Brooke says. "Maybe that's because I know I might die on this mission. Those people"—she points to the clearing where the refugees passed by—"they aren't actively putting themselves in danger like we are."

"True," I respond. "But they might if they were faced with the same situation as us; we were given a chance to make a difference."

"I felt like my life was just beginning when I went to Simon Lake." Brooke pauses. "I was finally doing something independent from my sisters. Even though this whole wilderness thing isn't *my* thing, I pushed myself to do it."

"That's impressive," I respond. "I—"

Brooke interrupts me. "It's not impressive compared to you, Josh. You push yourself with your running and other physical stuff all the time."

I shake my head. "What you're doing is harder. You're doing something new. I've been running for a long time and when I got to Simon Lake, I spent a lot of time running. If anything, I avoided doing anything new out there. You went way out of your comfort zone going to Simon Lake. I didn't. I was just doing the same thing in a different place. I didn't really realize that until now."

Brooke stretches her arms over her head and then nods. "But now we're both out of our comfort zones." She smiles, but it's not a happy smile. It's a we-share-this-intense-thing smile.

CHAPTER 79

I'VE GOT THE ROUTE FINDER in my hand, and we're all staring at it. "If we keep getting pushed off our target"—I point at the red dot—"we might need to cover some ground in broad daylight." The green dot, representing our location, has basically moved along the bottom of the screen. Instead of being closer to the red dot, it's farther away.

"I wonder if it's possible to go off the screen?" Derrick asks.

"That would be a poor design feature," Shannon responds. "Maybe it adjusts the scale to keep us onscreen."

"Orienteering for dummies." Derrick grins.

We talk a little more and decide to cut across the meadow and take the direct route. I keep the route finder in the palm of my hand as I stride through the clearing. The sun has set so it's about as dark as it's going to get—dusky.

I know once we get into the thicker forest on the other side, the going will be slower. But it'll also be safer with more places to hide.

When we hit the dense forest the mosquitoes immediately start swarming around us. Because of the special clothing and extra-strong repellent Sam gave us, they're not biting, but I'm programmed to wave them away like all Alaskans are.

I keep the arrow pointed at the red dot and take us through a thick patch of wild rose. The boots, combined with the clothing, provide a good barrier to the thousands of thorns we're brushing up against.

After a while the roses thin out, and now we're in a mixed-birch-and-aspen forest with a scattering of large spruce trees, which means there are a lot fewer places to hide.

We stop to drink some water and hear a bird trilling. Shannon tells us it's a varied thrush.

"Shouldn't it be a *constant* thrush?" Derrick asks. "The song is the same over and over and over."

"Varied refers to its plumage, not its song," Shannon explains. "They look similar to robins in size and shape, but they have more color variety. If you spot one, you'll see what I mean."

We keep walking, and the varied thrush song grows fainter and fainter until it disappears. The giant spruce trees, birches, and aspens are replaced by a forest of small, scraggly spruce trees growing out of bumpy, soggy ground, but at least our green dot has moved off the edge of the route finder and is about a quarter of the way to the red dot.

My boots sink into the swampy ground with every step. We walk and walk and walk. It seems like the route is taking us through the thickest part of the swamp. When I glance over my shoulder I see that I've pulled away from Derrick, Brooke, and Shannon, so I stop and wait. When they catch up, I pull a bag of peanuts out of my pack for all of us.

Derrick takes a handful and says, "What's with the miniature trees? The spruce back in the dry forest were huge."

"The trees in the swamp are black spruce. The trees in the dry forest were white spruce, and they're always bigger," I say.

Shannon finishes chewing some peanuts and swallows. "Generally white spruce *are* significantly bigger than black spruce. But these trees around here"—she motions with her arm—"are particularly stunted, most likely because of low nutrient content in the soil." She points to the ground. "There's probably permafrost—frozen ground—under a thin layer of nutrient-poor soil."

"Black spruce must be tough trees," Brooke says, "to survive harsh conditions."

We all nod in silence. I shove another handful of peanuts into my mouth and think about what Brooke and Shannon said. The tall white spruce appear strong, but they grow in ideal conditions and haven't been subjected to poor soil or permafrost like the black spruce. We're like the black spruce; we're scraggly compared to an army of trained fighters, but we've been tested in some harsh conditions.

But the harshest are yet to come.

We walked into the daylight hours to make up for lost time due to the detours we had to make at the beginning of the trip. Dusk came and went, and now the sun is just breaking over the ridge for the start of a new day. Through the trees I catch my first glimpse of the lake.

"We should lie low right here and wait till dusk," I say.

"That's almost twenty hours." Shannon takes off her pack. "Maybe we could inflate the boats, paddle the length of the lake to the outlet, and wait out the rest of the day there. That way, we can use the flat paddling on the lake to work out any kinks so we'll be super efficient when dusk sets in."

I nod. "I could live with that."

"We should stay here until the sun sets." Brooke takes off her pack. "We can't just keep breaking Sam's rules. He's counting on us. What if Russian soldiers on patrol see us?"

We all turn to Derrick. "Well, Frank," Shannon says, "what say you?"

Derrick yawns a big yawn. "Dudes, I like both ideas."

In the end, we compromise without having to do any random bottle-cap flipping. We agree to hike the quarter mile down to the lake and inflate the boats, but then wait until dusk to start paddling. We haven't taken two steps when movement at the lake stops us in our tracks.

CHAPTER 80

"SOMETIMES I STILL THINK, NO *way can this be real,"* I say to Shannon as I study the lake through my binoculars. We're on watch, peering down at the lake from a thick patch of spruce trees while Derrick and Brooke try to get some sleep. Mosquitoes buzz around us, but we've reapplied the insect repellent Sam gave us, so they're not biting.

"I stopped thinking that after Sam's camp was bombed." Shannon sets her binoculars down. "We may have to totally avoid the lake."

"That would slow us down more," I say. "And we're probably already taking more time than Sam thought we would because of all the people we've had to avoid."

"The other teams might be running into similar problems." Shannon waves her hand in front of her face to disperse the mosquitoes even though they aren't biting. "Maybe Sam accounted for having to avoid obstacles in his time estimate."

"It might take us from dusk to dawn to hike to the far end of the lake instead of paddling along the shore." I shift my legs because they're starting to tighten up. "I mean, who are those people going to tell if they spot us? We're in the middle of nowhere. I doubt they even know we've been invaded."

One red canoe and one green canoe. That's what we've seen so far in the partial view of the lake through the trees. Do those people live in the wilderness? Or are they on a trip? Are they going to float down the creek and then down the river like we're planning to? But if they float down the river and they don't know about the Russians, they could be surprised and gunned down. Plus, if the Russians spot them, it'll put them on alert and make it harder for us to carry out our mission, which would make it more likely that the United States will nuke Alaska.

When I share all this with Shannon, she swallows and says, "No matter what it takes, we've got to stop them from reaching the bridge."

I creep back to the tent, which is a couple hundred feet farther from the lake than our lookout spot, and tell Derrick and Brooke about our fear that the people on the lake will head down the river.

"We can't all go down there and confront them," Derrick says, "because if it doesn't work out, like if they turn out to be crazed murderers, or if they're Russian soldiers undercover, then we'll all be captured or killed, and we'll have no chance of pulling off this mission."

Brooke sticks her head out of the tent. "If *anyone* goes to talk to them, we should all go. The more of us there are, the less chance we have of being overpowered."

Derrick turns to Brooke. "That's a smart move if it works, but a dumb one if it doesn't." Then he shrugs. "I guess you could make the same argument for my idea."

"Sounds like we all agree that we need to do something," I say. "We—"

Brooke cuts in. "We need to beat them to the bridge."

Derrick and Brooke put their shoes on, and we all go sit with Shannon at the watch point.

"I think it's more a question of *when* they leave, not *if*." Shannon motions toward the lake. "As far as I can tell, there's two of them and they're camping. Even if someone was supposed to fly into the lake and pick them up, we know that's not happening now, so they'll have to paddle out."

"We should leave," Brooke says. Then she repeats her argument about how beating them to the bridge will solve our problem.

But then I come up with a different plan, which basically puts us all at more risk than the ideas offered up so far. But sometimes you have to risk big in order to have any chance of succeeding. And in our case, succeeding could mean the difference between saving Alaska and having it nuked by the United States.

CHAPTER 81

STAY HERE UNTIL HELP ARRIVES, *or you will die. United States Government.*

I've written this in big blocky print on a page that I've torn out of my journal. I've put the note into a ziplock bag that used to have peanuts in it, and I've stuck it inside one of my neoprene booties so the edge of the bag is sticking out just enough that I'll be able to grab it easily. The last part—*United States Government*—was Derrick's idea to make it seem official.

"You ready, Frogman?" Derrick grins and holds up a flipper, but I can tell he's nervous. Even though he's a stronger swimmer than I am, I can see his body quivering a little bit. We've got our dry suits on. At this point, there's nothing stopping us but ourselves.

I pick up my flippers. A half mile swim across—that's Derrick's best guess. For a long-distance runner, a half mile doesn't sound like much, but when I stare out across the water little shivers run up my spine. When you run, you can stop anywhere you want, and your feet are on the ground, but that's obviously not the case when you're swimming across a frigid lake. We don't have life vests, but, according to Sam, our dry suits have enough built-in flotation to keep us at the surface.

Brooke and Shannon took off an hour ago, making their way as silently as possible around the lakeshore to the left with the goal of positioning themselves in the woods behind the people's camp. Derrick and I have all four kayaks assembled and all our gear stowed in them. The kayaks are hidden in the brush close to the water, across the lake from the camp we're about to invade. Not only will Derrick and I have to swim to their camp and then do our part of the plan, we'll have to swim back, retrieve the kayaks and gear, and then each paddle one while towing another until we meet up with Shannon and Brooke, who hopefully won't have gotten caught, even though their part of the plan is to draw attention to themselves to the point that the people in camp pursue them through the woods for a while.

Derrick and I walk into the lake and sit down in the water like Sam told us to do. I fit one flipper over my neoprene bootie and pull until it's halfway on. Then I grip its heel and yank it with both hands, and it stretches around my heel in a tight fit, like a snake constricting a small animal.

By the time I'm done getting both flippers on, I notice my dry suit is filled with air and it's like I'm in a giant balloon with my head sticking out of it.

I turn and look at Derrick, and he's in the same predicament.

"Use your hand," Derrick says as he sticks his hand down his tight-fitting neck cuff.

Then I remember Sam telling us that we'd need to pull the neck cuff away from our skin to let the pressure equalize; otherwise, we'd be floating, helpless, like rubber duckies. I work my fingers under the neck cuff and create some space, and the ballooned-up air escapes. I keep the space open until I feel the suit pressing against me.

Now there's really nothing stopping us from swimming across, and I follow Derrick as he silently strokes away from the shallows. He's taller than me and a better swimmer, so I work hard to keep up with him. We're swimming breaststroke with our arms to keep our profile as low in the water as possible, but kicking like we're doing the crawl stroke to take advantage of having flippers.

We're aiming for the two canoes tied off on trees and floating in the shallows in front of their camp. Besides leaving them a note telling them to stay, we need to destroy their method of transportation in case they decide to ignore our warning.

CHAPTER 82

"TWO MORE MINUTES," DERRICK WHISPERS.

I nod. My arms are mush, but I just keep stroking forward. The red and green of the canoes are a blur in front of me. I hope Shannon and Brooke can see us so they'll know when to start their distraction.

My legs are tight, like I've just completed a hard run, except I'm not even halfway done with this job. Even though I'm wearing the dry suit, I'm starting to cool down. There isn't any ice in the water, but it sure feels like there is. If I had worn more clothing under the dry suit, I wouldn't be as cold, but Derrick thought we'd be too hot with all the swimming we'd be doing.

My feet hit the bottom and I want to stand up, but we need to stay as low as possible so I keep kicking. I see Derrick bump up against one of the canoes, and a minute later I'm next to him, breathing hard.

"Listen," Derrick whispers.

I take a couple of controlled breaths and focus on hearing whatever there is to hear. Voices. Too faint to make out words. I reach down and pull the ziplock bag with the note in it out of my neoprene bootie and hold it in my hand.

"I'm going to peek over the canoe," Derrick whispers.

"Okay." I scrunch my toes up and down because they're starting to go numb. I hope we don't have to wait too long.

"I see two people," Derrick whispers. "They're staring into the forest." Derrick holds up his hand. "They're walking away from camp into the forest. Go."

I creep around the green canoe, which is in knee-deep water, and extend my arm toward the shore and place the note on the shoreline. Then I crawl on my belly, pulling myself with my forearms. I catch a glimpse of Derrick doing the same thing, working his way toward the rope tying off the red canoe.

If only we'd thought to bring a knife, we could've cut the ropes and been on our way. At the tree anchoring the green canoe, I untie the rope and crawl back to the water. I wish I could stay on shore and just run the perimeter of the lake back to the kayaks, but we've got a job to do. Derrick's got the rope for the red canoe freed up, and he's crawling back to the shore when I hear shouts.

"Hey! What are you doing?" one voice yells.

"Stop right there!" a second voice shouts.

I shove the green canoe into deeper water and start kicking. I know Derrick is scrambling toward the shore.

"Son of a bitch," the first voice yells. "Are you crazy?"

"Don't let them take the red boat!" the second voice yells. "We'll be stranded."

"Crazy bastards!" the first voice yells.

I hear splashing noises.

Derrick yells, "Josh."

I turn and see Derrick struggling in waist-deep water with a man about as big as he is. I shove the green canoe away from shore and kick toward Derrick and the man, who are locked in a wrestling match for control of the red canoe.

The man is trying to hold on to the canoe and Derrick at the same time, and Derrick is trying to shove the canoe out into deeper water, and he's saying, "You don't understand. We're trying to help you. We—"

And that's when I barrel into the man at chest height and bring my fist down hard on the arm that's holding Derrick hostage. The other man is ten feet away and closing fast.

Derrick wrestles the canoe free and starts kicking away from shore, pushing the canoe in front of him.

I jump backward and start kicking my way toward the green canoe I've abandoned.

Now I can hear splashes behind me.

"We can't let them get away," the second voice shouts.

I keep kicking, then I feel a tug on one of my flippers, and I'm jerked backward. A sharp pain travels up my shin as I twist my body toward the tug.

Water streams off the man's head as he surfaces. With both hands, I shove his head down and hold it. He lets go of my flipper, and I kick away from him. I have the advantage with the dry suit and the flippers, but the man comes at me again and this time grabs my lower leg and pulls. My fingertips find the green canoe, and I use it as leverage and kick backward with my free foot.

"We're all going to die if you don't let go," I shout. I kick again with my free foot and catch his jaw. He lets go of my leg and goes under.

All I want to do is kick away from him and take his canoe with me, but I can't let him drown. I dive down, throw my arms around him, and lift.

Dead weight, I think. *I must've knocked him out.* I kick toward shore until my feet touch bottom. I keep kicking, and now I'm dragging him through the shallows. *Get him to shore*, I think. *Then leave him.*

I've got his whole body above the shoreline, and I lay him down. I can't stay with him, so I turn toward the water, and that's when I'm grabbed around the neck and dragged farther from shore. My legs with the flippers on my feet are useless. I'm flailing, my hands gripping the forearm that's choking me.

Then I hear a loud whack, and suddenly I'm free. I turn and see Brooke standing there with a large stick in her hand. Next to her the man is hunched over, his hands covering the side of his head.

"Just stay here," Brooke says to the man. Then she takes off into the woods.

I scramble back to the shore and swim out to the green canoe. I see the red canoe in the distance and kick toward it, pushing the green canoe in front of me.

When I catch up to Derrick, I say, "That was crazy, but we made it."

"We're not in the clear yet," Derrick says. "I saw movement on the shore where we left the kayaks."

CHAPTER 83

"WE NEED TO SINK THE canoes," Derrick says as he and I swim side by side, pushing the canoes along.

"Let's wait," I respond, "until we see if the kayaks are okay."

Derrick isn't sure what he saw prowling around the area where we hid the kayaks, but he's sure he saw something. Holding on to the canoe and kicking is easier than swimming, but it's still a long haul to get across the lake.

I wonder what the two guys we took the canoes from are doing. I hope they're okay, but I also hope they stay put. I wish I could've tried to explain why they needed to stay, and trusted them to keep their canoes, but the stakes are just too high.

My feet brush the lake bottom, and I keep kicking until I'm standing in waist-deep water.

"Whoever I saw must know we're here." Derrick points to the canoe in front of him. "This thing isn't exactly invisible."

We quietly guide the canoes until they're snug against the shore and tie them off on a couple of spindly spruce trees. I sit in the ankle-deep water and work the flippers off my neoprene booties, and Derrick is next to me doing the same.

The kayaks should be set back about fifty feet from the shore, but where exactly they are in relation to where we are, I'm not so sure. Did we cross the lake to the same spot we started from? When things got crazy on shore with the two guys, we could've gotten turned around. I was so focused on getting the kayaks hidden, and then swimming across the lake, that I didn't stop to consider having a point of reference.

"Do you recognize anything?" I ask Derrick. "I mean, do you think we're in the right place?"

"We're close," Derrick responds. "Right after we entered the water, I looked for a landmark. There's a big birch tree"—Derrick points to the left—"that's leaning into the lake close to where we stashed the kayaks. Once we were free of those guys, I searched for the tree and headed toward it. I didn't want to go right to it because I saw movement around it."

"You were always out in front, so I guess I just followed you." I think about not having my own landmark. How would I have ever found the kayaks without extensive searching if something had happened to Derrick? Even though my mistake is costing us nothing, I can't make any more like that.

I set my flippers down by the canoes and follow Derrick as we creep along the shore toward the big birch tree hanging over the water. I just want to get the kayaks and go, but even if we find them, we need to sink the canoes before we take off. I thought about just leaving the canoes tied off on this side of the lake, but if I were one of those guys, I'd hike around the lake to get my canoe back. We need to sink them.

Derrick puts his hand up, so I stop. He motions me forward, and I cover the few yards separating us, and now we're standing side by side. I follow Derrick's arm as he points toward the birch tree, which is about thirty yards away. Under the tree, I can just make out the light brown fur of a grizzly bear. How are we going to get the kayaks now? Derrick and I talk softly for a minute or so, and then we turn back toward the canoes—because we need them for the plan we just came up with.

CHAPTER 84

"I WISH THERE WERE PADDLES with the canoes," Derrick says.

I nod. "If the bear comes toward us, we'll just have to hang on to the canoe and kick like hell to get away from it."

We've got both canoes untied, and we've put our flippers back on. Derrick has the green canoe—our getaway canoe if need be—and I've got the red one.

I push off from the lake bottom with my flippers and kick. I keep the red canoe in front of me. Derrick is next to me but in deeper water a little farther away from shore, guiding the green canoe. We don't talk because we both know the plan. Under normal circumstances, like if we weren't trying to get our nuclear missiles back from the Russians before they decided to use them on us, this would be the absolute craziest, dumbest plan ever.

The canoe is about fifteen feet long, so I figure I'll have that distance for protection, that much of a head start to get to Derrick and the green canoe.

We pass the spot where we first spotted the bear, and a shiver runs up my spine as I see its brown fur under the birch tree. Is it sleeping? Whatever happened to the idea, *let a sleeping bear lie*? If we let this one lie and it woke up when we were getting the kayaks, then it'd be between us and the water.

Wake the bear up first. Try to scare it off before going for the kayaks, which are somewhere behind it. That's our goal.

I'm kicking as quietly as I can with my flippers. *Is there a better way?* I think. And then I take a breath and try to erase that thought from my mind. *Focus on the plan. Focus on the goal,* I tell myself. *You have to go all in,* I remember Theo saying, when we talked about doing new things and taking risks. We'd been talking about bold running strategies, like sprinting uphill in a race to open up a lead, something we'd both done with success.

But this plan with the canoe and the bear, it's different, because if it fails I could die, Derrick could die, Alaska could get nuked. The stakes are high for every decision we make.

Now I'm even with the grizzly. It's lying down right on the shoreline beneath the tree, and it still hasn't moved. I glance toward Derrick. He's got both hands on the stern of the green canoe and is treading water. He raises his eyebrows in a *what are you waiting for* gesture.

I nod and take a breath. Then I slowly turn the canoe so the bow is pointing toward the shore—toward the grizzly bear. I start kicking with my flippers, driving the red canoe straight toward the bear, aiming for its nose.

CHAPTER 85

THE FRONT OF THE CANOE scrapes against the bottom of the lake, but I just keep muscling it forward. The more momentum I have when I ram the bear, the more chance the bear will be persuaded to run.

I keep my legs straight back and just keep kicking.

Can a canoe scare a bear? I hope so.

I see the wall of fur begin to move as I close the final distance. I hear a snort and then a splash. I feel resistance as the bow of the canoe slams into the bear.

Run bear run, my mind screams.

I hear more splashes, and all of a sudden the canoe moves sideways, like it's been shoved by a giant. I leap backward, as if I'm doing a back-flip, and twist my body so I land on my belly, and then I'm swimming for my life, kicking with my flippers and pulling with my arms.

Then I feel pressure on my left foot, like something has clamped on to it, so I twist and pull. Something gives, my knee snaps toward my chest, and I keep swimming and reach for the green of Derrick's canoe. Now we're both kicking while we hold on to the stern of the canoe, moving farther away from shore. I don't know if the bear is still behind us and don't want to stop to find out.

My left foot feels funny, like it takes more kicks than my right foot to keep my pace steady.

"I think we're in the clear," Derrick shouts.

I stop kicking and twist around so I can see the shore. The red canoe sits on its side in the shallows. I scan the water between us and the canoe and then along the shore and don't see the bear. I know it could still be close by, but maybe we'll be able to get to our kayaks and get out of here and meet up with Brooke and Shannon down where the creek flows out of the lake.

We point the green canoe toward the red one and kick our way toward it. My left foot feels cooler than my right foot, and I'm still not getting as much kick from it either. The canoe starts to ground out, and Derrick and I stand up and scan the shore. We look at each other.

Derrick shrugs. "Seems like it's gone."

I nod. "Let's get the kayaks, sink the canoes, and get out of here so we can meet up with Brooke and Shannon."

"Sounds good." Derrick walks backward a couple of steps and sits down in the shallows to pull his flippers off.

I follow his lead and do the same, but when I bend my knee and reach for my left flipper I discover why I wasn't getting much kick from it. I remember feeling a tug and having to kick extra hard.

I take the flipper off, swallow the lump in my throat, and hold it up so Derrick can see.

"That bear took a huge bite out of it," he says. "One more inch, and it would've severed your toes."

I nod. Then I think about the blood and flesh the bear would've tasted instead of just yucky plastic and rubber. If it had tasted blood, it probably would've kept coming after me.

CHAPTER 86

I DIP MY KAYAK PADDLE into the lake and pull. Derrick and I are hugging the shore, so if we need to take cover we'll be able to quickly. The kayak feels sluggish, but the water is flat—without a current—and I'm towing Brooke's kayak, which has her pack in it. We sank the canoes as best we could, tipped them sideways and filled them with water. But they must have some built-in flotation because they didn't sink to the bottom, so we dragged them offshore a couple hundred feet and left them partially submerged. It'd be tough to get them without dry suits. You'd have to be in the water a long time, and it's cold.

Between fighting off the campers we stole the canoes from and almost getting my foot munched by a bear, for a little while I forgot that the Russians invaded Alaska and that our real challenge is to blow the bridge so Sam will have a better chance of taking back the missiles at Fort Greely.

Derrick's words cut into my thoughts. "I think I see the bear." He points with his paddle.

Down the shore a hundred yards, a brown clump of fur walks on all four legs. Is it the same bear? Maybe. Probably.

I remember the mess its mouth made of my flipper. "We should move away from the shoreline." I dig my right paddle into the water, and my kayak moves to the left, away from shore, and Derrick does the same.

We put about a hundred feet between us and the shore and then keep going. The bear keeps moving in the same direction we're paddling but doesn't show much interest in us. I feel exposed being this far from shore. Too visible from the air. But we don't have much of a choice.

The lakeshore is curving, and up ahead I think I see where the creek flows out. "Derrick," I say, "do you think that's the creek?" I point with my paddle toward a break in the shoreline.

Derrick nods. "I hope so."

"Should we head straight for the break?" I ask. "I mean, we're already exposed because of the bear. If we cut this corner off the lake, we'd save time."

"Let's do it." Derrick takes a couple of paddle strokes on the right side of his kayak so it points at the break.

We're paddling side by side, and we've picked up the pace, wanting to be exposed for as little time as possible. It's hard to tell distances on the water, but my guess is that we're about a half mile from where the creek pours out of the lake.

"Birds," Derrick says. "Straight ahead."

A sprinkling of white lifts off the water, and I hear the distant caws of gulls. "Something must've disturbed them. And they were sitting right where we're going."

"Could be the girls?" Derrick offers.

He keeps paddling, and I match his pace. The kayak I'm towing creates a little bit of drag, but it's tracking well, staying in line behind my boat.

The gulls resettle farther away from the start of the creek.

"I think I see them," I say. "Right where we're heading." On the shore next to what I think is the start of the creek are two gray bumps. "That has to be them."

Derrick lifts his paddle and waves in their direction, and we see the gray bumps move. I lift my paddle and wave, too.

The shore they've traveled has several small points jutting out into the lake, creating some bays. They probably didn't follow the shore the whole time because staying inland would save the time it would've taken to round all those points. As long as you could keep the water in sight, you'd be fine.

I dip my paddle into the water and dig. We're still exposed, and just because we've seen the girls doesn't mean that a Russian helicopter or jet won't suddenly appear over the horizon and attack us.

"Movement," Derrick says. "Off to the left on the shore."

I stop paddling and study the shoreline, and sure enough I can see two people working their way along the shore. "The canoe people," I say. "We've got to get to the girls before they do."

CHAPTER 87

I PICK UP THE PACE and pull ahead of Derrick, but having to tow a kayak is a literal drag and turns my attempted sprint to Shannon and Brooke into more of a controlled slog. At the same time, the guys on shore are running, making way better time than Derrick and me. I keep my eye on them for a few paddle strokes and know there's no way we'll beat them to the girls. We may tie them if we're lucky, but no way will we get there first.

Just focus on the girls, I think as I turn my head back toward the creek opening. But now I don't see Shannon or Brooke on shore. They must've seen the canoe people coming and realized, like I did, that we wouldn't make it in time. I must've slowed a little or else Derrick has sped up because now he's even with me and says, "Keep it in high gear, Josh."

When I refocus on the creek opening, I see Shannon and Brooke standing on the opposite side of the creek. They must've swum across, and Derrick must've seen them do it while I was focused on the canoe people. They don't have dry suits on, so they have to be soaked, but now there's a barrier between them and the canoe people.

I alter my course slightly, aiming for the side of the creek that Shannon and Brooke are on, and that's when I notice the bear still making its way down the shoreline toward the creek opening— toward Shannon and Brooke. And it's even closer to them than the canoe people.

CHAPTER 88

I'M PADDLING LIKE A WINDMILL in a tornado and Derrick is right next to me doing the same. My forearms are burning, and my neck is tight from leaning forward. Do they see the bear? And what will they do if the bear gets to them before we do?

The canoe people have rounded the final point, and now they're running a straight stretch of coastline toward the creek. If I knew they were going to pursue us, I'd have injured them more. Bear spray. That's what I would've used. And that makes me think about what we have for using on the bear, too. Derrick and Brooke still have full canisters while mine and Shannon's are mostly empty.

But the bear spray is probably inside their packs. I mean, I didn't see Derrick take his out. We were so focused on sinking the canoes and then paddling the kayaks that I didn't even think about protection.

We're about a hundred yards offshore, and the bear is bounding forward, covering ground twice as fast as it was a minute ago.

"Swim," I yell. "Swim to us. Now!"

I keep paddling.

Shannon and Brooke wade into the water and then dive and start crawl stroking toward us. At the same time the bear splashes into the water and starts swimming toward them.

Derrick is pulling a little ahead of me on my right, and I double down on my effort to keep even with him.

Fifty yards separates us from the girls, but the bear is still chasing them. *Come on*, I think. *Swim faster*. Then I remember that both of them said that swimming isn't one of their strengths, so I just keep paddling.

Derrick pulls ahead of me. Then he stops paddling and reaches toward his pack. I don't know what he's doing, but I blow by him, knowing that the main thing that will keep Shannon and Brooke from getting munched is getting to them before the bear does. Maybe we can scare it away if all of us are together.

Derrick pulls up next to me again, and I just keep paddling and we stay even. We've got fifteen yards to go to get to them, but so does the bear, which is coming at an angle from the right, closer to Derrick than to me.

"I'm going for the bear," Derrick shouts. "You get the girls."

He must've gotten his bear spray out of his pack, I think.

Left. Right. Left. Right. I keep digging my paddle into the water. We're going to need both of us to get Shannon and Brooke safely out of the water since our kayaks are tiny and made for one person each. But if the bear gets to them first, it won't matter. And if the bear injures Derrick and destroys his kayak and the one he's towing, we're all screwed.

The canoe people have almost reached the creek, but I don't care about them right now.

Derrick has turned slightly, but we're basically heading in the same direction because the bear has almost caught up to the girls and I'm heading straight for them.

Two gunshots slice through the air, and I jerk my head toward the canoe people as I continue to paddle. Are they shooting at us? Another shot rings in my ears, and I know it's not the canoe people because they're standing with their arms to their sides. Who's shooting?

"Yes," Derrick yells. "Yes!"

I turn to my right and see Derrick holding the pistol up. He's smiling as the bear splashes its way toward shore. I feel a bump on my kayak, and then Shannon's arms are draped over the side.

"Don't pull too hard, or you'll flip the boat." I lean in the opposite direction to counter the pressure she's applying. "Grab on to the back of the boat I'm towing, and see if you can crawl over the top."

Shannon's breathing hard, but she works her way to the back of the kayak behind me and crawls in.

"Are you okay?" I ask.

Shannon nods. "Just cold." She pulls one of her rubber boots off and pours out the water. "I couldn't have swum much farther with these dragging me down."

"We'll get you to shore, so you can get out of your soaked clothes and into your dry suit," I respond. I turn toward Derrick and see that Brooke is now lying in the kayak he's towing. "Let's get to shore so these two can change before they freeze."

I hear a snapping sound behind me and twist around. Shannon is holding up her paddle. She must've just snapped the two halves together.

"I'll stay warmer if I paddle," she explains.

I nod, wondering if I should untie her kayak now that she's got her paddle. "Shannon, I think—"

Derrick cuts me off. "Where are we supposed to go ashore?"

I turn toward the entrance to the creek. The bear has crawled out of the water on one side, and the canoe people are on the other.

Derrick waves the gun. "I scared the bear once, but I don't know if it'll scare again. And I don't want to shoot those guys."

"We'll be okay," Brooke shouts. "Just paddle down the creek between the two of them."

But the entrance to the creek is narrow enough that it wouldn't take much for a charging bear or an angry human to splash into the water and try to grab us—especially if they know we're coming, which they do.

CHAPTER 89

WE'VE UNTIED BROOKE'S AND SHANNON'S kayaks, and they both have their paddles assembled because there's no way we can go down a windy creek towing them. We're about forty feet from the canoe people—close enough for a shouting conversation—and set back from the creek so we won't get sucked into the current. The bear, which is on the far side of the creek and standing on its hind legs, is more of a threat to the canoe people than to us at the moment.

"We don't want to hurt you," I yell. "We're trying to save you. Just go back to your camp and wait, and we'll send a plane to pick you up."

"You sunk our boats," the bigger of the two of them yells. "Why should we trust you?"

"Think about it," Shannon responds. "We could've shot you." She points to Derrick, who holds up his gun. "We tried to take your canoes quietly. You saw the note."

"The four of you are nuts," the smaller man yells. "You won't get away with this. Send a plane or don't. I'll hike out of here and hunt you all down."

"What are you doing out here anyway?" I ask. "How long have you been here?" I glance toward the bear, which is back on all four legs but hasn't moved, like it's listening to the conversation. "And watch out for that bear. It's charged us twice now."

They back away a few steps from the outlet of the lake to put a little more distance between them and the bear. They tell us they're brothers from Woonsocket, Rhode Island, who inherited a remote piece of land from their grandfather years ago and are finally getting a chance to see it. They made the trip to Fairbanks, and then a bush pilot flew them into the lake about three weeks ago. They're camped on the land and were planning to make a trip of it, to float the creek and the river to the bridge, where they arranged to be picked up.

"Are you patriotic?" Derrick asks.

"As much as the next guy," the larger man yells.

"Stay here," Derrick says, "for the good of your country."

"We have to go," I yell. "I wish we could say more. If anyone approaches you, don't tell them you've seen us."

"What the hell is going on?" the smaller man asks.

"I'm going to tell them," I say softly, so only Brooke, Derrick, and Shannon can hear me. "Okay?"

Everyone nods, and I yell, "The Russians invaded Alaska, and we're part of a team trying to take it back from them. You get in our way, and you're a national security risk."

"Bullshit," the larger man yells. "Deranged losers. All of you!"

"Great," Derrick says softly. "Let's just paddle by these guys." We all nod, and he waves the gun. "We'll be leaving now," he shouts.

I paddle on the left side of my kayak, which causes me to turn to the right. I don't know if these men will try to stop us, but the farther away we can be from them when we enter the creek the better.

"You got a phone?" Brooke yells as we paddle. "That red screen is because of the Russians."

The two men look at each other and then back at us but say nothing. At the same time, they've stopped screaming at us and saying we're crazy. Maybe Brooke has gotten through to them. But we still can't trust them not to try something if we get too close to them. The risk is too great.

As we approach the creek, the bear stands up on its hind legs. Will it race into the water again, or is Derrick's gunfire embedded in its memory?

The big grizzly lets out a growl, drops back down on four legs, and then parallels us along the shore as we enter the current. The canoe people haven't moved from their position, so I paddle on the right side, which moves me toward the left bank—away from the bear. I glance over my shoulder. I see Brooke and hope the others are behind her.

We round a bend, and the creek widens. I stop paddling, and Brooke pulls up next to me. Then Derrick is next to her, and Shannon noses her boat between mine and Brooke's.

"If getting to this point was supposed to be the easy part," Derrick says, "I don't even want to think about what's coming."

"Let's paddle for a half hour or so," Shannon says. "We'll put some distance between us, the bear, and those guys, then wait for sunset. According to what Sam said about river distances, we should be at the bridge by the morning after next."

CHAPTER 90

"NO TENT," SHANNON SAYS. "LET'S just stay in our dry suits."

Derrick grins. "If the world ever gets back to normal again, this is how I'll camp. Pull up to a campground. Park it next to a monster RV, get into my dry suit, and just lie down in the parking spot."

We're in a clump of spruce forest on the right side of the creek, figuring the canoe people, in the unlikely event that they're tracking us down the creek on foot, would need to ford the creek to get to us. I doubt they're doing that—Brooke's talk about the phone seemed to really hit home—but the less risk we take the better. Now that we're almost at the bridge, the stakes for failing seem higher. We've put in all this time and effort to get this far.

I'm lying down next to Brooke with all these thoughts racing through my mind about trying and failing, or trying and succeeding, while Derrick and Shannon are on watch. I just want the time to pass and the sun to set so we can get on with this.

Brooke rolls over onto her side so she's facing me. Her gray dry suit makes it look like she's getting ready to board a spaceship or clean up a toxic waste site, but really it'll only protect her from the cold water. We've got all the right equipment to get where we need to go, but one soldier with a machine gun pointed at us could cut us to pieces. Do they make bulletproof dry suits?

I'm looking right into her eyes as I'm thinking all this. I reach out and touch her cheek. "I hope you survive. I hope we all do."

Brooke puts her hand on top of my hand and squeezes. "I keep picturing my family—my mom, my dad, my sisters—behind a big fence in some detention camp in Fairbanks."

A tear escapes Brooke's eye, and I scoot closer to her. "We're all we've got right now. And your family, and my family—we're all they've got right now, too. What we're doing, we're doing for them."

"Josh," Brooke says, "I'm ready to do what we need to do, but we're just one piece of a plan. And even if we succeed, there's no guarantee that the soldiers holding people captive in Fairbanks will just let them go. They may be ordered to gun them down."

"We can only control our part and our actions," I respond. I think about my parents, about not wanting them to get a divorce, about wanting to control what they do, but knowing I can't. "By doing our part, we're at least potentially giving everyone else a chance even if we die in the process. Like today, when you clocked that guy with a big stick. That allowed me to escape so I could keep going with the mission. If you hadn't done that, there might only be the three of you heading downriver. You did that."

The *whop whop* of a helicopter invades my ears, and I scoot closer to Brooke. I know we're invisible under the thick spruce, but then I think of Sam's hideout and how it was probably discovered by some kind of heat sensor, and I hope that we're not being targeted in the same way. Two people under a tree couldn't be much different from a moose, heatwise. Could they?

I just hope they aren't patrolling when we're paddling toward the bridge tonight.

CHAPTER 91

BY THE TIME THE SUN sinks behind the trees, we're finished packing our kayaks. My backpack is snugly strapped in the bow with my rubber boots and flippers strapped to the outside for easy access. I'm wearing my dry suit and my neoprene booties, just like everyone else.

We haven't heard any helicopters since the ones that flew over while Brooke and I were resting.

"The gun"—Derrick pats the top pocket of his pack—"is right here, along with my bear spray. I wish I could carry it on me while we paddle, but these dry suits don't have pockets. At least I can reach it in a hurry. And if something happens to me, you all know where to find it."

We all decide to put our bear spray, and the knives Sam gave us, in the top pockets of our packs. A shot of spray on an unsuspecting Russian soldier would be effective. I know from first-hand experience.

The sky is gray, and the air is heavy and still. Mosquitoes swarm around us, but we've reapplied the insect repellent on our faces and hands, the only exposed parts of our bodies. We've got these gray neoprene bathing caps on—all part of the attempt to make us the same color as the Tanana River, which is why we have to be extra careful paddling the creek to the river, because the creek is clear water—not glacier-silt gray—so we look like gray blobs resting on top of a sheet of glass.

"Let's try to stay together," Shannon says. "If last night's paddle is any indication, the creek will twist and turn, and we'll probably need to go single file a lot of the time. But let's not get too spread out."

"Do we need to settle on an order?" I ask.

"If it's okay with the rest of you," Shannon says, "I'd like to lead. I've got the most paddling experience."

"Genius out front," Derrick says. "Sounds good to me."

"The main thing to avoid," Shannon explains, "are sweepers. They're trees still rooted to the bank but hanging over the water, usually with their trunks bouncing on the surface and branches extending above and below the water." Shannon uses her hands to demonstrate. "If this is a sweeper"—she sticks out one finger—"and your kayak gets pinned on the upstream side of it"—she presses a finger from her other hand into the finger already sticking out—"the pressure from the current could flip your boat."

"Anything else?" I ask. I'm bouncing on my toes, ready to go.

Shannon tilts her head sideways and exhales. "The other main thing is that if you need to slow down, like if the current is taking you somewhere you don't want to go, or if you're unsure of where to go, just back-paddle and it'll slow you down and maybe even keep you in place, depending on how strong the current is."

"Coming down the creek last night wasn't so tough," Brooke says. "It was easier than I thought it'd be. Of course, we'd been chased into the water by a bear, so almost anything would seem easy after that."

We enter the creek and I follow Shannon as she paddles along, with Brooke behind me and Derrick behind her. A family of ducks scoots across the water in front of Shannon and disappears in some shallows on the opposite side of the creek.

We round a bend, and the first sweeper comes into view. I follow Shannon's lead and back paddle on the left side of my kayak, which turns my boat to the left. I paddle forward a few strokes, and now I'm in the center of the creek, easily avoiding the sweeper.

Shannon disappears for an instant but comes back into view as I round the main part of the bend, but now she's back-paddling furiously. Just beyond her I see why, and it makes my heart leap into my throat.

There's a moose standing in the creek, and it's not moving out of the way.

CHAPTER 92

"MOOSE!" I YELL, HOPING TO alert Brooke and Derrick, who are somewhere behind me, as I start back paddling. I keep windmilling my arms in reverse, but instead of going straight back my kayak is drifting to the left and not staying in the center of the creek. I haven't seen or heard Derrick or Brooke. Shannon has somehow worked her way upstream on the right side of the creek and has grounded out in some shallow water.

The water is deep where I am, so I keep back-paddling, but the current is relentless. Then I feel the back of my boat bump into something. *One of the sweepers we avoided when we rounded the bend a couple of minutes ago*, I think. At least I'm on the downstream side of it, but I can't go any farther back, and now my paddle is pummeling branches on the sweeper and I'm losing control and drifting toward the moose again.

I catch a glimpse of Brooke and Derrick across the creek with Shannon. No way can I paddle over there. The current would run me into the moose before I made it halfway across. As it is, I'm not sure how much longer I can keep this position. I'm basically back-paddling until I hit the sweeper, then the current takes me, then I back-paddle again when I have room to paddle. But my kayak keeps getting pushed sideways, and I don't know how to make it stay straight with the way the river is bending and the current is flowing. I'm a runner, not a kayaker.

I don't know what the other three are doing, like if they're making a plan about how to deal with the moose, but I need to deal with it now.

Theo's words pop into my head. *Sometimes the only way out of something is through it.* We were talking about choosing to run harder even when we felt more tired. I'm sure he wasn't talking about paddling full speed into a moose, but that's what I decide to do, because right now the choices are to slowly drift into it as I lose control of my kayak while back paddling or to charge it, and I'm going all in. I don't want to give the moose too much time to react. If I'm going to have contact with a moose, I want it to see me as a threat, as dominant, as not scared out of my mind and quivering with fear.

Don't get me wrong. I'm definitely scared.

I paddle forward and let out a loud scream. The moose is standing broadside to me. I keep screaming as I paddle toward the brown wall of fur.

The tip of my kayak bumps the moose's front leg, and it leaps sideways. I shoot by it and keep paddling, not giving it time to rear up and kick me unless it wants to chase me downstream. The creek is bending to the right again. I round the bend, glance over my shoulder, and see no trace of the moose. I take a breath and back paddle, waiting for everyone else to catch up.

I can feel the sweat underneath my dry suit. *Sometimes the only way out of something is through it.* Going through worked this time, but I could've just as easily died if the moose had chosen to stand its ground.

Surprise, I think. Sometimes surprise is the best strategy. I had to think fast and move fast. To have done nothing and drift into the moose would have given it all the power.

To be successful at the bridge, we might need to use an element of surprise, except there we could be met with machine guns instead of moose hooves.

Shannon, Derrick, and Brooke round the bend. I paddle forward so they won't have to slow down.

"Moose Man," I hear Derrick say from behind me.

"More like Moose Whisperer," Shannon says before I can respond.

I glance over my shoulder and catch a glimpse of Derrick grinning.

"I just did what I thought I had to do, and it worked out," I say. "It easily could've gone the other way."

Brooke's voice cuts in. "That was crazy, Josh." She pauses. "Cool, but crazy."

"I couldn't control my kayak the way Shannon did," I respond. "The way all of you did."

"Yeah," Brooke says, "but you had the guts to try something instead of just freezing up."

I back paddle and say, "I guess I did, but now I think Shannon should be back out in front. She's the best at avoiding obstacles in the current."

We could all learn from her. If only we had more time.

CHAPTER 93

A FEW HOURS LATER WE hit the broad, gray-brown waters of the Tanana River, dwarfing the small clear-water creek we've been paddling down. The overcast sky adds to the grayness, which is fine by me—the more we can blend in the better.

Shannon stops paddling, and I drift next to her and lay my paddle across my kayak. After another minute Brooke and Derrick are beside us, coasting in the current.

"We should press on," I say. "I mean, I know the sun is coming up behind those clouds, but it seems like good conditions for making some progress."

"I can keep going," Brooke responds.

Shannon adds, "Regardless, we should be at the bridge by tomorrow morning. Barring any obstacles."

"I don't know what we'd do without your memory." Derrick points at his head. "You know *what* to remember. For me, it's more of a lottery." He smiles.

"We won't have to paddle single file on every stretch of the Tanana," Shannon says, "but we'll have to watch for the same hazards—sweepers, moose, gravel bars, people. The river is wide, so we'll be able to see obstacles farther in advance, but since the current is faster, we'll have to make the right moves sooner to avoid them."

Shannon dips her paddle into the slurry of silt-laden water, and we all do the same, advancing downriver side by side.

Everything looks so peaceful. We're tiny blips, floating in the wilderness. Right now, it doesn't feel like we're on the edge of nuclear war.

My time at Simon Lake—running with Theo—seems like years ago, even though it's been less than a month since the earthquake and the Russian invasion.

The tiny particles of silt make a hissing sound as they collide with our kayaks. We're on top of a highway of swift-moving sediment, paddling boats and wearing clothes designed to look just like it. I doubt someone on the far side of the river could distinguish us from the water, especially in the dim light.

The river is making a broad turn to the right, and up ahead a series of small islands stretch across the water.

"We'll have to pick a channel," Shannon says.

"If we pick one of the middle ones," I explain, "we'll be less likely to see people."

"Why's that, Moose Man?" Derrick asks.

"People are more likely to be on the true shore than on an island in the middle of the river." I give everyone a glance. "Right?"

"That makes sense," Brooke responds.

"Stay with me." Shannon digs her paddle into the river on her right side twice, shifting the nose of her kayak so it's pointing toward the middle of the river.

We all do the same, and the islands come up faster than I anticipated. There are four. The top of each island is piled with driftwood, like the islands are strainers for anything coming downriver. If we just drifted and didn't paddle, the current would be just as likely to jam us into the head of an island as it would to push us through a channel between them.

Shannon is giving the tops of the islands a wide berth, and we're all right behind her doing the same thing. We float safely into the channel between the middle two islands.

"Why did you pick this one?" I ask, trying to learn something that may help me in the future.

Shannon rests her paddle across the center of her kayak. "I don't know what will be on the downstream end of the islands, so I figured being in the middle would give us more options if we're faced with having to make a quick decision."

"We should land on an island when we stop for the day," Derrick says. "I concur with Moose Man—less likely to run into people."

"Wherever we stop," I say, "we should get organized. As soon as we're close to the bridge, we need to be ready to act on a moment's notice."

We all paddle on in silence. The ends of the islands disappear behind us, and now we're in the middle of the Tanana, which stretches at least a quarter mile across, maybe more. We're just gray dots on gray water.

Then the screams of jets pierce the sky, and my heart tries to beat its way out of my dry suit. Hopefully they're flying too fast and too high to spot us. We're banking on the gray-on-gray camouflage.

We stop paddling and hold our bodies still, just drifting with the current, knowing that movement—like our paddle blades rising and falling—is the number one thing that could give away our presence on the river.

CHAPTER 94

THE ISLAND WE BEACHED OUR kayaks on a little while ago is brushy with willows, but in the center there's a small stand of spruce trees with less brush in the understory. After carrying our kayaks through the brush to conceal them, we've now got our gear spread out under the spruce trees.

"This island is less than a hundred feet across," Brooke says, "but it's the safest I've felt since before the earthquake."

"It's an unlikely spot to be found, that's for sure," Derrick says. "We could die and our bodies could turn to mummies before we'd be discovered by an archaeologist thousands of years in the future."

I crack a smile. Derrick knows how to exaggerate, but does it in a way that isn't outrageous or over-the-top.

We review how to set the explosives.

"Just to be clear," I say to Shannon, "tell me what happens after you and Brooke drop me and Derrick off. After you've towed our kayaks with you to opposite sides of the river under the bridge."

"When you and Derrick enter the water and start swimming toward the bridge," Shannon says, "we'll know it's time to set our explosives."

I nod. "Then after Derrick and I have set ours on the middle pylon, I'll swim to Brooke and Derrick will swim to you." I point at Shannon. "Then we'll all kayak downriver to get out of the way."

Brooke adds, "We'll make sure we've untied the kayaks so we can have a quick escape."

"Sounds easy enough," Derrick says, "unless there're snipers trying to pick us off. All we've got is this one gun." Derrick picks up the pistol. "Should we carry it in our bag with the explosive?"

"Sounds good to me." I don't know what we'll do if we get fired on. The one thing we have going for us is that we look like the river.

Sunlight filters through the trees, casting striped light and tree trunk shadows across our gear. I think about the jets we saw earlier and how they didn't see us. Or if they did see us, they weren't concerned. Or they've called in our location, and there's a patrol searching for us.

Brooke's words cut into my thoughts. "We should get some rest. Before we know it, we'll be back on the water."

Derrick lies down on his back. "Dry suit equals tent plus sleeping bag. Totally waterproof, too." He crosses his arms over his chest and closes his eyes, which are in a patch of sunlight.

We all follow suit and take Derrick's pose. I doubt I'll be able to sleep, but sometimes rest is just as good. I've had countless nights before cross-country and track meets where I've barely slept but I've rested, and I've performed fine.

At sunset, we'll start our biggest performance ever. I take a breath and think about the situation we're in. I go away to leadership camp to broaden my horizons, explore the wilderness, and come back a changed person. I've changed, that's for sure. I just hope I get to come back to a world that I know. To a world that's intact. And I hope I can do my part to make that happen.

CHAPTER 95

"WE SHOULD SEE THE PIPELINE before the bridge," I say, remembering what Sam told us.

While we rested away the day, two more groups of jets flew over us, but there was no way they could see us under the trees. And if they had some body-heat recognition technology, either it didn't work or they mistook the heat we were generating for moose or wolves or caribou. Now the sun is setting, and we're making our final preparations.

Derrick stuffs the rope with the carabiners into the waterproof backpack that holds the explosive I'll be carrying and says, "Gun, bear spray, explosive, communication device, waist straps, and rope—it's all in there now."

I take the pack and slip my shoulders through its straps.

"My pack's ready, too," Brooke says.

"Mine also," Shannon says.

"I'm going to wear my flippers." I point at them on the ground. "In case I need to jump out of my kayak and swim."

"Good idea, Moose Man." Derrick grabs his flippers and sets them next to mine.

"Do you think it'll matter that one of my flippers is barely a flipper?" I point to the flipper that was munched by a bear.

"If we were swimming a long distance, it would," Derrick says. "Or if we were swimming upriver, but we're not."

I nod. "Cool." The last thing I want is this mission to fail because of one of my flippers.

Shannon looks at Brooke. "Maybe we should wear our flippers, too. We'll have to take them off when we get to the bridge, but having them on while we paddle makes sense."

Brooke nods. "Just in case we come under attack and need to abandon our kayaks."

"We should all wear our waterproof packs with the explosives and our flippers, so if we do lose the kayaks, we'll still have what it takes to do the job," Shannon says.

The sun is dipping behind the trees. In my mind I go over our plan as I carry my kayak to the water's edge. Paddle to within striking distance of the bridge. Drop off Derrick and me upriver from the bridge, ideally on the right side from what we remember Sam telling us, and no more than a quarter mile away. Shannon paddles across the river to the left side towing Derrick's kayak and sets up under the bridge. Brooke tows my kayak and sets up under the bridge on the right side. Once we see Shannon and Brooke are in place, we press the button on the communication device and we wait for the signal.

I get my big backpack and rubber boots and strap them into the bow of my kayak. I scoot my kayak partway into the water, then I sit down and put my flippers on. I stand and pick up my paddle. It's featherlight, and gray, like the color of everything else we have.

I wait for everyone else to finish with their flippers, and then I say, "For the good of Alaska and all its people, let's go do this or die trying."

CHAPTER 96

IF WE HADN'T STUMBLED UPON Sam's camp, what would've happened to us? Would we have made it to the road and been captured by Russian soldiers? Would Sam be trying to pull off his mission by only blowing up two of the three bridges? I think about all of this as I dip my gray kayak paddle into the gray water and pull. A lot in life is left up to chance, but you can make a difference by what you do with the chances you encounter.

We work our way over to the right side of the river. I wish it would stay dusky like this for longer. We blend in better when the sun is down. Are the other teams already in position and waiting for us to press our button? The one thing I don't get is how Sam would know if a team got caught before they reached their end point. Maybe that communication device is also tracking us, and Sam can see our progress, so he has an idea of what's going on? He didn't tell us that, but he's got to be monitoring us or else he'd never know.

On a small muddy beach an old fish wheel rests, tied off right where the trees begin. It's about eight feet tall and has two long woven baskets.

Shannon says, "My great-grandfather had a fish wheel, but his was closer to Fairbanks. He shared it with a few other elders. I was little when he died. I don't know what happened to it."

"I saw one in action when I went to Old Minto," Brooke says.

"You went to Old Minto?" Shannon asks. "When?"

"Four or five years ago. My oldest sister was there as part of a class, and my dad and I took his friend's motorboat down there for a day to visit. I think he was worried about her because it was her first time away from home. Everyone there was super friendly. All the elders kept offering us more and more food."

"I've wanted to go there," Shannon says. "Maybe someday. Depending on . . . everything."

"What is it?" Derrick asks.

"Old Minto is a camp run by Athabascan elders on the Tanana River at an old village site," Shannon responds, "but it's way down-river from where we are. On the other side of Fairbanks, probably two hundred or three hundred river miles from here. It's remote—off the road system. University classes go out there for some type of cultural-awareness training, I think."

As the fish wheel fades in the distance, I say, "Do you think there're people out there now? If so, they probably don't even know about the invasion."

Shannon rests her paddle across her kayak. "If there're people out at Old Minto, they probably don't know. And they're probably a pretty low priority for the Russians. They wouldn't be a threat out there."

I think about being in a remote place and seeing a mushroom cloud. What would I do? What could I do? Would it even be possible to make sense of it? A lot of people live in remote places off the grid in Alaska. There must tons of people who have no clue about the Russians—like the two men who were canoeing.

Part of me thinks that it'd be nice to be living somewhere remote and not know. You'd just keep living your life up until the point when you were unknowingly killed by a massive nuclear explosion or you eventually came to town for supplies and found out that you no longer lived in the United States but now lived in a part of Russia. Would you be a citizen or a prisoner?

We round a bend, and I count four more islands in front of us. We decide to head for the middle channel, all agreeing that using the islands for cover is a good idea in case there are people on either shore. The set of islands is covered more with spruce trees than willows, like maybe the ground is a little higher on them than the island we camped on.

At the bottom of the channel, we see two people on the island to our left, dressed in military fatigues. We don't know if they're American or Russian, but they've spotted us and are raising their weapons.

CHAPTER 97

I DON'T KNOW WHAT REACHES me first: the sound of gunshots or the front of my kayak being pushed sideways as the bullet penetrates the fabric. I keep paddling, but the left front quarter of my boat is sagging from loss of air—listing to the left—so I lean to the right, trying to compensate as my arms work overtime in an attempt to get out of range of any more bullets.

Derrick, Shannon, and Brooke are all in front of me, paddling like crazy just like I am, but my partially deflated boat is slowing me down. They all round the point of the island, leaving the danger zone before me. Another shot whistles over my head, and I double down on my paddling, close in on my three partners, and yell, "My kayak's been hit."

They all stop paddling and turn toward me as I approach.

"Nailed the front of it." I point with my paddle.

"One shot sounded like it went right over my head," Derrick says. "Glad I'm not any taller than I am."

"Why did they shoot at us?" Brooke asks. "Are they Russians? Is our whole plan blown now?"

Shannon shakes her head. "If they were Russian soldiers, they would have had automatic weapons, but they were only firing single shots. Otherwise we'd have been Swiss cheese. I think they're part of one of those militias, and they thought we were Russian soldiers. We definitely look military, especially from a distance."

"That makes sense," I say.

"Everyone sees us as the enemy," Brooke says. "Great."

We all start paddling, and I work hard to keep up with the three of them. I'm thankful for the smart-wall technology that automatically isolated the front left section of my kayak.

"Is that boat going to hold up now that it's damaged?" Shannon asks.

"Stable enough for now," I reply, "but it's a lot slower. I just hope it's not too much farther to the bridge."

"If those Rambo idiots have a radio," Derrick says, "you can bet they're trying to communicate with their people."

I think of Brooke's phone and how the Russians have totally shut it down, and now I hope they've done the same for any basic radio equipment these backwoods militias might have.

"Why would they just start shooting if they didn't know who we were?" Brooke asks.

"If they know we've been invaded by Russia," I say, "then that's what they're expecting to see—Russians."

"We're assuming a lot," Shannon says, "but in this case I don't see how they could think we were anything but Russians and that they were bravely firing against the enemy."

"How'd they get to that island in the first place?" Derrick asks. "Do they have a boat, or did they get dropped off? Either way, we've got to be on the lookout for anyone and everyone."

"Until we get this job done," I say, "everyone is more or less the enemy."

The sky is starting to brighten, and I know the sun will be up soon. I think about almost getting shot, about how close those bullets came to putting holes in me, and I shudder. It doesn't matter who's shooting at you. Americans. Russians. Aliens from outer space. Bullets are bullets.

We round another bend, and, in the distance, we see two things spanning the river. They're still a mile or so away, but the pipeline, and then the highway bridge, connect the two riverbanks.

If everything goes as planned, only the pipeline will be standing after we're done.

We work our way over to the right side of the river and keep paddling in silence, searching for any movement anywhere. Are sentries stationed on the bridge? Or soldiers protecting the pipeline?

The sun is breaking over the horizon, casting shadows from left to right across the river, which works to our advantage because we can paddle in the shadows. Still, I feel more exposed now that the sun is up.

We all want to get into position, but doing it in daylight is risky. If we're going to stop first, let the day pass, and move again at sunset, we'll have to act soon, in the next few minutes; otherwise, we'll be too close to not get into position.

Up ahead, a jagged piece of land stretches about a hundred yards into the river from the right, forming a bay that's out of view of the bridge and the pipeline.

I point at the land formation ahead. "If we want to wait till sunset to get into position, there's a hiding spot coming up."

We all talk for a minute and agree to head for the bay created by the land jutting into the river.

We're almost on shore when we notice people standing just back from the trees. They emerge from the forest, and even though they're smiling, I'm scared out of my mind.

CHAPTER 98

"WE AREN'T WHO YOU THINK we are," Shannon says, with her arms raised just like the rest of us. "I'm Athabascan, like you."

The man pointing the rifle at us juts his head forward and nods, but doesn't put the rifle down. "Speak."

"We're not Russian," Shannon says. "We're trying to stop the Russians."

"They've been roundin' people up," the man says, "all people." He takes a step toward Shannon. "The Americans rounded us up using diseases and boarding schools, and we survived that. We even learned to live with them. But the Russians are holding people in pens, like they're animals." He spits. The two other men standing behind him spit, too. They have rifles but are holding them with the barrels facing downward.

"Will you please put the gun down?" I say to the man who is pointing his weapon at us. "We're not here to hurt you."

The man points the gun at Derrick. "Say something."

"Okay," Derrick responds. "Um . . . I don't want to say the wrong thing and get shot. Understand?"

The man points the gun at Brooke. "Say something."

"Don't shoot me," Brooke responds. "Please."

The man puts the gun down, and I let out a breath I didn't even know I was holding.

"I believe you," the man says. "I had to hear each of you speak to make sure all of you knew English. Understand?"

We all nod. Even though I know that his little test has its flaws—we could all be Russians fluent in English—I understand.

The man looks at Shannon. "Now, tell us what you're doing." And seeing that he and his two friends each have rifles, we all look at one another and nod, and decide to tell them everything.

I mean, if they hold us captive, we won't be able to complete our mission, and the best shot we have at being released by these three is to level with them.

We get out of our kayaks and pull them ashore. Then we carry them to the edge of the woods and put them just inside the trees, so they're invisible from the river. The sun is above the trees. It is full daylight now.

We sit down with the three men under the trees and recount our time at Simon Lake, our survival hike where we ran into Sam, and our commitment to helping him retake the missiles at Fort Greely by blowing the bridge spanning the Tanana River. We tell them that the United States plans to nuke Alaska to eliminate the missiles if Sam's mission fails.

The three men look at one another. Albert, the one who pointed the gun at us, motions for the other two to scoot toward him. They confer quietly, then Albert says, "We know this land. That's why the Russians haven't rounded us up. We can help you blow that bridge."

I think about what Sam emphasized—telling no one what we're doing. We've already broken that rule. But then I think about our ultimate goal of blowing the bridge and how there's no way that Sam could have anticipated every scenario we might find ourselves in. We tried to follow his directive to the letter when we assaulted the canoe people and took their canoes. But now that the bridge is in sight, and it's obvious these guys have way more experience in the woods than we do, the least we can do is hear what they have to say.

CHAPTER 99

AS THE SUN IS SETTING and we're moving our kayaks into position to put our plan into action, Albert's words fill my mind: *We'll be up on the bluff, watching. When we see you and Derrick start swimming, we'll create a distraction that'll draw their attention toward us. Since the bluff is downriver, it should make your approach easier because they'll focus their attention in the opposite direction from where you are.*

I've got the small waterproof backpack on with the explosive device, the communication device, the rope, the waist straps, and the gun inside. Shannon and Brooke are also wearing their waterproof packs—each with an explosive device inside.

Albert and his friends also told us that if we get into trouble on our initial approach, like if we get spotted in our kayaks while getting into position, or if it looks like we're going to get spotted, they'll provide a distraction right away. If that happens, we might have to place our explosives regardless of whether we get the signal from Sam, because then it might just be a matter of time before the Russian military closes in on us.

Albert and his friends left several hours ago so they could get to their position by sunset.

I look downriver, and just beyond the bridge on the right is a sheer bluff towering a couple hundred feet above the river. According to Albert, there's a way to climb the bluff from the backside even though, from the river, it looks unclimbable. Historically, the bluff was used as a lookout for the Athabascans. From the top you can see up and down the Tanana River and up the Delta River, which flows into the Tanana just below the bridge.

The trickiest part of getting to the bluff is having to leave the cover of the forest to cross the road. We haven't heard any gunshots, so hopefully they've made it. But the reality is, even if they haven't, we're still going through with our part of the plan.

"We'll pull off just before we get to the pipeline," Shannon says. "We'll drop you and Derrick, take your kayaks, and paddle our way to the bridge."

"The most dangerous part," Derrick says, "is when you"—he points at Shannon—"have to cross the river. I wish you didn't have to do that."

We all hate that part of the plan because Shannon will be so exposed.

"It'll be dusk," Shannon says softly. "Plus, Albert will be watching. If he sees something going on, he'll go into action. And if anyone on the bridge starts shooting at me, I'll dive into the river."

I already know all of this, but it still leaves me feeling lousy because the open crossing so close to the bridge is such a glaring weakness in our plan. We thought about having Brooke and Shannon both stick to the right side of the river until they got to Brooke's spot under the bridge, but then there'd be no way for Shannon to cross without getting swept downstream, because the current is so strong.

We paddle single file down the right side of the river, hugging the bank, until we're a quarter mile above where the pipeline crosses the river. Derrick and I hop out of our kayaks and tie them to the backs of Shannon's and Brooke's kayaks, leaving only a few feet between boats so they'll be easier to tow.

There's no time for a long goodbye, so I just say, "When you get to your spots, keep your eyes on us. As soon as you're in position, I'm pressing the button to alert Sam we're ready."

CHAPTER 100

DERRICK AND I SIT AT the edge of the willows, our gray flippered feet just touching the river. We work in silence as we snap our waist straps on. I lay the coiled gray rope between us, put the communication device on top of it, and then slip my arms through the shoulder straps of the backpack. The explosive, along with the handgun Derrick was carrying, rests in the middle of my back.

As I watch Shannon paddle across the river, in my mind I visualize swimming with the rope in one hand, rounding the middle pillar of the bridge, clicking the carabiner at the end of the rope onto the ring on my waist strap, meeting up with Derrick—who has the other end of the rope—and then having him get the explosive out of my pack, hand it to me, and then hoist me up so I can drill it into the pillar.

I whisper to Derrick, "Are you clear about the plan?"

Derrick nods. "Just try to stay calm when you're in the water swimming toward the bridge. You'll use less energy." He turns his head away from me and spits, then turns back toward me. "Sam presented this plan like it was obviously doable, but look at this river. It's going to be a bitch to stay in place while you're drilling."

"We can do it," I say, even though I have no clue if we actually can.

Now Shannon is a gray dot on top of a gray river. She's most of the way to the other side.

Brooke—also a gray dot—is a little farther downriver than Shannon but on our side of the river.

I think about Albert and his friends. Did they make it to the bluff, or were they caught en route? There's no way to know unless we hear gunshots. And even then, we can't be sure who's doing the shooting or from where. Or they could have been captured silently, without any gunshots.

"I think the girls made it to their spots," Derrick says, pointing downriver.

I study the far side of the bridge and can make out Shannon standing beneath it, but on our side of the river I can't see Brooke because the land juts out a little bit just before the bridge. "How do you know Brooke made it?"

"I don't know for sure," Derrick says, "but it should have taken her less time than Shannon since she didn't have to cross the river. Plus, we didn't hear any shouts or gunshots."

"We still don't know for sure," I say. "I think we should hike up the bank a little so we can get a view to check. I think—"

"Look," Derrick says, "I know you like her and want to protect her. She's awesome. But if we do that—hike up the bank—we might get spotted. And that'd be bad news for everyone, especially Brooke and Shannon, who are way closer to the bridge than we are."

I take a breath. "You're right," I say. "I wish you weren't right, but you are."

I pick up the communication device, a black box the size of an iPhone. I turn to Derrick, and he nods.

With my index finger I press the green button and wait.

I don't have to wait very long.

CHAPTER 101

"I HOPE SHANNON AND BROOKE can see us," I say as I grab one end of the rope and Derrick grabs the other.

"They'll see us," he says. "Even if they don't see us right away, they'll see us as we approach the bridge."

My heart is pounding like I've just completed a cross-country race, so I take a breath and try to focus on finishing the mission. We've made it this far, and I don't want my own panic to sink our effort—and be responsible for the nuking of Alaska and the start of World War III.

With my free hand, I chuck the communication device with the red glowing light into the river like Sam told me to do. I turn to Derrick, all decked out in river-color gray like me, and say, "Let's do what you said—keep the rope mostly coiled up until we get closer to the bridge."

"Roger that," he responds. "We should work our way to the middle of the river right from the get-go, so we'll have more room to maneuver when we get to the bridge. Just follow my lead. You're the runner. I'm the swimmer."

I hate the idea of being in the middle of the river on our approach because it'll be easier for someone to spot us, but I know Derrick's right.

On our bellies we slip into the river, just keeping our heads above the surface. Will Shannon and Brooke really be able to see us? At this point, I can't care because I don't have control over that. I only have control over what I'm doing. I try to swim so only my head from the nose up is exposed. I keep my legs hanging down and my shoulders and arms below the surface. If we were swimming upriver, this technique wouldn't work. As it is, the current tugs at the coil of rope in my left hand, and I can feel the water on the toes of my left foot because of the bear that bit off the end of my flipper.

For a split second, my thoughts jump to bears, hoping that Shannon and Brooke aren't having to deal with any. We made sure they each had our last two full canisters of bear spray before they headed for their spots.

About ten feet of rope separates Derrick and me. My hands are cold from the water, but there's no way we could be wearing gloves given what we've got to do. Sam assured us that we wouldn't be in the river so long that our hands would become numb, and he said that gloves would be one more thing that would just get in the way. I hope he's right. *When you plan a mission, you try to eliminate everything you can that could foul things up.* Basically, that's how you run a cross-country race, too. You wear the right clothes. You tie your shoes. You eat and drink what works for your body. The fewer variables or unknowns the better.

With the sun being down and my eyes just above the gray water of the river, things seem dark, but I know that if I were on the bridge I'd be able to see better. I hope the tops of our heads look like the river, or debris floating in the water. If they shoot us up and fill us full of holes, then we'll be real debris.

"Okay," Derrick says, "we're in the middle of the river. Now we just need to stay here and drift."

I really want to clip the carabiner onto my waist strap so I have no chance of losing the rope, but if I do that I'll have less control over where the rope goes while we make our way downriver and it could get tangled with my legs.

Don't clip in until you've rounded the pillar. You'll have way more control. If you drown, the world may die.

We pass under the oil pipeline, and now the bridge is looking bigger and bigger. The river narrows and the current picks up.

"We should start spreading out," Derrick says.

I let a couple of coils of the rope slide through my hand, and now I'm twenty feet from Derrick instead of ten. The conveyor belt of silty water keeps propelling us forward.

I want to glance up and study the bridge to see if there are people on watch up there, but the more of my head that is out of the water, the greater chance I'll have of being seen. I'm hoping, if the bridge is guarded, that there are just roadblocks on both ends with guards facing the road.

I tilt my head toward Derrick, and now he's about fifty feet away. He must've let more rope out from his side. I set a few more coils free, and now about seventy feet separate us. I don't even know how long the rope is.

Should I let the rest of it go and just hang on to the end? If I let the rope out too early, it might not stretch out and the current could tangle it up in my legs.

I clip the carabiner to the ring on my waist strap and then slowly start letting the rest of the rope out. I've got one coil left in my hand when I hear gunshots.

CHAPTER 102

I DIVE AND KEEP SWIMMING downriver, like Derrick and I planned on doing. I hope the shots are Albert exchanging fire with the Russians. I don't want Albert to get hurt, but according to him he's got great cover just below the top of the bluff, in a natural rock shelter that's mostly camouflaged by a wall of wild rose and alders.

I poke my head above the surface, and the middle pillar of the bridge sits in front of me like a giant's leg rising from the river. My heart leaps into my throat. I turn and start kicking furiously, trying to swim to the right. I must've been oriented a little to the left when I dove, and now I'm way too far to the left. I feel like I'm making good progress but then there's a yank on my waist.

The rope.

I turn and look for Derrick's head. I don't want to shout, which may draw attention to us, but if Derrick doesn't know what I'm trying to do—swim more to the right—he might unintentionally stop me by maintaining his current direction. I can't see his head, so I abandon my effort to find him and just keep trying to swim to the right, and now the rope is looser, like maybe he realized what I was trying to do and is swimming in my direction. The pillar is about a hundred yards away right now. Water flows around both sides of it in a rush, and I need to be in the rush on the right-hand side for our plan to work. If we both get sucked to the left, there's no way we'll be able to recover—to swim upriver and set the explosive.

A few minutes have gone by since Derrick and I entered the river, but it feels like this thing I'm doing—swimming toward the pillar—is all

I've ever done, like this has been my entire life. I'm not a runner. I'm not my parents' son. I'm not anything but this—a swimmer with an explosive in a backpack. And my whole purpose is to set that explosive, even if someone is shooting the arms off my body as I do it. Even if there is nothing left of me when I'm done.

I've got plenty of slack on the rope now, but I'm not sure how long that's going to last.

I start swimming the crawl stroke, kicking like crazy, not caring if anyone from above sees me. If I don't round the pillar on the right-hand side, everything I've done up to this point has no meaning.

I kick and kick and kick.

And pull and pull and pull.

I catch a glimpse of the pillar. I'm too close to it. Way too close. Like a final insult the current increases, making the possibility of me reaching my goal even more remote.

Dead center. I'm going to hit the pillar dead center. The river is a freight train, I'm stuck on the front of the engine, and it's driving me straight toward the pillar.

Even if I'm bludgeoned by my contact with the pillar and I die, if I can end up on the right side and Derrick on the left, then he can wrestle the explosive out of my pack and try to set it without me.

I lead with my left arm and leg, bracing for impact, trying to keep my head from bouncing against the concrete pillar.

Claw right. Claw right. Scratch your way around. Kick your way around. Crawl your way around, my mind screams above the rush of the river.

I'm going to make it, I think. *I'm going to make it. I'm going to make contact, but I'm also going to make it around the right-hand side.*

And now up close the surface of the pillar looks jagged instead of smooth. I'm going to make it around on the right-hand side, but not without a price.

CHAPTER 103

I THINK MY HAND IS going to be the first part of my body to make contact with the jagged cement pillar, but instead, the side of my knee slams into something under the surface, and the impact sends me spinning away from the pillar. Then I'm yanked back toward the pillar, and the jagged cement rakes across my forehead just above my eyes and below my gray bathing cap.

My forehead stings, like someone has punched a thousand needles into it at once. I'm trying to see through the blood that's dripping into my eyes.

I dip my face in the river in an attempt to get the blood out of my eyes, and it works. Now I can see the gray of the river and the end of the pillar, but I'm no longer moving.

I'm facing downriver and am pinned between the pillar and the current, which is treating me like any other obstruction, trying to flow through me and over me.

The rope is taut, like it's trying to pull me upstream. And then I know what's happened. Because I drifted left just before we got to the pillar, more of the rope went around the left side with Derrick, and now there isn't enough rope for me to cover the rest of the distance. I remember Sam saying, *You have a little leeway with the length of the rope but not much, so it's important to both start from as close to the midpoint as you can when you go around the pillar, so relatively equal lengths of rope flow on both sides.*

I try to scoot farther up the pillar, because right now the water is at chin level, and there are waves that come and go that are higher, that wash over my head. I could drown right here.

Can Derrick see me? Does he know this is happening? Where is he? Just around the edge of the pillar and out of sight? Is he waiting for me?

A big wave washes over me and totally submerges my head, and I hold my breath for what seems like forever, stretching my neck in a futile attempt to gain some height above the river. I think about unbuckling my waist strap and letting the current take me downriver. If I do that, I'll probably save myself from drowning, but then I won't be able to set the explosive. Now I'm seeing red and black dots, and my lungs are screaming for air worse than I've ever experienced. I reach for my waist strap.

I'll have to unbuckle before I black out, I think.

Then the water recedes and is back to chin level. I gulp air, and my lungs burn with relief. I'm still pinned to the pillar, but I've also still got the explosive.

A splash just downriver refocuses my attention. And there, maybe ten or fifteen feet away, I see a rounded gray shape emerge from the gray river.

Derrick's head.

He disappears and then surfaces right in front of me. He grabs me by my shoulders, which are still submerged in the water. "We've got to unhook you from the rope."

"I know," I say. "But if I unhook, we'll both be sucked downriver without setting the explosive."

"We'll have to try to swim to the spot just behind the pillar," Derrick says. "It might be protected enough to get the job done. I can't hang on to you much longer. The current is relentless. You've got to unhook."

"Okay," I say. "Don't let go of me."

"After you unhook, we'll hug the pillar as we're swept downstream by the current," Derrick says, "and then when we're in the calmest spot behind the pillar, we'll get the job done."

I reach for my waist strap and am about to unhook the buckle, but then I come up with what I hope is a better idea.

CHAPTER 104

"LET'S DRILL IT RIGHT HERE," I say. "Get the explosive out of my pack. Hand it to me and then boost me up."

"The only way I'm still here is because I'm grabbing your shoulders," Derrick says. "The current will sling me downriver the instant I let go, and I'll be dangling on the rope like I was before I fought the current to get to you."

"I don't want you to let go," I say. "Just get me above the water enough so I can do the job. Use me as your anchor."

"I'll get under you and lift," Derrick says, "but you'll have to wrestle the explosive out of your pack yourself."

Derrick's head disappears in the water in front of me, and then I feel his hands on my waist. He must be jostling around for leverage because I feel one hand leave my waist and then I'm yanked downward, but almost simultaneously there's this pressure between my legs and I'm being pushed upward. As soon as my shoulders are above the water, I wrestle the pack off my back, open it, and pull out the explosive by the handles. I lean into the pillar, using my body weight for leverage, position the drill as straight as I can, and press the power switch.

The drill bit churns, biting into the cement, the sound of the motor mixing in with the sounds from the rushing river. More blood from my forehead wound is running into my eyes, and I blink continuously, which allows me to see just enough to know the drill is working.

True to Sam's word, once the process is started, the drill continues deeper into the piling on its own and stops at some predetermined depth. I press the activate button, and it lights up green. We've got twenty minutes until this thing goes off.

"Done!" I shout.

The upward pressure below me disappears, and I'm back to being pummeled by the river with my chin barely above the surface. Derrick emerges upriver from me, and I realize he's holding on to the rope that's keeping me pinned to the pillar.

"Unbuckle your waist strap," Derrick shouts. "You go right, I'll go left, and we'll meet up with Shannon and Brooke."

I grab the plastic buckle with both hands and pinch the two release buttons, and the current immediately takes me downriver. I turn my body to the right and start kicking toward shore. I hope Brooke and Shannon are done setting their explosives and are just waiting for Derrick and me. The current is carrying me downstream, so I turn and try to swim upriver as I approach the shore, knowing that the plan was to meet under the bridge.

I hope Brooke can see me and will try to meet me with the kayaks wherever I end up. There's no way I'll hit the shore directly under the bridge, but I can walk upriver if she doesn't see me.

I don't want to stick my head too far above the water because I don't want to be seen by anyone on the bridge, but Brooke knows to be looking for my gray-capped head in this gray river. Maybe she even watched Derrick and me struggling to plant our explosive device.

My legs are working overtime, and I'm making progress toward shore. I'm still a couple hundred feet from land, but through the gray haze of the waves I'm encountering from swimming upstream I spot what I think are our kayaks just below the bridge. And up on the bank above them and just upriver, I see two Russian soldiers.

Instantly, I submerge and tread water, trying to stay in place and stay invisible.

Brooke, I think. *Do they have Brooke? Or did she get away?* I break the surface again, peering over the waves.

Soldiers? Yes.

Brooke? No.

I gulp air and submerge again.

Just because she isn't there doesn't mean she got away. But just because she isn't there doesn't mean she was captured. Maybe the soldiers are waiting, hoping to capture someone coming back for the kayaks, and Brooke spotted them first and slipped away.

I break the surface again but this time look toward the pillar where Brooke was supposed to set her explosive, and I see a tiny green light. Since the soldiers are just upstream from the bottom end of the pillar, they may not be able to see the green light, or if they can, they haven't shown any interest in it.

I submerge again.

Green light. The clock is ticking. How much time has gone by since the countdown began? What would Brooke have done after she set the explosive if she couldn't get back to the kayaks? If she'd seen the Russian soldiers but they hadn't seen her, or even if they had seen her, what would she have done?

My lungs are on fire, so I surface again and gulp air and then submerge again.

Swim, I think. *She'd swim for safety. Across the river and toward our meeting spot.*

Somewhere, Brooke must be alone in this big river, just like me.

I surface one more time, wishing I could know where Brooke went and when, or if, she's been captured. But since the explosive is set and the Russians aren't paying attention to it, I doubt they've captured Brooke, and I doubt they know about the explosive.

Enough thinking, I tell myself. *Do something!*

I submerge and then surface again, but now the soldiers are on the bank, pointing in my direction. One of them raises his gun, and I dive and start kicking my way across the river and downstream. I hear the muffled report of gunfire, but I'm a small target and invisible as long as I'm underwater.

The farther I get from the soldiers, the more my thoughts turn back to Brooke. I hope with all my heart that she is okay. I hope that she gets far enough away from the bridge before it blows. And I hope that I find her, or she finds me, and that we both find Derrick and Shannon.

CHAPTER 105

I POP UP FOR AIR and can see the Delta River entering the Tanana on the left and the bluff where Albert is supposed to be on the right.

Stay in the middle of the river for now, I think, *in case there are soldiers on both sides.*

I don't know how long it's been since Derrick and I set the explosive, but twenty minutes is all we supposedly have to get away, and I already feel like I've been in this river swimming away from the Russian soldiers forever.

I keep my head above the surface and continue kicking.

Around the first bend on the far side of the mouth of the Delta River, I remember. On the left bank, in the first patch of spruce trees big enough to hide in, by the mouth of a small creek that enters the river— that's where we're supposed to meet up.

It all sounded so neat and tidy. Brooke and I paddling our kayaks from one spot and Derrick and Shannon from another.

I hope those three are already there.

Those two soldiers under the bridge will probably die. Did they even want to be part of an Alaskan invasion or were they forced to by their government? People sign up for service to protect their country, but then they get sent on missions that have nothing to do with protecting their country, or even doing any good in the world. Do they even know they're sitting on a potential ground zero? Does anyone know except the United States government and us?

The swift water entering from the Delta River wants to push me back across the Tanana, so I double down on my kicking in an attempt to get out of the crosscurrent as quickly as I can.

I'm pretty sure my forehead is still bleeding, but I've pulled my gray bathing cap down as far as it will go to put some pressure on the wound.

I'm about to submerge and swim underwater when I catch a glimpse of something downriver.

An arm. No. Two arms. Swimming. Two gray arms swimming a couple hundred yards in front of me and a little closer to the right-hand side of the river. And a round gray head.

Brooke.

That has to be Brooke.

My heart does a little leap.

I want to scream and shout but know that would just bring danger to Brooke and me. She's following the plan, too. If Derrick and Shannon managed to keep their kayaks, they're probably already at the spruce grove because paddling has to be way faster than swimming.

I double down on my kicking because I want to catch up to Brooke. I want to swim with her to the meeting spot. I want to know how she got away without being seen while also managing to set the explosive.

The crosscurrent must be growing weaker because now I've got good downstream movement without being pushed sideways. I can see the bend coming up. There's no way I'm going to catch Brooke before she rounds the bend, but at least I know she survived.

Then my ears are assaulted by a loud *boom-boom-ba-boom*.

I turn and face upriver and watch in sick fascination as the three pillars crumble and huge sections of roadway and guard railing fall into the river. The jagged ends of the highway hang on both sides of the river with no bridge spanning them anymore.

Our part of the plan has worked. But has Sam's? Because if his hasn't, we're all going to get fried.

CHAPTER 106

"WE HAD TO SWIM, TOO," Shannon says. She recounts how she and Derrick had to jump from their kayaks when someone on the bridge started shooting at them.

"I'm pretty sure the kayaks sank," Derrick adds. "I mean, it was pretty heavy fire, and they were aiming at the kayaks. We dove and swam downriver."

"I don't even know if I heard anything," I say. "But I was on the opposite side of the river, and I was in the water—mostly underwater."

"I heard some shots," Brooke says, "but they sounded far away, and I guess they were."

We're sitting in the forest just back from the river in a patch of spruce trees, pretty sure that this is the spot Sam instructed us to stop at. Even if it's not, we had to get out of the water so we wouldn't get pummeled by debris from the bridge.

For the moment we all feel safe because the Russians would have to at least cross the Delta River and then round the first bend in the Tanana to come anywhere near us, and right now they're dealing with a blown bridge. Hopefully three blown bridges.

Then I say what I'm sure we're all thinking. "I wonder if Sam made it."

"We'll have to take turns keeping watch for mushroom clouds," Derrick says. He grins, but I can tell it's more nerves than actually joking around.

Our lives might be over in an hour or less if the United States launches a nuclear attack on Fort Greely. Standing in some isolated patch of spruce forest, exhausted beyond belief, and now we might die without any warning.

I say, "I wish there were some way Sam could contact us so we'd know."

"We can only see what happens," Shannon says, "as it happens."

"I want to know if these are my last minutes alive," I say.

"What would you do," Brooke asks, "if you knew you were going to die today?"

I look at Derrick and Shannon, and then I turn to Brooke and say softly, "I'd kiss you if you'd let me."

Brooke smiles. "Even with that jagged, bloody wreck stretching across your forehead, I'd let you." Her eyes bore into mine. "I'd kiss you back."

I cover the distance between us and we stand so we're face-to-face, our noses inches apart. She looks very alien with the gray dry suit and swim cap, but the serious smile on her face is all hers. My whole body is trembling. I'm more nervous than I've ever been running a race. A race is something you can plan for, but a kiss isn't—especially a kiss that could be your last.

With my hands, I softly cradle her cheeks. She tilts her head one way, and I tilt mine the opposite, and our lips meet. It's a silty kiss, but still, it's the sweetest kiss I've ever had.

After several seconds we break apart, and there, off to the side, I see Derrick and Shannon, and they're kissing, too.

Brooke tugs on my arm and I turn so I'm facing her again.

"Just be here," she says, and then starts kissing me again.

CHAPTER 107

"KISSES WILL ONLY SUSTAIN US for a limited amount of time," Shannon says, smiling.

The four of us are sitting under the spruce trees with our flippers off. My forehead has gone from throbbing to a steady ache. Rinsing it with river water only goes so far because of all the silt in it. I know there should be a creek just downriver from where we are, but I'm too exhausted to go searching for it right now.

"Maybe we're in the clear," I say. "I mean, we're still alive."

"Sam said to wait for three days," Derrick says. "He's supposed to come and get us or send someone."

"He probably assumed we'd have some food with us." Brooke says. "I was starving before I had to swim across the river."

"We can survive without food for a while," I respond. "It's not fun, but it beats getting picked up by Russian soldiers who may still be in control of the area."

"Even if they were given orders to retreat," Shannon adds, "if their friends were killed when the bridge exploded and they discover we destroyed it . . ."

"Life still sucks." Derrick raises his eyebrows. "Even in victory, we've got to watch our backs."

Through the trees I can see the river—relentless—as it keeps on flowing. Maybe there's tons of blown bridge debris just under the surface, passing us by right now.

I say, "If Sam doesn't show after three days, we're on our own." I turn to Brooke. "If that happens, then your idea about heading down-river toward Fairbanks may be our best bet."

"That was with kayaks," Brooke adds.

"You know," Derrick says, "if we do have to strike out on our own, going by river may be our best option."

"True," Shannon responds. "With footwear like this"—she holds up a flipper—"we can't exactly walk anywhere."

"Swim to Fairbanks?" I ask.

"We'd have the current on our side," Derrick says.

"Maybe we wouldn't have to go all the way," I add. "If people have been freed, there's a chance we'd run into someone in a boat."

Brooke says, "Can't we just swim across the river and work our way upstream until we get to where the bridge used to be? There must be people there."

"We can't unknowingly walk into what was, and still may be, Russian-held territory," Shannon responds. "We're unarmed. It's too risky."

"Even if Josh hadn't lost the gun when we set the explosive," Derrick says, "that pistol was no match for what the Russians were shooting at us with."

"We haven't been fried, and it's been hours since all of our *last* kisses," Brooke fires back. "We must've won."

"Even if we did win," I say, "the end of a war, or an invasion, or what-ever this is, is different than the end of a game, or a race, where everyone just goes home and goes about their business."

"Frank the Second"—Derrick points at my forehead—"makes a good case. My dad told me there was a Japanese soldier who fought for more than twenty years after World War II was over."

The mosquitoes find us, but since we have dry suits on the only places they can get at are our hands and faces, and it's pretty easy to wave them away or slap them if they land on us.

"So, we sit here and starve," Brooke says, "all because the enemy could be sore losers?"

"Maybe they were given strict orders not to give up," Shannon responds. "That's basically what happened with that Japanese soldier Derrick mentioned."

I stand up and wave my hands in front of my face. "Three days. Think of all we've been through. Surely we can handle three days of starvation while living in dry suits. Right? I mean, we may have helped to save the world from a nuclear war. Look at us! We did it. We carried out an almost impossible mission. I didn't do it so I could wander out on a gravel bar and be shot after the fact. I want to live."

The whine of a boat motor invades my ears. Somebody is coming, but we don't know who.

CHAPTER 108

"HOW DID YOU FIND US?" I ask.

Albert grins. "I knew where to look." He's snugged his flat-bottom riverboat up against the shore, and we've tied it off for him. A couple of rifle cases lie in the bottom of the boat along with four red gas cans. "You. All of you," Albert says, "did a good job on the bridge."

"Did anyone die?" Shannon asks.

"Some people did. Yes. But it saved lives. Not just our lives, but lots of lives." Albert swats a mosquito on his neck. "You people impress me. From high school students to high-stakes operatives in less than a month."

"You said you knew where to look to find us," Derrick says. "Could you see us from the bluff the whole time?"

"I could," Albert replies, "but I didn't have to."

"I don't understand," Brooke says, "but I'm glad you're here because that means we can leave, right?"

"Sam," I say. "You work with Sam. He told you. Didn't he?"

Albert shrugs, then he points to me. "You heard it from him, not me." Then he grins. "Get in the boat. We're heading to Fairbanks."

EPILOGUE

SCHOOL STARTED ABOUT SIX WEEKS later than usual this year, which means we didn't really have a cross-country season. But I kept running anyway, thinking of Theo as I sped up hills, and his life that was cut short by the landslide. My parents are still splitting up, but I'm thankful they're alive.

Brooke, Shannon, Derrick, and I had to spend a few days debriefing with Sam and a few people that work with him before we were allowed to see anyone else. It was unclear if Sam was their boss, or if one of them was in charge, or if they all shared power equally. We didn't meet at the army or the air force base. Instead, we met in a windowless room in the closed Kmart on Airport Way. The building is being used by the military as storage for vehicles and other stuff. All the windows are covered with plywood.

Mum's the word regarding the mission we were involved in. We aren't even allowed to tell our parents. We ran into Albert in the wilderness, and he was responsible for getting us back to town—that's our story. The Russian invasion—it's the talk of the town—but we didn't know a thing about it since we were at Simon Lake and then trekking through the wilderness without any contact with anyone, until we ran into Albert and he filled us in.

My friends keep telling me how lucky I am to have missed being rounded up by the Russians. How they thought they were going to die. I smile and agree because our real story, the whole *how close we came to getting nuked by our own bombs*, is classified information.

"Maybe in twenty years," Sam said, "or maybe in fifty, you'll get to tell that story. Whenever—*if ever*—it's declassified. Don't even discuss it among yourselves." Sam went on, "There are lots of stories that never get told. Stories that could cause more harm than good."

Brooke and I are hanging out at least twice a week, getting to know each other outside of being in an emergency situation. The more I get to know her, the more I like her. Since we shared such an intense experience, it's easy to be real with each other. I'm not guessing what she's thinking or feeling; I'm asking her and she's asking me.

We've gotten together with Derrick and Shannon a few times and it's just plain weird in the coolest way to see people in their everyday lives who you know secretly had a hand in saving the world from a nuclear disaster.

The reason our secret doesn't feel isolating is because we have one another. Even if we aren't directly talking about it, we acknowledge it all the time with eye contact, a touch on someone's arm, a hug, or a joke about Frankenstein or the *green thing*.

I'm not sure what my future holds, but I hope Brooke plays a large role in it. And I hope that Derrick and Shannon do, too.

ACKNOWLEDGMENTS

I wrote successive drafts of this book over the past two years as my father was facing several end-of-life health issues. While I was sitting with him in the comfort of his own home, by his bedside at the hospital, and then at the hospice care facility, and while flying between my home in Alaska and his in Indiana, I worked on this story when I was able.

I am deeply indebted to all my family members. Thank you to my brothers Carl and John, sisters-in-law Vivian and Sandi, and nephews Mark and Tim for your continual and comforting presence during this time.

Thank you to my mother, Dolores, who took excellent care of my father. Her deep well of love and compassion continues to nurture and guide our family.

A big thank-you to my agent, Amy Tipton, and my editor, John Morgan, for all the time and effort they put into this story. I feel fortunate to have you both in my corner.

Thanks also to Erin Stein, Natalie C. Sousa, Carolyn Bull, Jessica Chung, Melinda Ackell, Kerianne Okie Steinberg, and Raymond Ernesto Colón, and to all the other people at Imprint and Macmillan who helped bring this book into the world.

Thank you to my wife, Dana, for being there for me in all aspects of my life.